LITTLE WITNESS

BOOKS BY S.A. DUNPHY

LITTLE WITNESS

S.A. DUNPHY

bookouture

Published by Bookouture in 2024

An imprint of Storyfire Ltd.
Carmelite House
50 Victoria Embankment
London EC4Y 0DZ

www.bookouture.com

ISBN: 978-1-80314-721-5
eBook ISBN: 978-1-80314-720-8

For Andrew Vachss. A brother in arms.

PROLOGUE

LABYRINTH

1

Tessa Burns was scared and she knew it.

For a moment she couldn't make her legs work and just sat in her battered red 1984 Ford Capri, waiting for her heart to slow down and her breathing to return to normal.

Of course, that didn't happen. Not right away anyway.

Across the street, the crumbling warehouse looked like something the city had partially chewed and then spat out. Weeds and moss sprouted from cracks and crevices in its ancient structure, and most of the windows that dotted its high walls had long since lost all their glass to vandalism or the elements.

Tessa knew why she was scared. She was terrified of what she might find if she went inside that building. She feared who might be waiting for her in there. And perhaps even more so, who might not.

But being afraid was something Tessa was used to. She'd lived with fear of one kind or another most of her life, and she knew how to deal with it. This time was no different.

Darkness seemed to ooze from the empty window frames like dank fog, but there were no sounds or signs of life of any kind. The warehouse stood on its own amid several acres of waste ground, and Tessa could see no movement in any direction. She wondered if she might have misinterpreted the chain of clues that had led her here.

Could she be mistaken? She'd been investigating this case for three weeks now and was beginning to think her colleagues in the Special Detective Unit might be right: the trail had already gone too cold.

Tessa couldn't let it go though. The stakes were too high and the result of wasting even more time simply devastating.

Ireland's Special Detective Unit was dedicated to fighting threats to national security. They monitored persons and organisations deemed dangerous on both domestic and international fronts, and engaged in counter-terrorism – particularly targeting dissident Republican groups and Islamic extremists – and counter-intelligence across a number of fronts, including terrorism (political, eco- and cyber-), industrial espionage and keeping an eye on certain minority religious cults that might be a threat in the future if they ever became large enough. The SDU was also Ireland's main armed-response unit to serious incidents and provided security when weapons, ammunition and large quantities of money needed to be transported; they were in charge of operating Ireland's witness protection programme, and they provided bodyguards and protection to Ireland's presidents and any visiting diplomats, dignitaries and celebrities.

Tessa had performed all of these duties during her time with the unit, but where she excelled was as an investigator, and it was that skill that had brought her to this decaying edifice just outside Donabate, north-east of Dublin City.

Deciding there was nothing more to be learned from remaining in the car, Tessa, moving with a purpose she still didn't feel, opened the door to the Capri. Not even pausing to lock her beloved vehicle, she moved with rapid strides to where the rusted gates of the warehouse hung unevenly on their hinges. She could just about squeeze through the gap in the subsided metal structures and then she was inside.

Continuing to maintain her pace, she struck out for the rear of the building.

Tessa immediately realised she wasn't the first person there that day: it had been raining the day before, and something had pulled up the moss and scuffed the dirt that had accumulated on the worn asphalt of the yard, and you didn't have to be a detective to work out a vehicle of some sort was the culprit. Here and there, tyre tracks could be clearly made out.

Turning the corner at the far end of the yard, she spied a Transit van and a Skoda SUV parked out of sight of the road.

They might not belong to the people she was looking for; the team who had abducted five-year-old Bettina Watson, the daughter of the CEO of one of Ireland's most successful airlines. These vehicles could have nothing to do with the crew who were trying to force Jerome Watson to sell his controlling share of the company at a ridiculously low price.

Which, as the investigation continued and the child remained missing, he had done, despite the police warning that this might place the child at dire risk. While the kidnappers hadn't identified themselves, the SDU believed they belonged to an anarchist cell that had a history of similar abductions. In three of the four cases, the child that had been taken had been murdered within days of the ransom being paid.

Watson had sold his stock two days ago, and there had been no further contact from the people who'd taken her.

Tessa knew time was running out.

She pulled her phone from the rear pocket of her jeans.

'Sarge, it's Tessa. I think that lead might have paid off.'

'What do you mean, "might have"?'

Sergeant Maurice O'Driscoll was her team leader. He was a gruff man, but Tessa trusted him completely. He was one of the toughest people she knew and cared deeply about those under his command.

'There are two vehicles parked out back of the old Williams storehouse.'

'Which is supposed to have been abandoned years ago.'

'Yes, boss.'

'You're sure these aren't squatters? New Age hippies?'

'In 2019- and 2020-registered motors? I don't think so, boss.'

'I withdraw the question. Don't do anything. I'll send a car out with support.'

'You want me to stand down until they arrive?'

'I do. Return to your vehicle until your colleagues get there.'

'Copy that, boss.'

The line went dead, and Tessa was about to return to the Capri when she heard a sound that stopped her in her tracks. For a moment she froze all over again, and tears actually sprang unbidden to her eyes.

What she heard was a child crying: plaintive, lonely, bereft. The sounds echoed out of the broken windows of the old building, rising and falling for a moment before they seemed to dwindle away.

Tessa Burns knew the emotions that cry embodied all too well. She'd felt them at key moments in her own childhood, times when it seemed the darkness would consume her. And she couldn't ignore the little girl who was being held against her will in that devastated building, alone and afraid. Not for a moment longer.

The fear came back then in a surge of white-knuckle terror. But now she swallowed it down quickly, and something clicked in her head and she was no longer the day-to-day version of Tessa Burns, the woman who liked bourbon creams and listened to AC/DC at full volume and drank far too much Barry's tea. When that 'click' occurred, she was someone else, someone who felt the fear but was able to set it aside and deal with it later. Now she could do what needed to be done, whatever it involved.

Reaching inside her leather jacket, she took her Sig Sauer P226 from its shoulder rig and made for the nearest door.

There was no going back now.

2

The door was, of course, locked when she got to it.

Taking a step back, she aimed her right foot at a spot just below the handle and, using her heel as a battering ram, delivered as powerful a kick as she could. All this achieved was to send jarring vibrations right up her leg and into her hip, causing her to swear under her breath and limp about for a couple of uncomfortable seconds until the limb stopped throbbing and proper sensation returned.

Tessa was five feet six inches in height and weighed about 130 pounds – a little over nine stone. At first she thought the door had been built to withstand a blow from a much larger person, but then she realised it was a fire door, made of reinforced material, and probably would have held against a kick by the Incredible Hulk.

For a moment it looked as if this was going to be a completely ineffectual rescue attempt, but then Tessa, knowing there was no other option, pointed her Sig at the locking mechanism and fired three shots directly into it.

They'll know I'm coming now, she thought, *but they'd know quickly enough anyway.*

The door swung open, carried by its own weight, and she stepped inside.

The porch widened onto a long, narrow corridor, the floor tiles cracked and dusty, cobwebs that clung to the ceiling billowing in the breeze from outside. Tessa, her gun held in front of her in a shooter's stance, covered the length of the hall in four long strides. At the other end was an opening – Tessa saw when she got there that the door was missing.

She hung back, just inside the frame, and called: 'Hello? This is the Gardai. I am requesting you identify yourselves.'

No reply was forthcoming.

'I repeat, I am a member of the Garda Síochána – if you have weapons, put them down now. I'd prefer not to hurt anyone. Let's do this peacefully, shall we?'

Still no response.

'Okay, I'm coming in. Don't do anything stupid, all right?'

Instinctively she squatted and tentatively edged outwards.

Which was wise, because before she'd gone more than a couple of inches, a barrage of gunfire shattered the silence of the old building and tore up the wood of the door frame above Tessa's head.

She flung herself back the way she'd come, landing on her arse amid the dirt and debris of the floor. Her ears were ringing from the gunfire, and nervous sweat was running down her face into her eyes, and for a terrible instant she was both deaf and blind.

No, no, no, no, she thought, *it can't end like this. I will not go out like this!*

Somehow, above the echoing thunder of the shooting, she heard steps coming towards her. Using her sleeve to clear her eyes of the perspiration, she brought the Sig up so it covered the opening in front of her. The man who burst into the space was tall, lean and carrying a semi-automatic weapon.

She saw him raise it to his shoulder and fired instinctively, keeping her shots tightly packed and low, taking out his right knee. The man screamed and convulsed, firing a burst into the ceiling.

In a trice, Tessa was up, and she scuttled forward, grabbing the Heckler & Koch from the man and, almost in the same motion, clubbing him on the temple with the butt of the weapon.

This action took only moments, but they were seconds that might have killed her.

She had just straightened up when she heard a scuffling sound, and then she got a quick glimpse of a broad, dark-faced man in a black T-shirt and jeans who thudded into her, wrapping an arm about her shoulders and pinioning her arms. The force of the collision knocked Tessa backwards, right over his accomplice. For a second time, she landed on her back on the floor, and as well as the concussion, she felt a sharp pain in her midsection, and realised she'd been cut.

Fuck. He's fast, she thought and did the only thing she could think of at such close quarters: she drew her head back and headbutted her assailant, catching him on the bridge of his nose with a satisfying crunch.

He swore but didn't release his grip, instead shifting his weight so his right arm had more room to move, and there was another sharp pain and Tessa knew she'd been stabbed again. Panicking, she smashed her head forward once more, harder this time, and now she felt a wetness as the man's nose gave way and blood gushed forth.

Then he sagged, slumping onto his side.

Tessa, grunting with the effort, shoved him off her and struggled painfully up, taking a moment to examine her wounds.

Lifting her Metallica T-shirt, she saw there was a shallow slash across her lower abdomen and a deeper puncture wound just below her sternum. It was bleeding profusely, and she knew she had to staunch it or she wouldn't be any use to the child she was trying to help.

She shrugged off her jacket and used her teeth to rip the short sleeve of her T-shirt off, then tore a narrow strip off it. Rolling it into a ball but leaving one strand loose, she gritted her teeth and used her index finger to push the makeshift packing material into the hole the knife had made, as she'd been taught while in the army.

The pain was so great she thought she might pass out, and the world swam before her, but after a time the nausea and giddiness passed, and she thought she'd be able to remain upright. Taking a breath, she checked both men were unconscious before moving out of the safety of the doorway.

3

The room beyond was long and wide, taking up most of the ground floor of the building, and had once been used to store sheet metal. Now it was simply a wide, empty space that stretched into shadow at its furthest extremities. Tessa didn't like it – it offered no cover whatsoever, though neither could she see anywhere from which to launch a sneak attack.

So that was something.

Deciding that if the area had to be crossed, it was best to get it done quickly, Tessa broke into a run and sprinted towards the opposite end, at which she could see three doors and a stairwell that ran up the wall to what looked to be office space. The action caused the raw edges of the stab wound to grind against the packing, and the slash across her midsection stretched and clenched with the movement of her muscles.

The pain was shocking, but Tessa was in another place now and felt it only as a dull roar at the back of her mind. Her focus was elsewhere, because as she began to run, she heard the child again. This time the cries were even more urgent, and with a final burst of speed, she made it to the stairwell.

The crying seemed to be coming from somewhere above her, and this was the only access point she could see. Sweat beaded her brow and her T-shirt was sticky with blood, yet she took the stairs three at a time, and when she got to the top had to hold on to the rail for dear life to stop herself teetering backwards as her vision pinwheeled and stars exploded in front of her eyes momentarily.

She leaned over and threw up a mixture of blood and bile all over her boots, and then felt a bit better.

Gripping her gun with fingers moist with blood and sweat, she tested the handle on the door in front of her. It opened easily. Inside was the remains of an office – a desk, some empty document trays and an overturned chair.

Tessa stood in the dusty darkness for a moment, taking shallow breaths. The building had fallen silent, but then the child cried out again, the wail this time cutting out in a strangled gasp, and the detective rushed across the room to a door at the other side.

'Gardai – I'm coming in!' she shouted, banging on the door twice with her fist.

Her voice sounded odd to her, as if it was coming from somewhere far away, almost like it was drifting up through deep water.

Once again there was no response. Tessa stepped back, kicked open the door and lurched in, gun first.

And there was little Bettina Watson.

The child was small for her five years, and her dark hair was tied back in a ponytail, though strands had come loose and were sticking out at odd angles. She was wearing grubby pyjamas that had a picture of Paddington Bear on the front and was sitting on a stained duvet in the corner of the room, clutching a ragged-looking stuffed bear and, just briefly, Tessa wondered if it might be Paddington too. If so, his coat and hat were missing, and then she thought it was probably just a generic bear. After all, what was Paddington without his outfit? The same as any other bear, that's what.

Tessa recognised her thoughts were beginning to ramble and that probably meant she was in shock. She needed to get things resolved – and fast.

Sitting right beside the child on the duvet was a slim woman in a green tracksuit. She had long blonde hair, a sharp, chiselled face, and she was holding a knife to Bettina's neck. She smiled at Tessa and wiggled the blade back and forth for a moment in the air as a gesture of greeting, before placing it back against the child's skin.

To the left of the duvet, in the opposite corner of the room, was a tall, grey-haired man in a leather jacket and black jeans. He was holding a gun but loosely at his side rather than at arms, like Tessa. Which spoke of an arrogance that meant the man was either a serious threat or a complete liability to the woman with the child on the duvet. It was safer to err on the side of him being dangerous.

'You've come alone,' the woman said. 'That was dumb.'

'I'm just the front-of-house cop,' Tessa said, trying not to swoon. 'The others are just outside.'

'You're lying,' the woman said.

She had a foreign accent, Scandinavian perhaps, and Tessa could see, where the kidnapper's sleeve had pulled up as she held the knife, what looked to be the marks of a needle. Eyeing the woman more closely, the detective saw shadows under her eyes and how hollow her cheeks were. Was she sick? An addict? Self-harming? It was impossible to tell.

'They wanted me to come in and see what the situation was. Try to talk to you first.'

'And how has that gone for you so far?'

'I'm here, aren't I?'

'Though not looking very healthy.'

The world seemed to turn over on itself all of a sudden, and Tessa, in spite of herself, stumbled and would have fallen if her shoulder hadn't collided with the wall. The grey-haired man moved as if to grab her, and she brought the gun up.

'Get *back*,' she said, and her voice sounded steadier than she felt.

She kept her eyes on Grey-Hair but spoke to the woman.

'I'm not leaving without Bettina. So as a member of the Special Detective Unit tasked with bringing this matter to closure, I'm requesting you place her in my charge.'

'And are you going to arrest us?'

'All I care about is the child.'

'But we took her. Held her against her will. I mean, look, I have a blade to her throat. I could open her up at any minute.'

Tessa threw a glance at the little girl, who seemed to have lapsed into a catatonic state.

'I'm not leaving without her.'

The woman laughed – a dry, unpleasant sound.

'You're here alone,' she said, 'but I'll bet you've already informed the other little piglets that we're here, so they *will* be coming. Which means we should be on our way as soon as we can.'

'You'll be quicker without Bettina.'

'Do you think?'

'I do. And I won't let you leave with her. I said I'm not walking out of here without her, and I meant it.'

The woman smiled a wicked smile.

'I hear you,' she said, running a pale tongue across thin lips. 'George and me will make sure you both go together.'

Tessa saw the woman's arm tense as she began to put pressure on the knife, and the child wailed, and without pausing, Tessa shot the blonde woman in the head, knocking her backwards, the knife flying from her hand and across the room. As the detective fired, the grey-haired man did too, aiming at the wounded Tessa.

She was prepared, however, and as soon as she'd squeezed the shot off, she dropped to the floor and rolled. The bullet whizzed over her, thudding into the wall. Tessa came to a stop on her back, the Sig aimed upwards at her attacker.

She pumped three shots into his chest in quick succession, and he fell without a sound.

The shots echoed about the small, filthy room, reverberating like thunder, and finally they were gone, and all Tessa could hear was the sobbing of the child and her own raspy breathing.

She thought at first that she wouldn't be able to move, but she found the strength somewhere and rolled over, so she was gazing at the little girl.

'Are you okay?' she asked.

Bettina nodded. Tears were streaming down her grubby face, and there was a spray of red on her shoulder from the woman, but other than that, she seemed none the worse for wear.

'I'm a police officer,' Tessa said. 'I'm going to take you out of here and to your mam and dad, okay?'

That quick little nod came again.

Somehow, Tessa Burns got herself standing. She would have liked to carry the child, but she knew that would be way beyond her capabilities. So hand-in-hand they gingerly made their way back down the steps and across the huge storage area. The two fallen men were still as Tessa had left them, and then she and Bettina were outside, blinking in the sunlight.

'What in the name of all that is good and holy happened to you?'

Tessa turned slowly to see Sergeant O'Driscoll approaching her, resplendent in body armour and carrying a shotgun, five similarly clad detectives behind him.

'It became clear to me that waiting was no longer an option,'

Tessa said, and then her legs went out from under her, and the
sarge somehow managed to catch her.

   And she knew no more for a time.

4

The next twenty-four hours were largely lost to Tessa.

Most of it was merciful darkness, but there were frightening, uncomfortable periods where she came partly awake, and in those periods there were bright lights, and voices and pain. Somewhere in the recesses of her mind where her consciousness had gone to dwell, she knew she was in hospital and the doctors were working on her, but that didn't make these gulfs of time any more pleasant.

And at some stage during the ordeal, Tessa dreamed.

Which was odd in itself, because Tessa Burns rarely dreamed. But when she did, it was almost always the same one. Which wasn't really a dream at all. It was a memory.

A vivid recollection of her home, at least the one she'd lived in for the first part of her life. Of her father and mother. Both of whom had died when she was ten years old.

And the dream that was a memory was more than a memory. It's as if she is back there, and it's all happening again.

Tessa is sitting with her father in his office in the old house in Ranelagh, on the Southside of Dublin City. Her father is perched in a high-backed leather chair, clattering at the keys on a Hewlett-Packard desktop computer. Tessa is seated beside him in a chair her dad built for her himself, and they upholstered together using green felt that had orange stars dotted across it. Tessa thinks it very pretty but in a grown-up sort of way.

The room smells of cigar smoke – her father smokes one half-corona on Friday evenings, lighting up as he listens to gypsy jazz, usually something from the guitarist Django Reinhardt. For the rest of her life, Tessa will never hear jazz guitar without thinking of her father.

Paul Burns is a former Irish Army Ranger who's worked for the Department of Justice as a security consultant since he demobbed ten years ago. He often goes to his office after dinner to finish up whatever odds and ends of work he has to do, and Tessa usually goes in with him to keep him company. While he works, she pretends to do homework or some other project for school, but more often than not she's barely paying any attention to what she's supposed to be doing.

She's simply enjoying being in this room, with its framed photographs of soldiers on the wall, its shelves heavy with books, an antique musket hanging above the desk, its barrel filled with lead so it wouldn't be a danger to the boisterous young girl who (despite being told not to) has taken it down on more than one occasion just to be sure it can't be fired.

These evening sojourns are always relaxed, happy events, but tonight, Tessa can sense something unusual in her father's demeanour. He's on edge, nervous. She isn't sure how she knows this, because her dad hasn't said anything, and his eyes, dark under bushy eyebrows, remain on the screen as usual, his long slender fingers still dancing across the keys with easy dexterity.

But there's a tension in how he's sitting. He keeps checking his watch, and Tessa notes that every now and again he reaches into the drawer to the right of him, which is slightly open, as if to check something is in there. Eight o'clock passes, and for some reason, as if this is an important watershed moment, Tessa senses her father relax. She reckons that perhaps he's been waiting for an awkward phone call that is now not going to come.

Tessa knows her dad does difficult work. He doesn't talk about his time in the army much, but sometimes, when they're watching the news and a story about political unrest in some other part of the world comes on, she's conscious of something dark passing over him. It's as if a part of her father she doesn't really know comes alive, and it makes her sad, because she loves her dad dearly and hates to think of him unhappy or unsettled.

She's always mindful that the work her father does still brings him in contact with dangerous people and that a big part of his responsibilities involves keeping Ireland and everyone who lives there safe from things she's far too young to fully understand.

Tessa thinks that whatever has been bothering her father on this particular evening must have been related to this aspect of his work, but she's relieved to see the tension leave him and hopes he'll be finished in the office soon, so they can go out to the sitting room, where she knows he'll pull down a book from the shelf and read aloud to her before bed.

The book will be one of the adventure novels her father loved as a child: *Treasure Island* or *The Jungle Book* or *The Last of the Mohicans* or 20,000 *Leagues Under the Sea* or any of the rollicking stories he adored sharing with her.

And Tessa knows this is a special thing only she and her dad share.

No one else in her class knows who D'Artagnan is. When she'd tried to tell her best friend, Harry, about Allan Quatermain and explain what King Solomon's mines were, he'd looked at her blankly. And then she'd understood this was something niche, a sort of nerdy interest, and that had made her love these books and their exotic, richly textured tales even more.

Last night they'd begun *Tarzan of the Apes*, by Edgar Rice Burroughs. Tessa had seen the Disney animated version, but the story her father had started reading her was very different – much darker and more exciting. She's looking forward to finding out what happens to the infant Lord Greystoke when the Mangani, the tribe of great apes, adopt him.

She's just yawning, hoping her dad will notice and suggest they adjourn to the living room for their evening story, when the doorbell sounds.

'I'll get it,' Tessa says, jumping from her chair.

She assumes it's a delivery of some kind, or maybe someone collecting money for charity, and wants to get it dealt with quickly so they can get on with the adventures of the orphaned young Englishman, at the mercy of wild apes in the jungles of the Dark Continent.

'No!' her father says, his tone much sharper than she's used to.

It causes her to freeze, and she looks at him aghast, thinking she must have angered him in some way.

He recognises the hurt in her eyes and says, softening his voice: 'I'll go. Would you do something for me?'

'Of course, Da.'

'You know the cupboard over there, where I keep my files?'

She nods. There's a space about the size of an old-fashioned telephone box built into the wall right behind where they're sitting. It has three shelves, and her father uses it to store documents, boxes of papers and professional books about things like strategy and leadership and other things Tessa isn't sure she fully understands.

'Do you know what a bolthole is?'

She thinks about that for a moment. 'Is it like a hideout?'

'Yes, just like that. Would you see if there's space for us to build one in there?'

'You want me to look?'

'I want you to see if you can fit inside and close the door after you. Stay in there, and I'll check when I come back.'

Tessa shrugs. 'I can do that.'

'I think there's some boxes of old reports on the floor in there. Once you're in, you can pull those in front of you. They'll make it hard for anyone to see you when you're in there.'

The doorbell sounds again. Footsteps thud quietly on the stairs as Tessa's mother, who's been having a bath, begins to descend.

'I'll get the door, Bernadette,' her dad calls. 'I think it's for me.'

'Okay, love.'

'Off you go,' he says. 'I'll be back to check how you're doing in a moment.'

He opens the drawer and takes something from it, but Tessa doesn't see what it is, and then he walks briskly from the room.

The young girl trots over to the cupboard, opening the door and squatting down to peer inside. Her father is right – there are some cardboard storage boxes on the floor, but if she pushes them aside, there's certainly room for her to crawl in.

She does this, turning full circle to pull the door so it's almost closed. She doesn't want to shut it completely, as there would be no way for her to get back out, and even though she knows her dad will be returning, she still doesn't like the idea of being locked in there with no escape until someone releases her.

Once the door is as closed as she's comfortable with, she pushes the boxes back in front and waits. The space is almost completely dark other than a small crack of light from the door. It smells of dust and old paper, a not wholly unpleasant aroma. The lowest shelf is a couple of inches from her head where she's kneeling, so Tessa is reasonably comfortable.

Suddenly she hears raised voices: her father's and a man's she doesn't know. What are they arguing about?

She strains her ears, trying to hear. She discerns her father saying: 'No! This is not acceptable! I... we had an understanding!'

Tessa isn't afraid. She believes her dad can handle any situation, and at that moment is more curious than anything else. But then she hears something that does alarm her, a sound she's never heard before: it's her mother crying.

She crouches in the shadows, listening in horror, and is reaching to drag the boxes away so she can get out to comfort her mam when the first gunshot sounds. At first she doesn't know what the bang is, but then a second one rings out, then a third and a fourth. And by the time the house descends into an echoing silence, she knows what she's heard.

There are no more voices now. Just the ringing in her ears from the percussions.

She realises she is terrified.

Her heart is beating so hard, she's convinced it'll actually jump out of her chest. She has no idea it's even possible to be so afraid and still remain alive – it seems reasonable to her that she would surely die from sheer fright, but somehow, she doesn't.

There is no sound at all now. No voices, no movement, just the little bangs and sighs and thuds that an empty house makes.

She waits. She hopes.

Her father does not come back.

Finally, after what feels like forever, she gingerly pushes aside the boxes and, inching forward, edges open the door. Peering out, she sees the door to the study is open. Her father had closed it, and this strikes her as a good sign – surely it must be him who's opened it.

She crawls out of the storage cupboard and is standing in the open door, brushing herself down, when someone walks into her father's study with a calm assuredness.

This person is not her father.

He's tall, dressed in dark clothes and is holding a handgun, one which Tessa, at this stage in her life, thinks of as the kind of gun she's seen people on the television using but which she will later learn is called a Glock.

But that's not what frightens Tessa Burns to the point that she faints dead away.

What causes her mind to cave in upon itself is that this man has no face.

5

But that was in the past.

Tessa had much to deal with in the present.

Three weeks to the day she was admitted to hospital, Tessa Burns sat in a large, book-lined office in police headquarters in the Phoenix Park, Dublin. Sergeant O'Driscoll sat to her right, and on the other side of a huge dark wooden desk, drinking coffee from a mug which had the Wonder Woman insignia emblazoned upon it, was the Irish Police Commissioner, Dawn Wilson.

The commissioner was wearing the red-trimmed blue uniform of her office, and her red hair was tied back in a tight bun. She was seated, but Tessa had met her at a conference once before and knew she was over six feet in height, and had a reputation for being hands-on, not beyond throwing herself into the fray if she felt it was called for.

Dawn Wilson was known to be a crack shot and an expert in hand-to-hand combat. She was hugely respected among the rank and file, which was unusual for someone in her position.

'DS Burns, thank you for coming to see me.'

'Thank you for inviting me, Commissioner.'

'I trust you've recovered from your injuries?'

'I'll have a couple more scars, but I'm pretty much mended,' Tessa said. 'Do you mind my asking why I'm here? The sarge has been pretty tight-lipped.'

The commissioner grinned. 'Well, when one of my people puts their lives at risk to save a child from harm, I think it behoves me to bring them in for a cup of tea. Speaking of which, I haven't offered you any yet.'

'I'm fine, thank you, Commissioner.'

'Don't bullshit a bullshitter,' she replied.

She had a soft Northern Irish accent, which invested everything she said with a faint hint of irony.

'I've done my due diligence, and I hear on the grapevine you're a heavy consumer of Barry's tea.'

Tessa laughed. 'Guilty as charged.'

'Right, well let me get you fixed up. Sergeant, will you join us in something?'

'I wouldn't say no to a mug of coffee, Commissioner.'

'Coming up.'

Tessa expected Dawn to pick up the phone and order the drinks, but instead she got up and walked around the desk to a small table set between two bookcases behind them, upon which sat an electric kettle, a Nespresso machine and a mini-fridge, along with a ramekin with sachets of sugar and a large blue tin with a picture of the Justice League of America, DC's superhero team, on the lid.

'I suppose you know that Bettina Watson is doing very well,' Dawn said as she busied herself making the drinks. 'She's seeing a play therapist and still has some stuff to deal with, but she's a resilient wee thing and is bouncing back mightily.'

The Nespresso machine hissed as it did its business.

'I'm very glad to hear it,' Tessa said.

'There's no doubt at all in my mind she wouldn't be with us if you hadn't intervened,' Dawn went on. 'The two men you... incapacitated folded like nervous poker players under questioning. That little girl was to be killed before they disappeared into the night.'

'What was their plan in the long run?'

'To create chaos by bringing about another economic crash,' Dawn said. 'SuperFlight, the airline Watson pretty much owned, is one of the biggest and most lucrative companies based here in Ireland. By causing its stock to plummet, they thought they could tip us into a financial meltdown.'

'Couldn't they still do that?' Tessa asked.

'The forensic accountants and financial boffins are working on it as we speak,' Dawn said. 'There are people who understand the ins and outs of all that jazz, but I'm not one of them. I'm told the situation is salvageable. With Greta Bunchen dead, the head has been cut off the snake. They've been defanged, so to speak.'

'And who was the grey-haired man?'

'George Holmes. Bunchen's enforcer. As dangerous a bloke as you're likely to meet of an evening. Not many have seen his face and walked away.'

The commissioner strode over and placed a mug in front of Sergeant O'Driscoll and another in front of Tessa. A jug of milk and the ramekin of sugar were also deposited on the desk, along with some spoons and the blue tin, which, Tessa saw once the colourful lid was removed, contained a selection of biscuits, among which were her beloved bourbon creams. Tessa happily took one before adding milk to her tea.

'I've read your file, DS Burns,' Dawn said. 'But do you mind if I ask you some questions?'

'Not at all.'

'Good. Can we dispense with the formalities? I'd be happy for you to call me Dawn, but I'm told I shouldn't encourage it. So most call me boss. Can I call you Tessa?'

'Of course you can, boss.'

'Could you tell me about the circumstances of your parents' deaths?'

Tessa drank some tea and sighed. 'Boss, before I came to the Gardai, I was in the Irish Army. When I signed on, I was asked to talk to a shrink, and I did, and she found me okay to join up. I was with the armed forces for nine years, and I saw action in Kosovo and Iraq and Uganda. When I'd served my time, I applied to join the Gardai. It was during one of the recruiting drives. And I spoke to *another* shrink. And he found me okay too. I've never made a secret out of what happened to my folks. Why do you want me to talk about it now?'

'Commissioner,' Sergeant O'Driscoll said gently, 'I think what DS Burns is saying is that everything you want to know is already on her file. Maybe you have a specific question about some point of what happened?'

'Stand down, Sarge,' the commissioner said. 'Tessa, I want to know what makes you tick. I see a lot of myself in you, and I'm fascinated by it.'

Tessa took another biscuit and consumed half of it in one bite.

'My dad was in the army too,' she said. 'I think he was in the Rangers, but I'm not sure, because he didn't often talk about it. What I do know is that when he left the service, he set up a private security company, and he used to do a lot of work with various government agencies. He was involved with the Department of Justice, but he consulted with Defence too, and I seem to remember him looking at the safety protocols in the Central Bank at one stage as well. So he was important, was my dad.'

'Sounds like a good man,' Dawn said.

'He was. I loved him.'

'And your mum?'

'A schoolteacher.'

'That's important too,' Dawn observed. 'Maybe more so than what your dad did.'

Tessa shrugged.

'How did they die?' the commissioner asked.

'They were murdered.'

'And you were there,' Dawn prompted her.

'I was.'

'Did you see them being killed?' Dawn asked, almost as if she was talking to herself.

'No.'

'Do you know who killed them?'

'If you've read my file, you know I told the police they were murdered by a... by a man who had no face.'

Dawn pondered that. 'Do you mean he was scarred? That his face was damaged?'

'No. It was like... where his face was there was just... nothing. A blank space.'

The commissioner nodded. 'Have you given thought to the idea that you were so terrified, your mind has blocked out the man's features?'

'Of course I have. I've had loads of counselling, and all kinds of possibilities and theories have been put to me. And I don't rule any of them out completely.'

'Do you have a theory you favour?'

Tessa picked up her mug and had a long drink of tea. 'There are two that make a lot of sense to me.'

'I'm listening.'

'The first is that the person was someone I knew and trusted, and seeing him and knowing what he'd done was so devastating, my mind edited his identity out.'

Dawn Wilson nodded her agreement. 'Seems plausible. And theory number two?'

'My parents really were killed by a man with no face.'

The commissioner sat back in her chair. 'What did this Faceless Man do when he walked in and found you?'

'He stood there, very quietly,' Tessa said. 'I was so scared I actually fainted, and when I came round, I'd wet myself too. He just looked at me, even though he didn't have any eyes, and I suppose he must have turned around and walked out. I didn't hear the front door open or close, but when I came back to myself and plucked up the courage to move out of the room, he wasn't there anymore, and my mam and dad were both dead. They'd been shot, both twice, one to the head, one to the chest.'

'Whoever did it knew what they were doing,' Dawn observed.

'They did,' Tessa agreed. 'It looks like the work of a trained killer. I've often wondered if it was a contract killing. I was told later it was a robbery that went wrong. But I never believed that.'

'You were suddenly an orphan,' Dawn said, moving the conversation onwards. 'What happened to you?'

'None of my extended family were in a position to take me in,' Tessa said, 'so I was placed in care.'

'Foster care?'

'No. I was too old for anyone to be interested in having me join their family. I spent the next eight years in a series of residential care homes.'

'What was that like?'

Tessa shrugged. 'Sometimes it was okay. Mostly it was horrible. I survived. That's all that matters.'

'You joined the military right out of school?'

'Yes. Dad didn't talk about it much, but when he did, it was always with a lot of fondness. He called them his family. I didn't have one anymore, so it seemed a good idea.'

'I can see how it would,' Dawn said. 'Did you like it?'

'I loved it. It was simple, direct, all about setting clear goals and achieving them. I liked that. In care nothing was ever straightforward, and I could never work out how to please either the other kids or a lot of the staff. In the army, if you followed orders and looked after your kit, you were rewarded. Praised.

Accepted. It was a huge relief to me to finally find a place where people did what they said they were going to do, and hard work and consistency were the most valuable currency. And loyalty.'

'So I can take it those are qualities you value?' Dawn asked. 'Hard work, consistency and loyalty?'

'Those,' Tessa said. 'And kindness. I think kindness is probably the thing I value more than any other.'

'You bring all that into your policing?'

'She does,' Sergeant O'Driscoll said. 'I can attest to that without hesitation.'

'Do you like being a member of the force?' the commissioner asked.

'Very much,' Tessa said.

'Why?'

'I believe I can make a difference. Help people.'

'That's it? No spiel about upholding law and order, keeping the chaos at bay, making sure what happened to you doesn't happen to anyone else?'

Tessa smiled sadly. 'Well all of that is nice, but if I'm holding back a sea of lawlessness, I'm doing it one criminal at a time.'

'Don't be modest,' Dawn said. 'You just took out four single-handed.'

Tessa realised she was blushing and for the first time looked away from the commissioner. 'I was just doing my job, boss.'

'Oh, stop being coy,' Dawn said. 'So here's why I asked to see you. You're aware there was an investigation into the Williams warehouse incident.'

'Of course. I discharged my firearm a number of times, which resulted in two injuries and two deaths.'

'All of which were deemed justifiable by the investigators. So you, DS Burns, are cleared to return to active duty.'

'Thanks, boss. I can't wait to get back to the unit.'

Dawn held up her hand. 'Hold your horses, Detective,' she said. 'Are you sure that's where you want to be?'

Tessa narrowed her eyes at the commissioner. 'I don't follow, boss.'

'You're a hero now. I mean, I'm going to have to arrange some kind of medal or other. But in the meantime, I want to promote you. I'll need to process some paperwork, but I'm giving you the rank of detective inspector, and I'm also going to let you choose any job you want. Wherever or whatever that is.'

Tessa opened her mouth, but no words came out.

'You can take some time to think about it,' Dawn said. 'I know it's a big decision.'

'I... I don't need to,' Tessa said. 'I know what I want to do. I just... I just don't think the position exists is all.'

Now it was Dawn's turn to look puzzled. 'Well if you tell me what it is, I can tell you if you're right.'

So Tessa did.

And by the time she left the commissioner's office, a new post had been created for her.

PART ONE

THE WITNESS

6

At 8.30 a.m. on the day after Tessa Burns met Dawn Wilson and received a promotion and her new post, a Garda patrol car pulled into the front yard of a farmhouse just outside the village of Mullan in County Monaghan. The property, consisting of twenty acres of low-lying arable land, was owned by the Connolly family: Joe and Daisy, a young couple in their thirties, and Aisling, their daughter, who was seven.

The patrol car was driven by Garda Bob O'Connor, who that day was being shadowed by trainee Garda Fiona Mooney.

'A call came through to the station in Monaghan town at 0630 hours that there was something wrong out on the Connolly farm,' O'Connor said as he got out of the car.

He was a tall, stocky young man with a shaven head, his jaw showing the blue shadow of a beard.

'Did the caller say what they meant by that?' Cadet Mooney asked.

'No. But the dispatcher says they were in some level of distress.'

'Do you know the Connollys?'

'I've never had any dealings with them personally, but Joe

has a reputation for... well, he's known to produce a wee bit of moonshine. Rotgut, like.'

Cadet Mooney grinned. She was a slight, red-haired girl with a spray of freckles across her nose.

'He brews poitín,' she said, using the Irish name for home-produced whiskey. 'That's hardly a big crime now, is it? I mean, how many lads tried their hand at making their own beer or wine during the lockdowns? Like, it's more or less the same thing and doesn't make him a criminal mastermind, does it?'

'Whatever mine or your opinion might be, the production of poitín for anything other than your own use is against the law, so regardless of how many people are doing it, the Gardai don't condone the practice. And Joe Connolly was doing a bit more than making a few bottles to sip after his evening meal. He's rumoured to be making the stuff to a very high quality and on a grand scale.'

'Seriously?'

'The local vice squad has been on to him for a few years now but have never been able to pin anything on him. But word on the jungle grapevine is that he's supplying a lot of the new hipster bars all over Ireland; you know, the kind that serve artisan spirits and all of those trendy craft beers.'

Cadet Mooney whistled through her teeth. 'So we're looking at a high-end operation then?'

'Oh, we are. And it doesn't end there. One of the vice detectives, Robinson, thinks the Connollys have been exporting. Sending the stuff to specialist drinking establishments abroad. Which means they've established international lines of distribution.'

They were standing at the front door, and O'Connor rapped smartly.

The farmhouse was a three-storey affair, built from grey stone and standing at the end of a long driveway, about half a kilometre from the road. The fields the family owned spread out around it in a panoply of browns, greens and rust, and a low, whistling wind seemed to gust about the two police officers as they waited for an answer.

A blue Skoda Kodiaq was parked in a space to the left of the front door.

'That their vehicle?' Cadet Mooney asked.

''Tis,' O'Connor said.

'Do they own a second car?'

'Not that I know of, but they would have farm machinery. At least one tractor.'

'There are a few sheds in the field behind the house,' Mooney said. 'Will I go and check?'

O'Connor banged on the door again, louder this time.

No answer was forthcoming, so he opened the letter box and called in: 'Gardai! Is there anyone at home?'

All they could hear in response was the wind over the fields, whistling through the whin and bramble bushes that acted as boundaries to the land. There were four windows, two on either side of the front door. They opened onto what looked to be a study, a living room, a dining room and a sparsely decorated bedroom, probably a spare. None of these revealed signs of life.

'I don't think anyone's home,' Mooney said.

'Let's check around the back,' O'Connor said.

They followed the path that traced the perimeter of the building. The windows at the rear displayed an equally empty kitchen, utility room and pantry.

'They might have gone on holiday,' Mooney suggested. 'Got a taxi to town and then a bus to the airport.'

'Dispatch has been trying both of their phone numbers and they just ring out,' O'Connor said. 'I'm not sure that suggests a holiday.'

'Do we know who made the call to the station?'

Both Gardai were looking out over the fields that stretched into the distance behind the farmhouse. This part of the county was so flat, you could see for miles in every direction. Which would have been great if there was anything much to see: the landscape was an unending expanse of stubby grass and reeds, broken here and there by hedges of bramble and spiky whin. Pigeons dotted the pastures, every now and then rising into the air as something disturbed them – a fox or feral cat perhaps.

'A neighbour rang it in. Paddy Dorney.'

'And he was freaked out when he made the call, you say?'

'Yes. He's actually in the hospital now. Had some sort of meltdown. Isn't making sense.'

There was nothing to be said about that, so Cadet Mooney kept on looking out at the rambling, stubbled fields.

'Check the storage sheds,' O'Connor said finally.

'What are you going to do?' Mooney asked as she went off to do as she was asked.

'I'm going to break into the house and see what's what in there.'

'Aren't we supposed to have just cause to enter without the leave of the occupant?'

'I'll take full responsibility,' O'Connor said. 'I'm concerned, to be honest with you. It looks like the family have vanished, and I don't like it. Let's see what we can learn.'

7

Maggie Doolan surveyed the five people arrayed in front of her in the hall of the community centre in Ballymun, in Dublin. It was just after 8.30 a.m., and the self-defence class she taught every Wednesday before she went to work was almost finished.

What made this class different to most other martial arts training sessions was that students and teacher alike were all in wheelchairs. Not to mention the fact that a small black-and-white terrier-mix dog was watching proceedings from a pillow in the corner.

'Okay, let's go back over what we learned today,' Maggie said. 'First of all, what is our first line of defence against an attacker?'

Maggie was thirty-two years old, slim and angular, her auburn hair tied in high ponytail. Her face showed the deep laughter lines of someone who smiled often, and today she was wearing a grey tracksuit that did little to hide her bony knees.

Her wheelchair, which she had designed and worked on herself, was specially modified. A small computer sat on a platform at her right hand, and there was also a cradle for her mobile phone.

A middle-aged man put up his hand.

'Go on, Clark.'

'Our first line of defence,' Clark said, 'is that nobody expects us to fight back.'

'Spot on,' Maggie said. 'And if we *are* attacked, what is our most effective weapon?'

'The chair itself,' a girl with a frizz of curly hair said.

'Very good, Charlie,' Maggie said. 'Every single one of us has motorised wheelchairs, which are heavy and have low centres of gravity. They're also capable of rapid accelerations, and if aimed precisely can break someone's toe or crush their foot completely. But you can also strike an attacker in the shins with the footrest, which will hurt like hell, and armrests can be used to attack the groin area if you pivot the chair in just the right way. Of course, you don't need me to tell you that you only resort to these things if a quick escape isn't an option. Now, another important line of defence is to be prepared, so, if you have fine motor function and can use your fingers accurately, what can you do?'

A heavily set man raised his hand tentatively. His name was Cliff, and this had been his first session with Maggie.

'Have pepper spray?' he said uncertainly.

'Damn right,' Maggie said. She reached into a scabbard built into the right-side panel of her chair, one of its modifications, and produced an aerosol can. 'One blast of this into the face, and you'll stop most people in their tracks. Once they're distracted by the burning in their eyes, nose and mouth, you can make good your escape. Suppose you don't have good fine motor function though and can't use a can of pepper spray?'

'Use an alarm,' Billy, an elderly man said.

'Good man, Bill. I have one built into my chair,' Maggie said, indicating a button she had situated on the left armrest. 'And I recommend getting one installed. They're loud.'

She hit hers and for a second a deafening whistling sound

filled the hall. Everyone covered their ears, and Maggie shut it off quickly.

'But that will deter most attackers right away. If it doesn't, you can use the chair to break their toes while they're covering their ears, and then make good your escape.

'Okay, so let's say none of those tactics has worked and you're reduced to hand-to-hand combat?'

'Give yourself the advantage of having a weapon to hand,' Debbie, a girl with tight cornrows said.

'One hundred per cent,' Maggie said, producing a telescopic baton from a scabbard beside her pepper spray. She whipped it once, and it extended to its full length. 'I can carry one of these because I'm a police officer and have a permit, which most civilians do not. All it really is, though, is a stick, and there's no law against having one of those to hand. What it does is give us an extended reach, and we can bring the fight to an attacker.'

'I think I'd be scared to do that,' Debbie said. 'The other things you've taught I could probably do, but actually fighting someone...'

'I'm suggesting it as an absolute last resort,' Maggie said. 'To be fallen back on only when everything else fails.'

'What if they're faster than me or stronger than me?' Billy asked. 'I don't see how a stick would help.'

'Maybe I can help Maggie demonstrate,' a voice said and, turning, everyone saw a woman standing in the doorway from the street.

She was of average height, with strong, handsome features and shoulder-length dark hair, and was dressed in a green parka jacket over a Tenacious D T-shirt, jeans and brown hiking boots.

'Ladies and gentlemen, this is my friend Detective Sergeant Tessa Burns,' Maggie said, grinning.

'That's Detective *Inspector* to you,' Tessa deadpanned, coming inside.

'Congratulations,' Maggie replied. 'Nice of you to drop by now you've joined the big leagues.'

'How could I forget my closest friend and associate,' Tessa said and without warning lunged at Maggie, coming in from her left side and making as if to grab her by the front of her tracksuit top.

The movement was so rapid and unexpected a gasp went up from the students, and Debbie actually cried out in shock. Maggie, however, didn't seem fazed. In a single fluid motion, she unsheathed the baton and flicked it open, whipping it back so it came to rest over her right shoulder. Tessa had managed to get a grip with her left hand, and Maggie lashed the baton down, lightly, across her knuckles. Without losing momentum, she followed this by whisking the stick back up and stopping it just before it would have connected with Tessa's temple.

The pair froze.

'Do you see what I did?' Maggie asked. 'No real strength was needed, just the presence of mind to remember what you were taught. The entire altercation took less than five seconds, but I guarantee you any attacker would probably have fractured knuckles and a concussion. And you wouldn't even have broken a sweat.'

'And if it was a male coming at you,' Tessa said, 'use your low height to go for a direct blow to the groin.'

She demonstrated by standing up again, and Maggie drove her elbow into where her friend's testicles would have been, had she possessed any.

'Remember, your elbow is always more effective than a fist. It's harder, can be propelled with much more force, and you won't break a finger or dislocate your thumb.'

'Couldn't you really hurt someone by doing that though?' Clive asked.

'That's kind of the point,' Maggie said. 'If you're in this situation, they want to hurt *you*. It's not time to start getting scruples over how to defend yourself. You've been chosen as a victim because someone thinks you're an easy target. They would think nothing of leaving you hurt and helpless on the side of the road. In circumstances like that, you need to do what you have to.'

There was a pause, and then Debbie started to clap, and soon everyone joined in.

The little black-and-white dog sat up straight for a moment, as if he was puzzled by the noise, then lay back down again.

'Okay, everyone, thus endeth the lesson,' Maggie said. 'See you all next week.'

The group filed out. As they did, Maggie said to Tessa: 'Thanks for that. A lot of people with physical disabilities find the idea of using force, even to defend themselves, a terrifying concept. They're conditioned by their condition and how society views it to be mild and passive. I spend a lot of time in these classes trying to get my students to unlearn that lesson.'

'Not easy,' Tessa said.

'No. So, what brings you here? Not that I'm unhappy to see you.'

The dog had got up and wandered over, and was nuzzling Tessa's hand.

'Hey, Pavlov,' the detective said. 'I'm here to offer you a job, as it happens.'

'I already have a job. I'm a family liaison officer.'

'I've got something really exciting,' Tessa said. 'For you and Pavlov. Let's go and get a cup of coffee and I'll tell you.'

8

Garda Bob O'Connor used the handle of his torch to break a glass panel in the front door of the farmhouse and then carefully reached in and turned the handle, marvelling that for a family that was allegedly so involved in a criminal enterprise, security was so poor on their farm: no alarms sounded, not even a dog barked. He stepped inside the hallway and knew immediately from the sense of the house that no one was there – that nervous, edgy feeling buildings get when they're unoccupied was very much in evidence.

He moved through the rooms quickly, every now and then calling out to identify himself. There were mugs in the sink in the kitchen, and upstairs he found clothes on the bedroom floors, in both what was obviously the parents' bedroom and the room that had to have been the little girl's.

There was a trapdoor in the ceiling on the second floor. O'Connor found a hook leaning against the wall on the landing and used it to pull it open, and a folding staircase came down with it. He climbed up and found an attic space, tidily stacked with all sorts of odds and ends. Much of it seemed to be the usual boxes of papers, old electrical gear and some stuff (bottles and piping) he took to be orphaned bits of distilling equipment. And there, right against the south wall of the house, stacked up into the roof space, was a pile of suitcases.

Whoever had put them there and had arranged the other detritus in the attic had done so with an eye for detail, packing everything in so not a bit of space was wasted. Each suitcase and bag was in its place, and none had been removed so far as O'Connor could see. He carefully checked the rest of the piles stored there, but could see no other signs of luggage.

Climbing back down to the second floor, he went back into the bedrooms to see if any might have been kept there, but there didn't seem to be any in evidence.

A look through the wardrobes and cupboards didn't suggest any clothes had been taken, and the bathroom revealed three toothbrushes, and nothing seemed to be missing that should have been there. O'Connor knew some people kept separate wash gear especially for trips, but he didn't think the Connollys were that type of family, although with their alleged export trade, who knew.

He heard Cadet Mooney coming in downstairs and went down to meet her.

'If a tractor or any other piece of farm machinery that might be used as transport has been taken, I can't see from where,' she said.

O'Connor nodded and wandered into the living room.

'They're gone,' he said. 'But they've taken nothing. In fact, they seem to have just upped sticks and gone without warning or preparation.'

'Think they might be running from something?' Mooney asked. 'The business they're in might be dangerous.'

O'Connor considered this, and as he did, his eyes fell on the mantle over the fireplace.

'Maybe they didn't run...' he said and, leaning in, saw that there, on the place where the mantle met the wall, was what looked to be a bloody handprint, as if someone had hung on there to prevent themselves from falling.

As he examined the area, he saw that the wall and the fireplace itself were all spattered with a fine spray of blood.

'What are you saying?' Mooney asked.

'I think they were taken,' O'Connor said. 'We'd better ring this in. And, Fiona, touch nothing else, okay? We're now standing in a crime scene.'

9

Tessa and Maggie went to a café up the street from the community centre. The young guy behind the counter greeted the family liaison officer by name and didn't seem to have a problem with Pavlov sitting under the table at their feet.

'So what's this big, exciting opportunity?' Maggie asked when she had a hot chocolate, complete with whipped cream and marshmallows, in front of her and Tessa had a pot of boiling water, into which she put a Barry's teabag she pulled from her pocket – she'd learned she couldn't depend on places to stock the brand of tea she favoured so always brought her own along.

'I'm forming a team,' Tessa said. 'I want you to come and work with me as part of it. You and Pavlov, of course.'

'What exactly is this team going to do?'

'We're going to specialise in cases involving children or vulnerable adults,' Tessa said.

'As in kids who've committed crimes?' Maggie asked, spooning cream and melting marshmallows into her mouth. 'I mean, don't the usual police force deal with that, and then social services and the juvenile liaison office steps in? What exactly do you see us doing?'

'No. That's not it at all. I'm talking about cases involving missing kids, or children who've witnessed crimes, young people who've been accused of criminality but who are foundering in juvenile detention and shouldn't be there, maybe even cases where children have died because the system has failed them. I mean, you and I both know what it's like to be at the mercy of a bureaucracy that doesn't give a damn about you one way or another.'

Maggie smiled at her friend. 'This is a real passion project for you, isn't it?'

'It's what I've always wanted to do. You know that. No one was ever there to help me. I had to learn to do it for myself. I want to make sure the kids we encounter know there's someone on their side.'

'Like you were for me,' Maggie said.

Maggie had first met Tessa when they were briefly in the same residential unit. Tessa had been sixteen at the time, and Maggie ten. The unit specialised in kids who were intellectually gifted but had 'external problems' that impeded their capacity to learn. Tessa was there because of her history of residential placements breaking down due to her wilful conduct and refusal to follow rules she considered unfair or – as she was prone to put it at the time – 'just plain stupid'. Maggie had been sent for a brief stay to receive physical therapy due to her cerebral palsy, the condition that necessitated her being in the chair. The form of the disorder Maggie lived with was called ataxic cerebral palsy, which meant she had poor balance and coordination, though her intellectual functioning was unaffected.

In fact, her being in the unit meant she had, actually, tested in the top two percentile in the country. This fact seemed to have been lost on some of the other residents, however, who chose to bully Maggie terribly.

Tessa had ignored the jibes and name-calling the younger girl received, though it did surprise her that the staff appeared disinclined to do anything about it. When the attacks became physical, however, she could turn a blind eye no longer.

It happened in the playground.

Tessa had been sitting on the wall, thinking about what the therapist they had her seeing might like to hear so she could get out of this place and back to the usual crappy centres she'd become accustomed to. She was just reaching the conclusion she might have to start playing ball with the shrink when, from the corner of her eye, she noted Maggie trundling out of the main building in her chair.

In those days, the wheelchair Maggie was using was manual, so she had to turn the wheels herself. Her type of CP meant that her movements weren't precise (physiotherapy and a huge amount of determination helped Maggie to get the spasms she suffered largely under control as she grew older) and the chair moved in a lurching, stop-start motion as she painstakingly drove it forward.

Tessa noted the girl's presence and went back to her musings, but then she heard some shouting and a clattering sound and saw that a tall girl whose hair was dyed electric purple – Tessa thought her name was Patricia – had knocked Maggie out of her wheelchair and was leaning over her fallen victim.

'We all know you're faking it, spaz,' Patricia was shouting. 'Every one of us has seen you walk.'

'I can go short distances,' Maggie was saying, her voice teetering on the brink of tears. 'But even then I sometimes fall. Do you think I want to be in this thing?'

'You're a lazy fucking *spastic*,' Patricia intoned and delivered a kick to Maggie's stomach.

That was when Tessa decided she'd had enough.

She crossed the yard in seconds, and before Patricia had time to deliver a second blow, Tessa had spun her around and was nose to nose with her – well, almost, as the purple-haired bully was a head taller than her. Such things didn't bother Tessa. She'd brought down bigger during her six years in care. You just needed to know how.

'Leave her alone,' she said. 'The kid has a condition. Every single one of us is here for something, hers just happens to involve a wheelchair.'

'Go back to your wall,' Patricia said. 'You're only here as a charity case anyway. No one here gives a shite what you think, Little Orphan Annie.'

Tessa sighed and shook her head. 'I'm going to ask you one more time to leave Maggie alone.'

'And if I don't?'

'Then I'm going to have to make you.'

Patricia threw her head back and laughed, and Tessa hit her three times, fast, like a drumbeat, in the space just below her ribcage, causing her diaphragm to freeze. The air exploded from Patricia in a gust that smelled of cherry cola, and she fell to her knees, trying to suck air into lungs that, temporarily, didn't work.

Tessa stepped around her and righted the wheelchair, then helped Maggie get back into it.

'Jesus, what did you do to her? I think she's going to pass out,' one of Patricia's friends said in horror.

'Oh, don't be so dramatic,' Tessa replied and thumped the girl in the centre of her back with her fist, shocking the diaphragm back into action. The girl sucked in a deep breath of air with a sound that was almost a scream.

'Remember,' Tessa said, leaning down by Patricia's ear, 'I can do that to you any time I choose. So you don't want to piss me off. And if you lay a single finger on my friend Maggie here again, that will *seriously* piss me off.'

Winking at Maggie, she wandered back over to the wall and

hopped back up. Maggie watched her for a moment then trundled over too.

'Thank you for helping me.'

'No worries. Patricia needed to be taught a lesson in good manners. I was happy to do it.'

'No one has ever stood up for me like that before.'

'Maybe you need to learn to stand up for yourself,' Tessa had said.

Maggie hadn't known it at the time, but that was a big moment in her life. It changed everything.

She'd only stayed at the unit for another fortnight before returning to her parents, but she and Tessa had kept in touch and, as the years passed, had become close friends. In fact, Maggie thought of Tessa Burns as her best friend.

Other than Pavlov, obviously.

'I'll give you that,' she said. 'And this idea of yours has been approved?'

'By the police commissioner herself.'

'Who else is on board?'

'As of now, just you and me.'

'I haven't said I'm in yet.'

'No, but you will.'

'Okay. Supposing I said I was interested. Would you be *allowed* to have me? The only job on the force that will permit the employment of people with special needs is family liaison officer. Do you think the commish would agree to having me seconded?'

'You have a skillset the team needs,' Tessa said. 'You have degrees in psychology and sociology. You're a qualified therapist and, as we both know, you can kick ass too. The job you already do to a very high level proves you're great with kids. You are a no-brainer, as far as I'm concerned.'

'But will the commish sign off on my position?'

Tessa grinned. 'She already has.'

Maggie snorted and gave her friend a hard look. 'How did you know I'd agree?'

'You're painfully predictable,' Tessa said. 'Anyway, I'm only using you to get to Pavlov.'

'Everyone does,' Maggie said dolefully.

10

Forensics arrived to examine the farmhouse. Monaghan was approximately two hours' drive from Dublin, but it still took them six hours to get there after O'Connor made the call.

By then the Connollys had been missing for ten hours.

The living room was cordoned off with crime-scene tape and the blood spatters and handprint photographed before samples were taken for analysis. The rugs were combed for fibres and the furniture examined under black light for further fluids, and then pored over a millimetre at a time to find any other traces of who might have been there on the morning the family vanished.

Each room in the house was investigated with the same attention to detail, and as this was being done, another team, led by O'Connor, was searching the twenty acres of the property in the hope of finding some trace of the Connollys.

O'Connor broke the area down into grids of one square metre, and, moving forward in a line that stretched across the length of each field, members of the force, augmented by volunteers from the Garda Reserve, carefully searched every inch of the land the Connollys had lived on and farmed.

Every now and then someone would shout: 'Halt! Object in situ!' and the line would stop as the exact location of the find was marked with a small numbered plastic cone, and the item, whatever it was, was bagged and logged to be examined later. Most of these finds would prove to be junk, but you never knew what might offer a clue that could lead to the missing people being located.

Another team checked the storage sheds in the field right behind the house, and it was here that a further sign was found that suggested the Connollys might not have left voluntarily.

When they moved a large combine harvester, a trapdoor was revealed beneath it. It had been locked, but the padlock seemed recently broken, the wood pale and unweathered where the bolts had been ripped out. A steep metal stairwell led to a series of cellar rooms, which had obviously once been used for distillation but were now in complete disarray: tables over-turned, bottles and jars smashed, tubs of fermenting grain spilled and mixed with raw alcohol, and papers and other docu-ments torn and strewn about the place.

No one could tell if it was an act of wanton vandalism, if it was an attempt to put the Connollys out of business, or if the perpetrators were looking for something.

And if they were, had they found it?

11

Danny Murphy lay on his back and stared at the ceiling.

He was in a cell in the police station in Arklow, the station he had, up until the day before, been based at as a uniformed Garda. He doubted he would be called upon to return to that position, and in fact fully expected he would be spending at least the next couple of months in a prison cell.

Why he hadn't been moved to one before now he wasn't certain.

Danny wasn't naïve. He knew prison would be hell for a former cop and fully expected he was destined for the hardest time it was possible to serve. He knew he could survive: he was six feet four and weighed 240 pounds, putting him at a little over sixteen stone, all of which was muscle. He just didn't know if he wanted to.

All his life had been about being a cop. As a kid, he'd looked up to members of the force, seen them as people to be respected, emulated. Now he'd brought shame on the institute he'd been so proud to serve.

The light changed in quality as afternoon became evening. Danny didn't move. In the normal run of things he was a very active man, physically and mentally. If he wasn't working, this time of day would see him catching a hurried dinner before going to the gym or one of the many evening classes he liked to attend. Danny had a passion for criminology and read voraciously on the subject.

He'd hoped to one day become a detective and believed having an intricate knowledge of the history of crime and the myriad ideas about why people engaged in it could only be a valuable asset.

Such hopes were, he suspected, vain in the extreme now. Danny was pretty sure his career in law enforcement had come to an untimely but definitive end. All that was left was to learn what his fate would be. He hadn't been charged with anything yet, which seemed odd. There was no doubt he'd committed the crimes for which he was being held. He knew they could keep him for thirty-six hours, and that time was almost up.

He figured he'd be taken to his old sergeant's office before lights out and formally charged. He'd be brought to court the next day and transferred, probably to Wheatfield Prison in Dublin – Mountjoy, Ireland's main prison, would be too dangerous for him as a former Garda, although he knew Wheatfield would be no walk in the park either.

He closed his eyes and dozed for a while and was awakened by keys rattling in his cell door.

Here it comes, he thought. *Time to go and face the music.*

'Someone to see you, Murphy,' Garda Sykes, an old colleague of his said.

Sykes could barely make eye contact with him. Danny knew he was considered a Jonah now by his old co-workers; someone who'd permitted the darker aspects of the job to poison him and turn him into a weapon.

He rolled off his bunk, still wearing the blue shirt and woollen trousers of his uniform, and stood in stockinged feet –

they'd taken his boots – while Sykes handcuffed him and then padded up the corridor behind the other officer.

The sarge's office was situated just behind the station's front desk, and to Danny's surprise, the old man wasn't there. Instead, a woman who looked to be in her late thirties was sitting where the sarge usually sat. She was dressed in a green parka jacket over a T-shirt with some band name on it he didn't recognise.

'We can lose the cuffs, I think, Garda Sykes,' the woman said.

'He's a fucking wild man, ma'am, if you pardon my language,' Sykes said contemptuously.

'I'm known to be pretty wild myself when the mood takes me,' the woman said, her eyes on Danny the whole time. 'Are you going to give me any hassle, Garda Murphy?'

'I think I'm in enough trouble as it is,' Danny said.

'There you go,' the woman said to Sykes. 'Docile as a spring lamb.'

Muttering darkly, the older Garda removed Danny's restraints. 'Will I stand outside? Just in case.'

'I'll holler if I need you,' the woman said, and Sykes gave her a look of disdain and left them to it.

'Sit down, Garda Murphy.'

'I don't think I should be addressed by that title anymore,' Danny said.

'Have you been divested of your rank?'

'Not yet, but I reckon it's a matter of time.'

The woman flipped open a file and began to read aloud. 'Garda Daniel Murphy, you've been on the force for five years and have served with distinction during that time. It says here your parents died in a car accident when you were four years old.'

'I grew up in foster care,' Danny said.

'One family or several?' the woman asked.

'The first placement ended because Eileen, my foster

mother, got cancer. The second placement was with an older couple, and I think they just got fed up having a boisterous kid about the place. The third placement, which I went to when I was eight, kept me for the rest of my childhood, and I still consider them my family.'

'Did they support your decision to become a guard?'

'All the way. They're going to be... this is going to kill them.'

The woman pursed her lips and continued to riffle through his file.

'I didn't catch your name,' Danny said.

'I'm Detective Inspector Tessa Burns.'

'I haven't seen you in Arklow before.'

'I don't usually work here. I have, up until yesterday, been part of the Special Detective Unit, based out of Harcourt Street.'

'Why are the SDU involved in this?' Danny wanted to know.

It made no sense. His actions had been bad but not enough to create a national incident or untether the fabric of Irish society. Or at least he hoped they hadn't...

'The Special Detective Unit don't have a stake in your case. I'm not currently assigned to them.'

'Are you here to charge me then?'

'Tell me about what happened.'

'You've got my file in front of you.'

Detective Inspector Tessa Burns looked up at Danny, and her facial expression told him he'd better start talking.

'The day before yesterday my partner, Garda Tracy Jones, and I brought in a man, a Mr William Ennis, for questioning regarding the death of a neighbour's child, a three-year-old lad named Neil McGuinness.'

'I read about that in the newspapers,' Tessa said. 'The child had been missing for a few days, hadn't he?'

'He had. A man who was walking his dog came upon Neil's

body lying in a ditch half a mile from the housing estate where he lived. The medical examiner found that he'd been strangled to death, but before that he'd been... he'd been beaten and sexually assaulted.'

'Poor kid,' Tessa said.

'Tracy and I did the door-to-door. When we talked to William Ennis, he seemed like any concerned neighbour. Stated he'd seen the lad out playing on the street but had no dealings with him other than that.'

'I take it this proved not to be the case?'

'Have you ever investigated a death in a housing estate?'

'I have.'

'Then you know people are slow to open up. It was late on the first day that someone mentioned that William Ennis used to bring the kids into his house for ice cream.'

'Nothing so awful in that,' Tessa said.

'No. Nothing. We made a note of it and kept on with our investigation. But as the second day wore on, Ennis's name came up more and more often in relation to being overly familiar with the local kids. One mother told us her son, who was two, had disappeared and she'd spent hours looking for him and was about to call the police when one of the older kids informed her Ennis had taken him into his house. When she knocked, the man presented the kid immediately, but she told us the child was upset.'

'That's enough to warrant another chat with Mr Ennis,' Tessa said.

'We called again, and this time he was less welcoming. Tried to cut the interview short.'

'As is his right as an Irish citizen,' Tessa said.

'As I was leaving, I spotted something,' Danny continued as if she hadn't spoken. 'He had a pile of junk under the stairs. Odds and ends of cushions and bits of broken furniture. He'd tacked a bit of a blanket across the space to hide it, but a corner had fallen down and I caught a glimpse of what was behind.'

'What did you see?'

'What I took to be a child's T-shirt.'

'Did you think it belonged to Neil?'

'No. He had all his clothes on him when he was found. But I'd looked at the files of other children who'd gone missing in the area – there were two going back fifteen years, and that was about the time Ennis had moved there.'

'Interesting.'

'I thought so. It was enough for us to get a search warrant.'

'Anything worth finding in his house?'

'The T-shirt didn't belong to any of the local missing kids. But it did belong to a kid who'd been reported missing a month previously in Galway.'

'That's the other side of the country.'

'I know. But William Ennis would be missing from the estate for days at a time every couple of months. He was unemployed and never told anyone where he was going.'

'Did he have a vehicle?'

'A Ford Transit van.'

'Was a vehicle matching the description seen about Galway around the time the child went missing?'

'It was, and Ennis's van passed through the toll bridge on the way into Galway City the morning the disappearance was reported to the police.'

'So you brought him in for questioning.'

'I was asked to interview him along with one of the detectives from the station here.'

'They probably assumed your size might intimidate him,' Tessa said.

'Yes. Probably.'

Tessa sat back for a moment. 'You don't seem pleased with that suggestion.'

Danny shrugged. 'It's something I've had to deal with my whole life. I've always been big.'

'But you don't like it.'

'I don't think about it.'

Tessa shook her head. 'I reckon you do. You're sitting kind of hunched over, to make yourself seem smaller. I noticed you slouched your shoulders forward when you walked in, which made your height less noticeable.'

'I prefer to put people at their ease,' Danny said.

'Why would you assume your size would bother me?'

'It bothers most people.'

Tessa grinned. 'I'm not most people. Shoulders back, sit up straight. That's what we were taught in the army.'

'I've never served.'

'Which is probably a pity. You'd have brought a lot to the table. So anyway, you interviewed Ennis.'

'By the time we began, we already had confirmation that Neil McGuinness's DNA had been found in Ennis's home, in a spare bedroom, to be precise. We let him know we knew, and that we'd found the Galway boy's T-shirt.'

'How'd he react to that?'

'Of course he denied everything at first. Neil had been in his house with the other kids playing, which is how his DNA was there. He'd bought the T-shirt at a car boot sale. That kind of thing.'

'Which I'm sure you took with grave seriousness.'

'The gravest. I think he finally realised we had him when we told him there was now legal precedent for trying him based on circumstantial evidence alone. That he could easily be convicted just on the information we already had.'

'Do you think you could have made a case like that stick?' Tessa asked.

'It annoyed me to think we might have to try,' Danny

agreed. 'But sure, we didn't have to go there. He caved. Confessed he took the boy from Galway.'

'Was the lad still missing?'

'Yes. And he wouldn't say what he'd done with him or where he'd taken him. He wanted to make a plea and at that point asked to see a lawyer. My colleague went to see if he could arrange one. And while he was gone...'

Danny paused. His eyes had suddenly become moist, and he was afraid he'd start to cry. He didn't want that. He had to face what he'd done.

'You okay?' Tessa asked.

'Yeah. I just... if I could go back and do it all over again... I don't know if I'd be able to do it any differently.'

'What happened?'

'He asked me if I'd ever seen a photograph of Neil McGuinness before he'd been murdered. I told him I had.'

Tessa was watching Danny very closely, listening intently.

'He said to me: "Don't you think he was a beautiful boy?" and then he did something with his face. It was like... like he was *leering*, d'you know what I mean?'

'I think I do,' Tessa said.

'He saw it upset me, and he started to laugh. It was... it was more than I could cope with. I lost my temper and I... I hit him. And I... I kept hitting him. I hit him until he wasn't laughing anymore.'

'I'm not surprised he wasn't,' Tessa said. 'It says here you broke his jaw – you completely unhinged it actually – as well as knocking out four of his teeth.'

'I'm not proud of it. But... this was a bad man, Detective. I was afraid that when his lawyer arrived, he wouldn't tell us anything. I had to find out where that boy was.'

'And he told you.'

'He did. I told him I'd break his arm.'

Tessa nodded. 'You could have done far worse. I'm guessing you were pretty gentle with Mr Ennis, all things considered.'

Danny couldn't look at her. 'I wanted to kill him.'

'But you didn't.'

'He couldn't have told me anything if he was dead.'

Tessa gave a loud, hard laugh at that. 'The lad has been found. He's recovering in hospital. He'll live to fight another day, thanks to you.'

'Was he...' Danny asked, his lower lip trembling. 'Did Ennis... y'know...'

Tessa shook her head. 'There's nothing in that for you. The lad is safe. Be thankful.'

Danny nodded and sat back, wiping his eyes on his shirtsleeve.

'Garda Murphy, your instincts and intentions were good,' Tessa went on. 'Your execution, on the other hand, was absolutely bloody dire.'

'I know that.'

'You've a temper on you, don't you?'

'Most of the time I can keep it under control. Sometimes though... it gets away from me.'

'You probably need some help with that,' Tessa mused.

'I'm sure there'll be therapists in prison,' Danny said.

'What?' Tessa asked, as if shaken from her reveries.

'I can get therapy where I'm going,' Danny repeated.

'I'm not here to charge you or take you to Mountjoy,' Tessa said. 'I want you to come and work with me. I can help you channel that anger. We can make a difference. Bring the fight to them.'

Danny Murphy blinked. 'I have no clue what you're talking about.'

So Tessa told him.

In Monaghan, the search of the Connolly land continued through the night.

At 11.46 p.m. Garda O'Connor took his first break since arriving at the farmhouse that morning, sitting down in the mess tent the Garda Reserve had set up on the lawn of the property to have a cup of tea and a cheese sandwich. He was chewing the first bite when his radio crackled.

'Boss.'

It was Mooney.

'What is it, Fiona?'

'I think you're going to want to see this. I've sent a pin to your mobile phone.'

'Okay. I'll be right there.'

Taking a last large bite and chasing it with some tea, he started out across the fields, using his torchlight to pick out a path through the scrub and his phone as a guide to navigate to the spot where his team were situated.

It took ten minutes to get there, and when he arrived, he saw that the group were clustered about a copse of trees.

'What's up?' he asked, trying to keep the exhaustion from his voice.

'We've found something.'

'I gathered that all by myself,' O'Connor said. 'Are you trying to build suspense?'

Mooney motioned with her head and led him around the cluster of trees. Behind it, illuminated in the light of the two Gardas' torches, was a long shipping container. In the darkness it was difficult to tell if the structure was blue or purple, but what O'Connor could see was that the door was open a crack.

'Have you been in?'

'I had a look. It's another distillery. Whoever trashed the other one mustn't have found it.'

O'Connor pulled open the door and shone his torch inside. Sure enough, the space was a maze of barrels, tubes and tubs of sodden grain. It was obvious that this was a live still – the smell of fermentation was rich in the room. It wasn't unpleasant: a yeasty, beery, bready kind of aroma.

'I don't know who we should even call to get this stuff packed away,' O'Connor said. 'Should it be forensics? Do we have, like, a science department? Do I call vice?'

'Beats me, boss,' Mooney said.

'It's above my pay grade,' O'Connor sighed. 'I'll call the sarge and let him decide.'

He ran the torch slowly along the banks of equipment. It all looked new and top of the line. This was no makeshift operation. No expense had been spared.

The inside of the container felt like a tomb. The ever-present breeze could be heard through the open door, but other than that all was silent.

'I don't think there's much more we can learn here,' O'Connor said to Mooney. 'Whoever it is that's going to take this stuff apart while trying to detect whatever it is they can detect from it will probably be out tomorrow. In the meantime, let's shut it up and continue the search.'

He was about to switch his torch off when, almost subliminally, he noticed a slight movement in the very far right corner of the container. O'Conner later wondered if he would have missed it if there had been more light – the beams from the torches exaggerated the shadows and made tiny movements seem bigger.

Whatever the reason, he jerked his torch in that direction. There was a large copper still barrel set up right in that part of the container, and whatever it was (if he hadn't imagined it) had shot into the space behind it.

'Did you catch that?' O'Connor asked Mooney.

'What, boss?'

Stepping into the makeshift distillery, he walked forward very slowly, keeping the beam of his torch focused on that corner.

'I don't know whether an animal has got in or...'

There was a scuttling sound, and something skittered rapidly across the back wall, low down, almost at floor level.

'*What the fuck was that?*' Mooney shouted.

The two cops had only caught a glimpse of it, but the thing was pale and had moved at quite a speed. They'd both seen, however, that whatever it was, it was too big to be a rat or a fox.

'I don't know, Fiona, but I have a suspicion.'

'Care to share it with me?'

'Maybe *I'm* building suspense this time. Stay in the doorway. I don't want her getting out.'

'Her?'

O'Connor held up a hand to Mooney and they both paused. He stooped down and peered through the gloom.

There, cowering in the corner, was a small girl. From what O'Connor could see from the light of his torch, she was very dirty, her hair tangled and lank, her cheeks filthy and tear-streaked. The child was clutching some kind of stuffed toy to her thin chest, and her wide eyes and trembling frame told the guard she was scared out of her wits.

'I think,' Garda O'Connor said, 'that we've found Aisling Connolly.'

PART TWO

THE BURNS UNIT

While O'Connor and his team were finding the child in the shipping container, Tessa Burns was sleeping a mercifully dreamless sleep in the small flat she kept on Mayor Street, just off Dublin's North Wall.

The flat had been described to her by the letting agent as a 'studio apartment'. What Tessa found when she actually went to view it was a bedsit, a single room that contained a bed, a small table that could accommodate two people if they didn't need a lot of room to eat, a two-seater couch, a small TV that hung on the wall, a two-ringed cooker by a tiny sink, and a single bed.

Tessa shared a bathroom with a Nigerian gentleman named Njulo, who worked for Google and occasionally brought her bowls of jollof rice that she adored, and while most people would have considered her living quarters cramped and uncomfortable, they suited her needs.

Having spent her childhood from ten to eighteen years sharing bedrooms with sometimes as many as four other young people, she was used to making do with very little space and had developed the ability to live with few possessions.

Her wardrobe, for instance, consisted of five T-shirts, three pairs of jeans, two shirts, five pairs of socks and five pairs of knickers, an Aran-knit jumper, one pair of Doc Marten boots and one pair of red Converse high-top trainers, a green military-style jacket and a leather biker jacket. She kept all of these items in a suitcase she stored under her bed and simply cycled through them, washing the used items in the sink and drying them on the radiator overnight. She found that if she stretched everything out carefully, she had no need for an iron.

She rarely watched the TV, preferring to relax by listening to her beloved eighties and early nineties metal and rock classics while reading popular fiction. She occasionally heard about a film that sounded interesting, and she could usually find it online somewhere, but more often than not she was content to let such cultural touchstones pass her by.

She had other things to spend her free hours on.

This particular night, Tessa was woken by her phone ringing. Assuming it was work, she answered without even looking at the screen to see who was calling.

'Tessa Burns here.'

'Tessa, it's Bill.'

She knew the voice immediately. It belonged to a man she'd come to think very highly of – Father Bill Creedon, a Roman Catholic priest who ran Homeless Project on the Dublin Quays. Father Bill wasn't a... *typical* priest. A former boxer, he'd grown up in Dublin's inner city among working-class people, and had been close friends with individuals who'd gone on to become major players in the city's criminal underworld. Father Bill maintained cordial relations with them, not afraid to call in favours if he thought it might help his flock.

And Bill's flock was made up of the drug users, rough sleepers and desperately poor who populated the area in increasing numbers and availed of the services his project provided: beds for the night but also meals, endless cups of tea, and perhaps most importantly a listening ear and a friendly face.

Tessa had got to know Father Bill and his team due to the fact that a large number of people who ended up on the streets had spent time in care during their childhoods. And Tessa made it her business to stay in touch with as many of her fellow care veterans as she could. They had, after all, been the only family she'd known for close to a decade.

'What's going on?' she asked, throwing her duvet off and sitting up.

'I've got a man in some distress down at Eden Quay,' the priest said. 'He's asking for you.'

'I'm on my way.'

Eden Quay was situated on the banks of the River Liffey, the waterway that bisected Dublin, and about a hundred yards from O'Connell Street, considered the capital city's main street. It was close to 1 a.m. when Tessa got there, and she spied Father Bill's tall, lean figure leaning against the railings as she emerged from the Ford.

The priest retained a boxer's build: broad shoulders tapering to a very slim waist. His light brown hair was cut short, and he was grey at the temples, but there was a sense of youthfulness about the cleric that made it difficult to put a precise age on him. The fact his nose had been broken more than once didn't take away from the fact he was extremely good-looking in a rakish kind of way.

He looked up as Tessa approached. 'Thanks for coming. He's in my car.'

Tessa saw the priest's Honda Civic parked in the mouth of an alleyway and made a beeline for it, Father Bill taking up the rear.

'He's on the back seat,' the priest told her. 'I should warn you, he's not in a good state. He'll need to be seen by a doctor.'

'I can take him. Do you have a bed in the project?'

'No. We're full by seven every night these past six months.'

Tessa could see a dark shape slumped in the shadows. She knocked once and then pulled open the door slowly.

The person inside woke with a start, and Tessa raised a hand. 'Take it easy. It's me, Tessa Burns. I hear you've been looking for me.'

'What... Tessa? Is it really you?'

The figure, who'd clearly been asleep, sat up and moved into a beam of light from a street lamp, and Tessa could see who it was.

'Jesus, Jimmy,' she said, her eyes involuntarily filling with tears, 'you're a sight for sore eyes.'

The young man peering back at her was perhaps five years younger than Tessa and had sustained a pretty serious beating. He was dressed in a camouflage jacket over a khaki-coloured T-shirt and combat trousers. The detective could see he had a military-style kit bag on the seat beside him, which he'd been using as a pillow.

'You on R & R leave, or has the army released you back into the wild?' Tessa asked him.

'I'm out,' Jimmy said. 'Did me time. I qualified as a mechanic. Thought I could get a job doin' that.'

'Not as easy as you'd think though, is it?'

'No. You can't get places to rent without references, and after I got out of care, I went straight into the army, and I've been with them since. I... I couldn't find nowhere to live, and without an address, you can't get a job.'

'So you ended up on the streets,' Tessa said.

'I had the money they gave me when I demobbed. But that all got used up. I stayed in hotels first, but I knew I couldn't keep that up. The last couple of weeks I stayed in hostels, but even that got too pricy. I reckoned I'd slept in worse places than doorways and under bridges when we were deployed overseas, so I thought I could handle roughing it for a bit.'

'What happened?'

'Four fuckers jumped me while I was asleep. I tried to fight them off, but... well, you can see for yourself.'

'If they'd come at you when you were awake, it would have been a different story,' Tessa said.

'They took what little cash I had left. Me mobile phone. All I've got left is a few jocks and socks. I don't know what I'm gonna do.'

'How'd you know to ask Father Bill to call me?'

'I met a guy when I was sleepin' near Connolly Station. He said he'd been in care, and that you'd helped him. Said I should get in touch with you. I... I didn't want to. I was... I was embarrassed. I wouldn't want you thinkin' I'd fucked things up so bad.'

Tessa shook her head and wiped a tear away. She was looking at a man in his thirties, but what she saw was the kid she'd known in care. Jimmy had only been a little over ten years old when she'd first met him, and it was hard for her to think of him as anything other than that: a scruffy, scared kid who'd lost both his parents to drug overdoses on the same night and was struggling to adjust to being an orphan in the care of the state.

'Jimmy, what did we agree all those years ago?'

'If I was ever in trouble, I could call you.'

'And did you not think this qualified?'

'I got the priest there to get you, didn't I?'

'Only after you'd nearly been beaten to death.'

'Well better late than never.'

Tessa looked at the man she'd once thought of as a little brother and bent over and gave him a tight hug.

'Ow,' he said, but he returned the gesture.

'I'm going to take you to the hospital, and then you're

coming to stay with me. I've not got much space, but you can have the bed for the moment and I'll put the couch cushions on the floor and sleep there. In the morning, I'll make some calls and see if we can't get you sorted out with a place to stay and a job.'

'Just like that?' Jimmy asked incredulously.

'Let me make the calls. If we don't try, we can't succeed, can we?'

It took Tessa four phone calls the following morning to get Jimmy a job, over the short term at least, in the Garda motor pool, and by the end of the following day, he'd moved into a room in a boarding house owned by a former sergeant of hers.

This story had a happy ending. Tessa was painfully aware many others she was involved with did not.

But that wouldn't stop her trying to help.

14

They arrived in Monaghan town separately two days after Aisling Connolly had been found: Tessa in her vintage Ford Capri, Danny in his black Volkswagen Golf GTI, Maggie and Pavlov in her specially modified Ford Focus.

The town was small, its population not reaching 8,000 souls, but it was unquestionably pretty, its streets resplendent with nineteenth-century architecture, its town centre made of four interconnecting squares that gave it a sense of openness and space.

Maggie had booked them all rooms in the small but centrally located Westenra Arms Hotel (she told the owners Pavlov was a support animal, otherwise he wouldn't have been permitted on the premises), and they met in the bar once their luggage had been stowed.

'It's great to see you all,' Tessa said when everyone had a drink in front of them. 'This is the first time the four of us have been together, so let me make the introductions. Maggie, this is Danny; Danny, Maggie and Pavlov.'

'It's very nice to meet you,' Danny said.

He was dressed in a leather jacket, a denim shirt and blue

jeans, his dark hair cut close to his head, his face clean-shaven. Tessa noticed he seemed ill at ease and hoped she hadn't made a mistake with him.

'Likewise,' Maggie said, bumping fists with the big detective.

Danny made a half-hearted attempt to offer his hand to the dog, expecting it to be licked or sniffed, but to his surprise, the animal offered a paw in return, and Danny, feeling a bit incredulous, shook.

'Danny, Maggie is a family liaison officer and a therapist. She and Pavlov are going to be looking after the... well, the emotional end of the cases we get. She's also a good researcher and has a pretty good head for tech. You and I will be doing the investigating. Your old sarge tells me you're a keen observer and have a good head for detail. I'm good at looking at the bigger picture, and my time in quite a number of care institutions growing up has left me with contacts in lots of interesting places. So between us, I think we've got things covered.'

'If you say so,' Danny said, still very unsure of what was going on.

'Oh, and you're a detective now, by the way,' Tessa said to the huge cop.

'I'm a what now?'

'You're a detective.'

'I beat up a suspect during an interview and instead of getting fired, I get bumped up the ranks and given a job on a specialist team?'

'That's about the shape of it, yes.'

Danny shook his head. 'It doesn't seem right.'

'The deal I cut states you're on probation for the next six months. But as long as you don't shave your head, climb a building and start shooting civilians during that time, the promotion stands and you're in the clear.'

'I'd stop complaining and take the lucky break,' Maggie said.

'Okay,' Danny agreed. 'Thanks, boss.'

'No bosses on this team,' Tessa said. 'I don't work that way. Yeah, on paper I'm team leader because that's how the guards work, but in reality, I want both of your opinions on anything and everything we do. If a casting vote is required, it will be from whichever of us is the most knowledgeable of whatever issue is up for consideration. So speak up and don't be afraid to disagree with me or with each other. I'll fight my corner on anything we're discussing, and I expect you to as well.'

'Okay boss,' Danny said. 'I mean... Tessa.'

Tessa grinned. 'You'll get used to it. Right. Do you both know why we're in Monaghan?'

'I had a quick look at the file,' Maggie said. 'A couple of nights ago a seven-year-old child was found in a shipping container on an abandoned farm in the arsehole of nowhere. No one's sure if her parents abandoned her or if they were taken by competitors in the illegal hooch-brewing business.'

'Moonshine is a big deal around this part of the world,' Danny said. 'There's a long history of it going back a couple of hundred years.'

'We don't know their involvement with making poitín has anything to do with what happened to little Aisling's parents,' Tessa said.

'Isn't it a good bet though?' Maggie asked.

'That really depends,' Danny said. 'The legal response to poitín-making isn't exactly consistent and seems to depend on which judge you get, and what the local police force think of it too. I mean, in 2009, the Gardai here in Monaghan raided a shebeen just outside Ballybay and confiscated €15,000-worth of distilling equipment and €25,000-worth of illegally made spirits. Yet the following year an elderly man who had almost €10,000 worth of poitín in his shed was cleared of all wrong-doing because he claimed it was for medicinal purposes and the judge decided to believe him.'

'That seems like a lot of medicine,' Maggie observed.

'He said he was arthritic and was bathing in it,' Danny explained.

'Wouldn't the fumes knock you out?' Tessa wondered aloud.

'I'd have thought so.'

They all sat for a moment and thought about the logistics of bathing in what amounted to rubbing alcohol.

'Aren't some forms of poitín legally sold now?' Maggie asked.

'According to the research I've done, true aficionados turn their noses up at the stuff you can buy in the airports,' Danny said. 'Poitín, by definition, is illegal and can't be formally sold. What you get in those fancy shops in presentation boxes is a form of white Irish schnapps. Not the same thing at all.'

'I think part of the thrill for people is getting it from a guy who knows a guy who knows a guy,' Tessa said.

'So this family, the Connollys, they're known to be serious producers?' Maggie asked.

'They've never been charged,' Tessa said. 'Neither Joe nor Daisy has a conviction, and I'm half-wondering if they've fallen prey to the rumour mill. I mean yeah, they clearly dabble in distilling, but that's not unusual for farmers and smallholders. We've all heard of people making their own nettle beer if they come across a big crop of the stuff, or pear cider from a windfall.'

'No one disappears because they made beer from nettles though,' Danny said. 'There have been well-known feuds between rival poitín distillers. One was fought between several generations of two families in the Sligo mountains in the nineteenth century and got seriously vicious. Several people died, and one entire shipment of liquor was poisoned by mixing it with a caustic agent, metal hydroxide – most farmers call it lye.'

'We're all discussing the ins and outs of what might have

happened, but we have a witness,' Maggie said. 'What's Aisling, the little girl, saying?'

'That's part of why we're here,' Tessa said. 'She's not saying anything. Apparently since she was found in the shipping container, she hasn't uttered a word.'

'And what are we supposed to do about that?' Maggie said.

'You've boasted to me for many years now that you and Pavlov have a magic touch with traumatised kids,' Tessa said. 'How about you go and visit her in the hospital and work some of that magic?'

'You're not asking for much, are you?' Maggie asked.

Tessa winked. 'Nothing more than a miracle.'

'And what will you and Danny Boy do?'

'I was thinking Danny could chat with the neighbours,' Tessa said, 'while I have a word with the local Gardai.'

'Why?' Danny wanted to know. 'We've all read the case file.'

'I always find that what's left out of the file is sometimes even more important than what gets put in,' Tessa said.

'I don't think I know what that means,' Danny said, looking puzzled.

'Don't worry about it. We all know what we're doing. Let's find Aisling's parents and catch us some bad guys.'

15

Danny parked his black Golf GTI outside St Davnet's Psychiatric Hospital near Rooskey, just outside Monaghan. He was there to see Paddy Dorney, the neighbour who'd called 999, alerting the police to the Connollys' disappearance before having a complete mental breakdown.

No one seemed clear as to exactly what it was that had inspired the man to make the call, nor what had caused his psychotic episode, so a visit seemed timely. Danny just hoped he would be able to learn something useful.

The building was made of red bricks and had a homely feel that was probably unusual for facilities designed for the mentally unwell. Danny was met at reception by a middle-aged nurse named Cora, who had platinum-blonde hair and an open, friendly face that put him at ease immediately.

'You're here to see Paddy,' she said as she shook Danny's hand.

'He's not in any trouble,' the big detective told her. 'He made a 999 call a few days ago, and I'd like to know what caused him to do it.'

'Isn't wasting police time something that will get you in trouble?'

'He didn't waste anyone's time,' Danny said. 'Two people are missing and a little girl is in the hospital. The police are curious as to what Paddy saw that made him so frightened.'

'Well he is certainly that,' Cora said. 'He's been suffering from anxiety for years, has poor Paddy, since long before we even called it that. When I started working with people like him, we would say he suffered with his nerves. But it all boils down to the same thing.'

'Can he communicate?'

'Oh yes. But I don't know if you'll be able to understand what he'll say to you. Severe anxiety causes the brain to skip, like a scratched record. Paddy's conversation is inclined to jump about a bit, so keeping track of it can be a challenge.'

Danny grinned. 'I'll do my best.'

He met Paddy in the visitors' room, a wide high-ceilinged space set out with tables and chairs. Cora brought them tea and then left them to talk.

Paddy was in his early sixties with a shiny bald head and a face that expressed a rapid turnover of emotions, as if the entire gamut of human feeling passed across it every couple of moments.

'Paddy, I'm Danny. I'm with the Gardai, and I was wondering if you could help me with something.'

The older man looked at him solemnly. 'Joe and Daisy,' he said. 'And wee Ash. It's about them, isn't it?'

'Ash is Aisling?' Danny asked.

'Ash, yeah.'

'You rang 999,' Danny said. 'You said there was something wrong out at the Connolly farm.'

'Yes. There was trouble. Big trouble.'

'What kind of trouble?'

'The kind where people... where people *die*,' Paddy said, looking about him as if someone else might be listening.

Danny noticed that there was a sheen of sweat on the man's head now, and his leg was jiggling up and down rapidly.

'You're completely safe here, Paddy. So you can tell me what you saw.'

'You won't tell them?'

'Tell who?'

'I... I liked the Connollys. They were my friends. Lotta... lotta people don't want to be my friend because sometimes I'm not okay in my head, but they did. Daisy would sometimes make me a plate of dinner and drop it down to me. Her and Joe didn't mind when I came to visit, and I liked being with Ash. She's a nice little girl. Friendly, like. A sweet kid.'

'You visited them a lot?' Danny wanted to know.

'They were my friends.'

'Did anyone else call to see them?'

'Lotsa people did. Joe had the ones who worked on the farm... and the ones who did the *other stuff*.' Paddy whispered these last words.

'Do you mean how Joe made poitín?'

Paddy nodded, putting his finger to his lips. 'Don't tell the guards, okay?'

'I am a Garda, Paddy. I already told you that.'

The older man tapped the edge of his nose and nodded conspiratorially.

Poor guy is completely out of it, Danny thought.

'Who came to talk to him about the "other stuff"?'

'A man from the island,' Paddy said. 'I didn't like him. He scared me.'

'The island?' Danny said, puzzled. 'Monaghan is land-locked. I mean, it doesn't have any beaches. Was this man from the Aran Islands? The Blaskets? Did he travel to see them?'

'There was always lads there about the cratur,' Paddy said,

using the old-fashioned phrase for moonshine. 'Folks from all over. I knew a lot of them weren't good people. Not God-fearing, like. But the man from the island, him and his people... they were worse than any of them.'

'Do you know their names, Paddy?'

'Bad men, they are. Real bad men.'

Danny nodded. 'I hear you. They were bad news.'

'Very bad,' Paddy said, and now he was tapping a rhythm on the tabletop too, in counterpoint to the jiggling of his leg.

'Was the man from the island there the morning you called the police?'

Paddy blinked at the detective, but didn't respond.

'Was he there that day?' Danny tried again. 'Do you think he did something to the Connollys?'

Paddy continued to stare at Danny but didn't utter another word.

He was still sitting gazing into space when the Garda went to get Cora to take him back to his room.

'I think I broke him,' Danny said ruefully.

'Don't flatter yourself,' the nurse said. 'Life did that to him decades ago.'

16

Tessa met with Detective Inspector Jeremiah McEvoy, of Monaghan's vice squad, in a coffee shop on Market Street.

McEvoy was about six feet tall and broad, dressed in a brown leather jacket and dark blue jeans, what little hair he had gelled back tight against his head. He was clean-shaven and had a strong, rugged face.

'My guess is that the Connollys are dead,' he said without preamble. 'I don't know why they sent you and your cronies, to be honest.'

'Isn't it worth putting whatever resources are available into a case like this?' Tessa asked. 'There's a little girl in Monaghan General who could do with having her parents found, and if there's even the slimmest chance...'

'Has it occurred to you that wee lass might be better off without them?'

The coffee shop was quiet in the early afternoon. A waitress sat on a stool by the cash register reading a fashion magazine. An old lady was dozing over a cup of tea at the back of the room, her head slumped forward on her chest.

'You're telling me the Connollys were abusive? Neglectful?'

'I'm saying I believe they were in league with some very serious – and yes, very dangerous – criminals.'

'You believe?'

'Isn't that enough for you? One copper to another?'

'Trust but verify,' Tessa said. 'What's your opinion based on?'

'I've been chasing Joe Connolly for a long time,' McEvoy said. 'He's not from Monaghan – you know that, don't you? Neither is his missus. Both of them blow-ins, him from Limerick, her from Dublin. And the pair of them had connections with all kinds of scumbags before they arrived in my corner of the world to try and set up shop on their own.'

'As moonshiners?'

'As makers of poitín, yes.'

'I've been told there are... mixed views about the seriousness of poitín-making in this part of the world.'

'Not by me. It's against the law.'

'So you chase everyone who's doing it?'

'Look, we're a small force here,' McEvoy said. 'Vice in Monaghan is basically me and one uniformed lad who doesn't know his arse from his elbow yet. He'll learn, but it's gonna be slow. So no, I don't pursue every single backwater farmer who decides to ferment a few gallons of wash.'

'How do you decide who to go after then?'

'I'm interested in the ones who're making either most of or a good part of their living from illegal booze. That, Detective Burns, is profiting from a criminal enterprise.'

'Tessa.'

'What?'

'Call me Tessa.'

'Oh. Okay. Well, Tessa, the laws around distilling and selling intoxicating liquor are very simple. If you want to set up a distillery in Ireland you need a distilling licence, and if you wish to sell your product on the open market you need a manufacturer's licence. If, as many distillers do, you wish to establish your own bar – a shebeen – you need a publican's on-site licence to sell beer or spirits, depending on what it is you're peddling. Needless to say, the Connollys, who produced *a lot* of liquor, did not possess any such licences, and seemed to think they could operate with complete impunity.'

'And this is what they'd done before coming here? They made poitín?'

'Joe did anyway. I think they met initially through criminal connections. Their previous address as a couple was Limerick, and my sources there tell me Joe was involved in making spirits for a collection of shebeens one of the gangs own.'

McEvoy was referring to what rural Irish people called a speakeasy, an illegally run drinking establishment.

'So he had experience.'

'Joe Connolly has a degree in fucking chemical engineering,' McEvoy said. 'He could have used his skills for the betterment of mankind. Instead he devotes his talents to making eighty-per-cent-proof rotgut whiskey. Go figure.'

'Which gang did he work for?'

'The Donegans,' McEvoy said, contempt dripping from each syllable. 'Daisy is the daughter of Jim Reville, enforcer for the Shiggins Mafia out of Tallaght.'

'We're dealing with quite a criminal vintage then,' Tessa mused.

'The worst,' McEvoy said. 'And for the past year, all kinds of thugs were travelling here from their boltholes to talk to Joe. I think he was planning something.'

'What?'

'I don't know. He was always tinkering about with recipes and formulas. In the past we've intercepted quite a few different types of 'shine we believe were his handiwork.'

'Was he any good?'

'The stuff didn't taste like paint stripper, if that's what you mean. I could believe people would pay good money for it in some of those new hipster bars that have sprung up all over. The last one we got our hands on was some kind of elderflower gin. It's not my cup of tea, but some of the younger lads said it could stand up to the best of the artisan varieties.'

'Why not just buy one of those legally then?' Tessa asked.

'Because Joe's was *way* stronger. He specialised in making spirits that tasted mild but would blow your socks off. More bang for your buck.'

'You can buy very strong liquors,' Tessa said. 'I've heard of vodkas and whiskeys that are ninety-five-per-cent proof.'

'Joe's not a fool,' McEvoy said. 'He uses ingredients that metabolise a lot more slowly than that stuff, so you can sip away and not pass out immediately. His liquors don't come in over ninety per cent. They usually have a mild taste and can be taken in shots or even used as a sipping whiskey. He makes powerful drinks that can be consumed in a civilised way.'

'Isn't that a contradiction in terms?' Tessa asked.

'It's a dangerous lie,' McEvoy said. 'Joe Connolly might not have been cooking meth, but he was still making poison. And I think some of the guys he was trying to partner up with got sick of how good he was at it and had him killed.'

17

Maggie, with Pavlov trotting along behind her, steered her chair into Aisling Connolly's room on the children's wing of Monaghan General Hospital.

The little girl was sitting up in bed, reading a comic book that had a picture of a dog wearing a fireman's helmet on the cover. Beside her on the pillow was a very sad-looking, threadbare stuffed rabbit that might have once been white but was now a dull grey. The child looked up when Maggie came in, gazing at her with huge, liquid eyes.

'Hi, Aisling. My name is Maggie, and I work for the police. And this is Pavlov. He's my friend, and I thought he might be your friend too.'

The dog wagged his tail and in a motion that seemed to require no effort at all jumped into Maggie's lap.

'Would you like to pet him?' she asked.

Aisling eyed the dog for a moment, then tentatively, almost too gently to see unless you were looking very closely, nodded.

'That's great – Pavlov loves being petted,' Maggie said and rolled a little closer, though she was careful not to invade the child's space.

If Aisling wanted to stroke Pavlov, she could reach over and do so, coming to Maggie rather than the other way around.

And that's what happened. Seeing that the family liaison officer wasn't going to come right up beside her bed but planned to leave a little space between them, Aisling scooted up so she was on her knees and, scooping up the rabbit in one hand, reached over and gently scratched Pavlov behind the ears with the other.

'Oh, he likes that,' Maggie said.

Pavlov made a gentle moaning sound, an expression on his face that looked for all the world as if he was smiling.

'The nurses tell me you don't much feel like talking,' Maggie said. 'And that's okay. It really is. Do you know that when I was a kid, I didn't talk until I was almost four years old?'

Aisling gave her a look that seemed to say: *Really? That's kind of weird.*

'I have a condition called cerebral palsy, which means my muscles don't work as well as they should. That made everything I had to do much harder. So I didn't much feel like talking for a long time. It was just too hard for me. So I know how you feel.'

The little girl nodded and ran her hand down the dog's back. He stretched out, as if he was giving her more surface area.

'Do you know what though? I'm here to try and help find your mam and dad, and the only person we have who probably knows what happened to them is you. Now, I know that must be really scary. It's a big responsibility, isn't it?'

Aisling didn't nod or shake her head, but she did seem to shrink a little bit, dipping her shoulders and sagging, which was in itself an answer.

'It would be great if you wanted to tell me what happened, but it really is okay for the moment if you can't. I'm going to be here, and whenever you feel like talking, we can talk. And if you don't ever feel like it, there are other things you can do to tell me things.'

Aisling looked up at her, and to Maggie's delight, she smiled.

'That's it exactly,' the family liaison officer said. 'Just like that.'

DAISY CONNOLLY

It was dark and it was cold.

Daisy couldn't remember ever having been this cold before. It was as if she was in a refrigerator that had been set to a level that would keep her chilled but not quite frozen. To keep her fingers from going numb, she clenched them between her knees and used her own body heat to warm them. It worked for a while, and she even managed to sleep for short periods, but then she would snap awake, her teeth rattling from the cold, goosebumps standing out all over her body.

Her hands, while not warm, wouldn't be frigidly cold, but all down her back, right along the rear of her thighs, right to her ankles, would be frozen. She wished she could curl into a foetal position – she felt that would help to conserve what heat she could – but the restricted space she was in made that impossible.

Lying against the side of her prison, pressing her back against it, seemed to create a bit of warmth, but eventually cold seeped through from the outside, and Daisy found the process ultimately counterproductive. So she had no option but to remain on her back, her hands clenched between her knees, her chin tucked to her chest, and try to focus on keeping the panic at bay.

She didn't know where her husband was. The last she'd seen he was being restrained as she was dragged away. Daisy had no idea if he was dead or alive. She didn't know if she would ever see daylight again. Maybe they would leave her here. She wore an old-fashioned digital watch on her left arm, a gift from her grandfather when she'd gone away to college. She'd initially thought it was naff, but when the old man, whom she'd loved dearly, had died, it acquired a sentimental importance for her, and she was never without it.

By pressing one of the tiny buttons on the watch, a light came on and she could see its readout.

It told her she and Joe had been taken two and a half days ago. She'd been in the darkness now for twelve hours.

She had no idea where their daughter, Aisling, was. If she was safe. If the awful men who'd kidnapped and then tortured and detained her and her spouse had her child in their evil grip also.

The thought made her sob with despair, and crying made her take deep gulps of air, and that made her head swim and, weak from lack of food and dehydration, she tried to get her feelings under control.

She had to hope.

She had to believe someone knew she and Joe were gone and would come looking for them.

Hope was all she had left.

18

Other than Paddy Dorney, who lived in a cottage two kilometres from the Connolly homestead, the family's nearest neighbours were an elderly couple called the Drews, who had a small sheep farm five kilometres the other direction.

Danny called to their old stone-clad house after he left the hospital.

'Joe and Daisy were a grand young couple, so they were,' Benjy Drew told him. He was a broad bear of a man with hands like shovels and a thick red beard that had two patches of grey down the front, almost as if they'd been painted on. He was sitting in a huge, scuffed leather armchair and smoking a black briar pipe, which gave the room a sweet, savoury kind of feel.

Danny was aware of the health hazards of passive smoking, but he couldn't help liking the fragrance of pipe tobacco.

'Joe was a good neighbour, always happy to help out if we needed an extra pair of hands. I'm right sorry to hear him and his good lady might be in trouble.'

'Do you think they might have had to leave in a hurry?' Stella, Benjy's wife asked. 'There's all class of gossip being talked about it.'

'What kind of gossip?' Danny asked.

'Most people seem to think the family got into some kind of trouble with some very bad people. That they had to get the hell out of Dodge before something bad happened.'

'If they did, they left their little girl behind,' Danny said. 'Does that seem likely to you?'

'No,' Benjy said definitively. 'They doted on that wee girl, both of them. I don't think I ever seen Joe without her bein' with him. She was a proper daddy's girl, so she was. Could wrap him around her little finger, of course, but then, daughters learn to do that to their fathers early on, don't they?'

'Well our Maria certainly did,' Stella said, placing tea and all the fixings on a table in front of her husband.

Benjy grinned. 'That she did, that she did. Could buy and sell me by the time she was three years old.'

'Do you know of anyone who would want to hurt the Connollys?'

Benjy sat forward to pour the tea. Danny really didn't want any, having had four cups so far that afternoon between the chat with his new colleagues in the bar and his visit to see Paddy Dorney, but he was well aware that the presence of a mug of something in the hand could make conversation flow much more easily than without.

'No,' the big bearded man said, 'I couldn't begin to think of why anyone in their right mind would want to harm Joe and Daisy.'

Danny took the proffered mug and added a dash of milk and one sugar. 'No reason at all?' he asked, leaving the last syllable hanging in the air expectantly.

'No. None.' Benjy puffed on his pipe forcefully, sending up a plume of smoke as if this somehow drew a line under the conversation.

Danny, however, was not to be so easily dissuaded.

'So their distilling wouldn't draw any unpleasant attention their way?'

Stella came to sit in a chair beside her husband, and he threw her a glance.

'I don't know what you're talking about,' he said gruffly. 'We'd have no interest in that class of thing around here.'

'Now you're hardly what I'd call a teetotaller,' Stella said, patting the back of her husband's hand. 'Stop playin' silly buggers and tell the detective what you know. That wee girl is without her mam and dad, and that's more important than any code of secrecy. We've gone beyond playin' hide-and-seek with the peelers.'

'You know we don't talk to the polis about the mountain dew!' Benjy said indignantly.

'You're not squealing to the Gardai,' Stella said firmly. 'You're helping wee Ash. That's far more important.'

Benjy heaved a deep sigh and stood up, going to a cupboard above the ancient TV set that sat in the corner. He returned with a Kilner jar that contained a clear liquid and three shot glasses.

'This is what Joe liked to call his private batch,' Benjy said, pouring a measure into each glass.

'I'm driving,' Danny protested, but the big man only tutted.

'Take a sip. You can talk about this up and down, theorise about what Joe was doing on his land, wonder about why someone would have tried to take what he had away from him. Until you *taste* it though, experience it for yourself, you'll never really understand.'

He passed a glass to the detective, one to Stella and took one himself.

'To Joe and Daisy,' he said. 'May they be safe and in good health wherever they are, and may they be returned to their daughter with all speed.'

Then he and Stella knocked back the contents of their glasses. Danny rose his to his lips and took a small sip.

It was a remarkable experience.

The flavour was almost impossibly complex. Danny wasn't a big drinker and certainly had very little experience consuming straight spirits – his usual tipple when he went to the pub was a pint of pale ale – so he was unprepared for the drink Benjy had just given him.

What surprised him was how pleasurable it was.

There was a spiciness to it that wasn't overpowering and caused a tingle at the back of his tongue. He could taste caramel and vanilla, but it wasn't cloyingly sweet. There was a hint of raisins and dark fruit, but this was overlaid with a smoky, savoury quality that reminded him of barbecues or dried wood.

All of these thoughts ran through Danny's head in the space of a couple of seconds, and had he been asked, he probably wouldn't have been able to articulate them. He liked to cook and actually considered himself something of a gourmet. But this was a wholly new experience for him.

Benjy watched him closely. 'It's quite a thing, isn't it, lad?'

'It's... it's not like anything I've ever tasted,' Danny agreed.

'This is just one example of what Joe could do,' Benjy said, pouring himself another. 'He is, to put it in the plainest terms possible, an artist. And while he chose to operate his business outside of the bounds of accepted legal practice, that doesn't mean he ignored his civic responsibilities.'

Danny looked at the old man quizzically. 'How so?'

'There were times when he had a big run on a particular batch,' Benjy replied. 'When that was happening, he would employ lots of local people to help out.'

'Was much help needed?'

'Not if you're doing it on a small scale.'

'But the Connollys weren't?'

'No. They were operating on a... well, I wouldn't call it *industrial*, but...'

'They had a large-scale business,' Danny finished the sentence for him. 'And they employed a lot of people within the community.'

'They did. So when you say who would want to hurt them, I'd have to tell you that I reckon most people love them,' Benjy said. 'They're good employers. Okay, so it was seasonal work, they took people on at times of peak business, but as things took off for them, that happened more and more.'

'You're saying they'd been getting more successful?'

'Oh yes. Joe and Daisy were doing big business.'

'You tell me Joe's the artist, the talent behind making the spirits. What does Daisy do?'

'I would say she's the ideas woman,' Stella said. 'She comes up with what kind of product they're going to produce and then Joe makes it happen. She always kept her finger on the pulse. Knew the trends in what people wanted. Joe was always able to bring her ideas to life.'

'And she designed the labels and all of that,' Benjy said. 'She came up with the name they used too.'

'Their company had a name?' Danny asked.

'Oh, it surely did,' Stella said. 'Drumlin Spirits. After the rock formations on their property.'

'Almost poetic,' Danny said.

'I'd say it was *very* poetic,' Benjy replied.

Danny didn't know what to say to that.

Joe and Daisy Connolly were, it seemed, criminals with artistic souls.

And he didn't know if that helped him or not.

19

Tessa left the café and pulled her mobile phone from her pocket as she walked back to the Capri. It took her a few seconds to find the contact she was looking for – it was a number she hadn't dialled in a long time.

'Hiya, Noel,' she said when her call was finally picked up.

'Tessa Burns,' the voice said at the other end. 'What the fuck do you want?'

'I need to pick your brains.'

There was a pause for several beats. 'Maybe I don't want to have my intellect turned over by the likes of you.'

'Aw, come on now, Noel. You and me go way back. Surely we can set aside our differences.'

Noel made a noise that sounded like a growl. 'All the way back to that shithole of a care home.'

'My recollection is that we helped each other out more than once. I kept some of the scumbags away from you, and you were able to get your hands on a few items I needed.'

'You wanted books,' Noel scoffed. 'It wasn't like you were looking for me to smuggle in heroin!'

'I was still grateful.'

'Your gratitude didn't stop you arresting me when we met under different circumstances.'

'I don't recall as you gave me much choice, Noel. You stuck a gun in my face.'

'And you took it away from me and threatened to stick it somewhere very uncomfortable.'

'I gave you a chance to walk away.'

'Yes, but I wanted to drive away in the BMW I was trying to steal.'

'It was your call. Can I drop by? I really do need to know some things, and they're the type of things you usually have some expertise in.'

Noel sighed deeply and said: 'You know my address?'

'I do.'

'Even though I've moved since we last crossed paths and I didn't inform you of where I was going?'

'Noel, you're insulting me now.'

'I'll put the kettle on.'

'Good.'

Noel Randall lived in a mobile home that sat on breeze blocks in a small field down a narrow lane off a byroad – a tributary from a secondary road that sustained so little use, grass grew in the middle of it.

Unless you knew exactly where you were going, this made him exceedingly difficult to find, and this was exactly the way he liked it. County Monaghan offered enough barely populated regions to make it an ideal hideaway for a man who made his living in legally dubious ways.

He was two years younger than Tessa's thirty-eight, but he looked ten years older, his sandy-coloured hair thinning on top and a pronounced pot belly hanging over the belt of his ill-fitting jeans.

'So to what do I owe this distinct displeasure?'

'It's good to see you too, Noel.'

He scowled. 'Best come in. Let's get this done quickly.'

Inside, the mobile home was surprisingly clean and organised: a small dining table was already set with tea things, and Richard Thompson was playing through a small speaker, singing about the fact that waltzing is for dreamers and losers in love.

'How have you been, Noel?' Tessa asked as she sat down on one side of the table.

'In the five years since I got out of the Joy? I would say I've been tolerable. I'd have much preferred it if you hadn't got me stuck in there, but I suppose beggars can't be choosers.'

'You been busy?'

Noel spluttered out a raucous laugh. 'Do you seriously expect me to give you the honest answer or the one that won't get me locked up again?'

'How about you be honest but not specific in the details?'

'Well in general terms, I'm doing very well, thank you so much for asking.'

'You've been in Monaghan a couple of years.'

'Your sources are as keen as ever.'

'Tell me about the Connollys.'

'The distillers?'

'Yes.'

'That's all I know. They make hooch for a few gangs who run illegal drinking and gambling establishments.'

'Which gangs?'

'As far as I know they were both connected before they came here.'

'And they haven't expanded?'

'Tessa, you know I'm a thief, right? And a damn good one? Since when have I been involved in the 'shine business?'

The detective drank some tea.

'You got Barry's,' she said.

'I always drink Barry's. Who in their right mind would drink anything else?'

'Noel, if there's something criminal going on in a fifty-kilometre radius, you're going to be in it up to your neck. So the fact you now live in a county with a reputation for the production and sale of illegal alcohol leads me to believe you have, in some way, involved yourself in that industry.'

Noel looked at her impassively and said: 'Okay. I might have been at a couple of meetings at the Connollys' property.'

'Recently?'

'No. It all got too rich for my blood.'

'In what way?'

'Joe and Daisy wanted to set up shop on their own. He was producing a whole line of top-quality independently produced artisan spirits that, because the buyers didn't have to pay taxes or duties on them, could be traded for a fraction of the price the standard stuff trades at. As you probably know, there are also limits on how much establishments can legally purchase, particularly of spirits with very high alcohol content. *All* of Joe's is really strong, but because it all comes in under the radar of customs, he can sell as much as anyone wants to buy.'

'And he was exporting?'

'When I was there, he was just starting to and it was in small quantities, but he wanted to expand. Well, I got the impression it was Daisy who was the brainchild of the whole thing. She did most of the talking at the meeting I was at.'

'Why were you there?'

'Naw,' Noel said. 'You don't get that. I'll help you because we have a history no one else would understand. But I'm *not* incriminating myself.'

'Okay. Who else was there?'

'Representative from the Donegans from Limerick.'

'Joe's relatives,' Tessa said.

'Yes. There were people from the Shiggins crew, out of Dublin, too.'

'Daisy's people.'

'There were some Eastern European gentlemen as well. Now, I hadn't dealt with them before, but I believe they were Ukrainian.'

'Lots of Ukrainian gangs in Ireland,' Tessa said. 'Do you know which one?'

'I don't. And I really don't. My role didn't require me to be privy to that kind of information.'

'Why were they all there? Gangs from different parts of the country don't usually work with one another.'

'It was all Daisy's idea,' Noel said. 'The concept was simple. Joe would produce a branded line of spirits especially for the European market, everything from Scotch to a version of Jäger-meister, tequila to cognac. He'd come up with versions of every-thing, to be exported as cheaper, but very high quality, alternatives to the legal stuff, and all dressed up as highly desir-able, trendy booze from a craft distiller. The Limerick guys were going to bankroll the operation, help Joe source materials and buy the extra equipment he needed. The Dubs were going to help out with the transportation. The Ukes were all about distribution. They ran a lot of bars and night clubs all over Europe and the Mediterranean where the stuff Joe was going to make would sell by the truckload.'

'And everyone got a cut,' Tessa observed.

'That's my understanding of it. Nothing brings people who would usually hate each other together like money.'

Richard Thompson was singing about how someone was a rare thing now.

'A lot can go wrong where three gangs are trying to work together.'

'Hell of a lot,' Noel said. 'Which is why I got my ass out of there.'

'A pity the Connollys didn't before it all blew up in their faces,' Tessa said.

'Great ability doesn't always come with great common sense,' Noel said, pouring them both some more tea.

'You've got very philosophical in your old age,' the detective observed.

'Prison will do that to you,' the thief replied without a hint of irony.

'Looks like I did you a favour then,' Tessa shot back.

Noel gave her a look that suggested he didn't wholly agree.

'Other than the Connollys, who's the biggest mover of illegal liquor in the county?'

'The biggest mover or the biggest producer?'

'There's a difference?'

'A distinct one, yes.'

'I suppose I want to know who the biggest power player is now the Connollys are gone. Who's going to benefit from their removal.'

'That would be Elias Two-Toes.'

'Seriously?'

'Not the name he inherited from his father obviously. He used to do some work for a paramilitary organisation based north of the border. During an attempt to plant a device underneath the vehicle of a representative of the Royal Ulster Constabulary, he managed to blow three of the toes on his right foot off.'

Tessa thought about that. 'Three fingers I'd understand,' she said, 'but three toes?'

'He's very sensitive about it,' Noel said. 'If you meet him, I'd avoid raising the issue if I were you. Elias is now primarily an importer and exporter of various... products and substances. He does a fairly significant trade in alcohol though. All of it of the duty-free variety.'

'Doe he create any of it himself?'

'He dabbles, but I would say not on a very serious basis. Tessa, Elias Two-Toes is a deeply unpleasant individual. I would be very careful around him. People who piss him off tend to wind up losing fingers and toes themselves. It's kind of his trademark.'

Tessa grinned. 'I'll keep that in mind. Now, when can you introduce me?'

20

Purely by chance, Danny and Tessa arrived at Monaghan General at the same time, just before five in the evening.

'How'd you get on?' Tessa wanted to know.

Danny quickly filled her in, and she brought him up to speed on her own progress.

'So we're thinking one of the gangs they were working with decided they wanted all the profits for themselves,' the burly cop said when she'd finished.

'I'd say yes, but for the fact that everyone is saying what Joe could do was something really special and highly skilled,' Tessa said. 'Killing him doesn't make a lot of sense.'

'Maybe they got his recipes or whatever and have someone else who can do the cooking?' Danny suggested.

'I'm not sure it works like that.'

'How does it work then?'

'Maybe that's something we need to find out more about,' Tessa replied. 'How about we go and see how Maggie and Pavlov are getting on?'

As they strolled across the car park, they could both hear a bit of a disturbance: someone shouting and laughing coarsely, and what sounded like another voice raised in protest. Peering about, Tessa saw that the ruckus was being caused by a group of people parked at the other end of the car park. There seemed to be some kind of disagreement between a couple of men and a young woman, who was holding a small child by the hand.

As they watched, one of the men stepped forward and gave the young woman a shove, sending her staggering.

'Okay,' Danny said, 'that's enough of that.'

'I'm with you, partner,' Tessa said, and the two of them set off at a jog towards the scene of the altercation.

The aggressors must have seen them coming, because before the pair got close, they jumped into a battered-looking green jeep and roared away, doing a full lap of the car park before screeching out the gate. Tessa caught a glimpse of two long-haired, skinny individuals – the one in the passenger seat grinned and waved out the window as they tore up the road.

'Did you get the number of the jeep?' Tessa asked Danny.

'You already know I did.'

The woman was comforting her son.

'Are you all right?' Tessa asked her.

'Yes, I'm all right,' she said, though her voice was tremulous. 'That pair. They were making comments. Inappropriate things in front of my son here.'

The child looked to be perhaps three, a little blond boy with huge blue eyes.

'We're both police officers,' Danny said. 'If you want to make a statement, we could follow it up for you?'

'Thank you, no. I'd prefer just to put it behind me.'

'If you change your mind, here's my card,' Tessa said.

'Thank you,' the woman said, and the detectives left her to it.

'We won't hear from her again, will we?' Danny asked.

'Nope. And those shitkickers will continue to be a blight on the face of civilisation,' Tessa said.

'Maybe we'll run the plate later and pay them a visit,' Danny said. 'I'd like to have a proper chat with them. I hate bullies. I *really* hate them.'

Tessa patted him on the arm. 'Maybe we will. For now though, we have another kid to worry about who doesn't have a mother around to comfort her.'

'You're right, boss,' Danny said.

'Tessa. You're right, *Tessa*.'

'Sorry. Reflex.'

'I know. But I'm going to keep correcting you until you get used to it.'

'You're going to ruin me for the next job I get, you know that?'

Tessa grinned. 'What can I say? I'm a bad influence.'

21

When they got to Aisling's room, the child was sitting on the edge of her bed cuddling a stuffed rabbit, with Pavlov perched beside her, Maggie in front of the two of them.

'Hey, Ash, I want you to meet my two friends. This is my oldest and best friend, Tessa, and this is my newest friend, Danny.'

The little girl looked at each of them in succession and nodded gravely. Tessa noticed the big detective kept behind her and didn't offer his hand to the child. He was doing that thing where he hunched his shoulders again too, trying to make himself seem smaller than he was. She let it go for then but told herself she would mention it to him later.

'Tessa and Danny have been out this afternoon trying to find out what happened to your mam and dad.'

'It's really good to meet you, Aisling,' Tessa said. 'Should I call you Ash? Is that how people usually say your name?'

The girl nodded.

'Okay then. Ash it is.'

'Pull over a couple of chairs,' Maggie said. 'I was just about to tell Ash the story of how Pavlov here found me, and how we became a family.'

'Um...' Danny said, looking awkward suddenly. 'I saw some chairs out in the corridor. I'll go and get them.'

He clattered out, returning with the two items, and when he and Tessa were both seated, Maggie began.

'A few years ago, I was out one night doing a quiz in a pub, in Dollymount, in Dublin,' she said. 'You know what a quiz is, Ash? It's like a test – you have to answer questions and get them right, and the team who get the most answers right wins a prize. Well, my team came paddy last, and I wasn't in a very good mood when I came out at the end of the night. I was on my way back to my car, scooting along, when I passed a bin, and I heard a strange sound coming out of it.'

Pavlov was sitting very still, his ears pricked up and his dark eyes fixed on Maggie.

'He loves this part of the story,' she said to Ash. 'The sound was kind of like something crying. But it was very quiet and very squeaky. Sort of a "wah, wah, wah". Do you think you could make that sound? I probably didn't get it right.'

To everyone's delight, Ash, a look of fierce concentration on her face, tried to mimic what Maggie had just done.

'You know, that's a lot better than my impression. What do you think, Pavlov?'

The dog lapped Ash twice on the nose, and she hugged him tight.

'Well I stopped quick smart, and I wheeled back to the bin and I looked in, and do you know what I saw? It was a plastic bag, and it was moving, and the crying sound was coming out of it. So I picked it up, and took it out of the bin and put it on my lap, and I ripped it open, and inside I found four tiny black-and-white puppies. Three of them weren't moving at all, only just breathing, but one of them was still squirming around and wailing, and that was Pavlov. I brought them to my car, and when I got there, I looked on the internet to see if there was a vet that stayed open late, and I brought those puppies in to be looked after, and then I went home.'

Pavlov made a kind of whining sound, and Maggie reached over and rubbed his head.

'The next day I got a phone call from the vet and he told me that three of those poor puppies hadn't lived through the night, but one had, and he was going to need a home and someone to look after him, and feed him, and love him, and the vet wondered, seeing as I'd brought him in, if that person might be me.'

'And you said yes,' Ash said in a very tiny voice.

Maggie, grinning from ear to ear, nodded. 'I said yes, and Pavlov and me have been a family ever since.'

'Pavlov's a funny name,' the little girl said – it seemed now she'd started talking, she was determined to continue.

'I suppose it is,' Maggie said. 'It's the name of a scientist who's famous for teaching his dogs to do interesting things. When I got this little guy, I saw very quickly that *he* was training *me*. He knows I love him so much it's very hard for me to say no when he wants something. I called him Pavlov because it seemed to suit.'

'I like it,' Ash said. 'I don't know no other dogs called that.'

'I don't either,' Maggie said. 'There's only one Pavlov, that's for sure.'

22

They got back to the hotel around 9.30 p.m.

Maggie headed straight to bed, but Tessa and Danny opted to have a drink at the bar before turning in.

'How'd you feel today went?' Tessa asked when she had a Bushmills Irish whiskey in front of her, and Danny a pint of Galway Hooker Irish pale ale.

'I couldn't tell you,' the newly appointed detective said. 'I did my job. I'm satisfied I did it as well as I could. I don't know if we're any closer to finding out what happened to that little girl's parents...'

'Aisling,' Tessa said. 'She likes to be called Ash.'

'Yeah, I know.'

'Why didn't you call her by her name then?'

The big man shrugged.

'And you were barely able to make eye contact with her today. It's interesting, because you were *totally* at ease when we were in the car park and you wanted to step in and protect that woman and her kid, but when you were face to face with a little girl who's all alone in the world, you fell to pieces.'

Danny stared at his drink. 'I don't think I fell to pieces.'

'You nearly got stuck in the door on the way out you were in such a hurry. What's the problem?'

'You know what the problem is!' Danny said, looking at her with annoyance.

'I really don't.'

'A little kid like that isn't going to want a big lug like me hanging around her! I must have scared her half to death!'

'Danny, I was there and I did not see a scared child. She didn't give you a second glance!'

'That's because Maggie was doing so well with her. If she hadn't been, I think you'd have seen a very different picture.'

Tessa sipped some of her whiskey. 'What is it with you and this persecution complex?'

'I don't have a persecution complex.'

'Yes you fucking do. You, Danny Murphy, do not like yourself very much. Now, I see the value you bring to the table, and I know Maggie does too. Pavlov seems to like you, which is always a good sign. Hell, I bet if I asked Ash, she'd tell you she's happy you're along for the ride. But I have to tell you, my friend, that if you don't begin to see the value in *yourself*, your time on my team is going to be short-lived.'

Danny heaved a deep sigh, and Tessa wondered for a moment if the detective might be close to tears.

'I don't think I know how to do that.'

'Okay,' Tessa said. 'What is it exactly that you dislike so much about... about your size?'

'Sure, look at me!'

'I am looking at you.'

'I'm a feckin' freak, like.'

Tessa shook her head in incredulity. 'You're a big bloke, but if you pardon my candour, I've seen bigger. There was a guy in the army when I was there who was six foot five, and we were all *delighted* to have him on our teams when we were on patrol. *No one* wanted to fuck with him.'

'Yeah, because he looked like the Incredible Hulk!'

'I thought he was pretty damn hot, if you must know. And I wasn't the only person in my unit who did, guys and girls alike. Danny, haven't you ever read a Jack Reacher novel? A lot of ladies go crazy for big strong guys. They're certainly not seen as ugly or repulsive.'

'I got picked on all the time in school for being big.'

'Kids are horrible. I grew up in residential homes, believe me, I know what it's like to have to fight your corner.'

'They used to call me Frankenstein and Sasquatch. Told me I was a monster.'

'They were being arseholes,' Tessa said. 'Just cause some little dicks told you you're a monster doesn't make it true.'

'My second foster placement, I heard my foster mum tell my foster dad that I was big and ungainly. They sent me away soon after that.'

'If your placement broke down because of *that*, they didn't deserve to have you in the first place.'

'It wasn't just them or the kids who saw me like that. The teachers did too. When I did fight back at school, everyone said *I* was the bully. I got more detentions because of it than anyone else in my class. In the end, I just kept my head down and put up with it.'

'That's shit,' Tessa said. 'No wonder you hate bullies.'

'I applied to be a cop because there was one who used to walk a beat near where I grew up, my last foster placement. He would let me walk with him sometimes, and when I did, no one would say a word to me, because I was with him. People respected him. I knew that was the job I wanted to do. And my size would be a benefit. If criminals were scared of me, then that had to be a good thing.'

'I can see you're down with the idea of your size making people afraid, but has it occurred to you it might also make people feel safe?'

Danny looked at her as if she might have taken leave of her senses. 'What do you mean?'

'I guarantee you that Ash sees you as someone who can protect her. You're big and strong, but show her that you're also kind and gentle. You didn't do anything so awful today, other than fall over yourself a bit and not say a whole lot. The next time you're with her, take the time to let her know you're her friend and are there to take care of her and protect her. I promise you, she'll be delighted and will feel much better knowing you're around.'

'I don't know, Tessa. Maybe I'd be better sticking with the investigative stuff and leaving the touchy-feely stuff to you and Maggie.'

'I'm afraid that's in breach of your job description.'

'You never gave me a job description.'

'Yeah well, you'll just have to take my word for it then, won't you?'

23

Tessa was woken from a deep sleep, and at first she didn't know where she was or what had woken her, but then she realised her phone was ringing and picked it up.

'Yeah?'

'It's Jeremiah McEvoy,' the voice said.

'What can I do for you, Detective?'

'It's more what I can do for you. There's been some deaths, and I'm pretty sure they're linked to your case.'

'Why's that then?'

'Because the people killed are known poitín makers.'

'Can you send me the address?'

'I already have done. See you shortly. And, Tessa, I'd best warn you in advance, this isn't pretty.'

'Murder never is. What makes this different?'

She could hear the sound of muted conversation in the background, the ambient sounds of the crime scene.

'It's a family,' McEvoy said. 'Just like the Connollys, in fact, except the daughter is a bit older.'

'I'll be there as quickly as I can.'

Tessa rang Danny and Maggie as she dressed.

. . .

The address McEvoy had sent was for a farm that was really more of a smallholding on the Louth/Monaghan border. Maggie drove, deftly navigating the winding country lanes, many of which seemed even darker than usual due to the fact the upper branches of the trees that grew on either side of the narrow roads seemed to have reached out for each other and become entangled, forming a kind of natural roof above, blocking out even the pale moonlight.

The last stretch they traversed was pocked with potholes so deep, Tessa was sure one might swallow the car whole if they drove into it.

'Are you sure we're not lost?' Danny asked, peering nervily through the window at the very rural setting.

'Only if Mr Google has steered us wrong,' Maggie said. 'I'm following his instructions.'

'It doesn't look like anyone lives here,' the big cop grumbled. 'And shouldn't there be other police vehicles?'

Suddenly the lane began to widen, and it broadened out into a cobbled yard that contained a large shed, from which the lowing of cattle could be heard, a long building that Tessa assumed was a milking parlour and a small house that had light emitting from each of its windows. An array of police cars and Mariahs were parked here and there about the farmyard. Maggie parked her Focus up beside an unmarked Toyota with a blue flashing light still revolving on the roof, illuminating the darkness.

The house looked as if it had been built sometime in the nineteenth century. It was small, made of solid concrete bricks and had a high, vaulted roof. The front door was open, and light spilled out in a long rectangle.

They all disembarked, put on protective white overalls, foot protectors and masks to prevent their leaving any of their own

DNA behind, and gingerly stepped inside. Maggie produced a bottle of disinfectant and, with Tessa's help, carefully scrubbed down the wheels of her chair.

McEvoy, as if he'd been waiting for them, appeared out of a room to their left.

'Medical examiner isn't here yet,' the detective said when the trio were gathered in the hallway of the cottage. It was low-ceilinged, the walls decorated with floral wallpaper that seemed far too busy for the narrow passageway. 'Bodies are still where they fell.'

McEvoy stopped, his eyes suddenly falling on Pavlov.

'That mutt can't be here. Come on, you fucking know that.'

'He won't move from my lap,' Maggie said, 'and he is, actually, a member of the force. Pavlov is a registered member of the dog unit.'

'Seriously? If he's a sniffer dog, I've never seen one like him.'

'He works with me and he will not contaminate the crime scene,' Maggie said firmly. 'That's all you need to know.'

McEvoy shrugged. 'Have it your way.'

'What happened?' Tessa wanted to know.

'Family were called the O'Neills,' McEvoy said as he led them up the hallway to the stairs, which were steep and curved to the east, as was the custom in cottages built in the nineteenth century. The floral wallpaper continued here, and Tessa noted there were family photos hanging on the wall on the way up the stairs: a dark-haired man whose smiles didn't seem to reach his eyes, a blonde woman with rosy cheeks and an auburn-haired girl, shown at different ages in the pictures: a toddler, a grinning, gap-toothed child of about seven, and a surly pre-teen were all featured.

The friendly family scenes seemed at odds with the tableau the police officers were now faced with.

Someone had put a tarpaulin over a shape that lay about halfway down the stairs.

'From what we can see, the killer kicked in the front door, made their way upstairs,' McEvoy explained. 'The noise seems to have woken Tony, the dad. We figure he got up and was coming to see what was going on. Met the intruders on his way down. His wife, Rita, was found shot to death on her bedroom floor. They had a teenaged daughter, Susan, and she was shot in her bed. Must have been a deep sleeper. Didn't seem to wake up through it all.'

'Or the poor kid was so scared she just froze,' Maggie said.

'Maybe,' McEvoy agreed. 'I could show you but...'

He looked at Maggie's chair and then helplessly at Tessa.

'We don't need to see,' Tessa said. 'Not right now, anyway.'

'I could probably manage the stairs if I had to,' Maggie added. 'But I appreciate your concern, Detective.'

'I... I'm sorry if I've come off as awkward,' McEvoy said. 'I've never met a member of the force with... with physical challenges before.'

'That's quite all right,' Maggie said gently. 'Can I just advise you that if you're not sure when it comes to people's levels of ability, it's always best to ask?'

'I'll remember that, thanks.'

'Were they clean kills?' Tessa asked.

'One shot in the chest, one in the head,' McEvoy said, seemingly relieved to have the subject of the conversation changed.

'Execution style,' Tessa said, more to herself than anyone else.

'Yes. I suppose so,' McEvoy agreed. 'Whoever did it was confident. We've not found any brass, but there's no reason to believe he missed. Seems pretty straightforward.'

'Were these people large operators too?' Danny asked.

'Not particularly,' McEvoy said. 'I mean, I knew Tony had a still, but he only made a few bottles for himself and his pals. He was barely even on my radar.'

'Is it possible he started to expand recently?' Tessa asked.

'It's possible. But it's fucking unlikely. I just can't see it.'

'Why not?'

'Because Tony O'Neill wasn't very good. The stuff he made was... well, it was *awful*. The kind of poitín that people used to say would make you go blind if you drank a lot of it.'

'I thought that was just something they said to stop people imbibing,' Tessa said.

'It was really, but some of the stuff you'd come across is pure poison,' McEvoy replied. 'And O'Neill's batch was pretty close to it.'

'So why shoot him and his family? It doesn't make any sense.'

'Damned if I know. All I can tell you is that two people are missing and a family has just been butchered. And something needs to be done about that. It can't go unanswered.'

'So let's answer it,' Tessa said. 'In the plainest language possible.'

24

They got back to the hotel at 5 a.m. and sat in the reception lounge.

The night porter, a rail-thin man with a bald head and a frizz of grey about his ears, brought them tea and a bowl of water for Pavlov, and told them breakfast wouldn't be served for another hour but that he'd be happy to bring them some toast if they wished.

'Just the tea will be fine,' Tessa said. 'You're very good, James.'

The man nodded and withdrew.

'Where the hell does this leave us?' Maggie asked.

'We've been basing our case on the hypothesis that the Connollys have either been killed or abducted or gone on the run because of a disagreement between criminal partners over profit-sharing,' Tessa said. 'We weren't sure what the logic behind the whole thing was, but it seemed reasonable to assume the events out at the Connolly farm were all rooted in a business deal gone wrong.'

'But now we have a triple homicide,' Danny said. 'Another

family, another distiller, but at the complete other end of the market.'

'Is it possible McEvoy has missed something?' Maggie asked. 'Are the O'Neills much more influential than he thinks? Maybe Tony has improved his skills a lot over the lockdowns and is now shit-hot.'

'So the murders could be about knocking out a competitor?' Tessa mused. 'But why kill the daughter? That seems very heavy-handed.'

'It looks like an execution,' Danny said. 'There's no emotion in it – it's pure business. Completely impersonal.'

'And yet about as personal as you can get,' Maggie said.

'Could we be looking at a cull of all the distillers in the area?' Danny asked.

'Wipe out the competition...' Tessa said. 'That is possible. But is it feasible? In a county with so many?'

'How many can there be?' Maggie pondered. 'I mean, we're not looking at the chap who just makes one batch a year. We'd surely have to consider only people who do it commercially.'

'The O'Neills barely seem to qualify, but yes, I'm with you,' Tessa said.

'I'll bet McEvoy has a list of all the active distillers who would fall into that category,' Maggie replied.

'We need to get them under guard,' Danny agreed.

'That could be quite an undertaking,' Tessa said.

'Easier than having to investigate dozens of murders!'

'I'll give you that.'

'So who's going to call to tell him?' Danny wondered.

'It was your idea,' Maggie and Tessa said in unison.

'I knew not having a boss would come back to bite me sooner rather than later,' Danny grumbled.

25

McEvoy didn't hide his distaste but listened to Danny's suggestion and asked that the team meet him at the station in an hour to look at the files he kept and determine who might require protection.

They gathered in a conference room at the back of the main Garda building, by which time McEvoy had already filled the long table with brown cardboard folders.

'Well if it isn't the Burns Unit,' he said as they came in.

'I see you're not computerised yet,' Maggie deadpanned.

McEvoy snorted. 'We've only recently discovered digital watches out here in the sticks. This is as good as it gets.'

There were twenty-two bundles on the table.

'What constitutes a professional-level moonshiner?' McEvoy asked. 'Like, I'll give you that the Connollys were hardcore, but Tony O'Neill might have produced twenty, thirty bottles a year, most of which were hardly better than furniture polish. I want to be clear: I had no evidence he was selling the stuff and no cause to arrest him.'

'No one's blaming you for what happened to that family,'

Tessa said. 'You didn't drop the ball here, Jeremiah. This is something none of us could have seen coming.'

She felt the detective was perhaps being a bit oversensitive about the whole thing and wondered if he'd been pulled up before for dereliction of duty.

'What you can do is help us make sure no one else gets hurt,' Maggie said.

'I can do that,' McEvoy said. 'So what are we looking for?'

'I suppose we take the O'Neills as a baseline,' Tessa said. 'So anyone producing the same or more than they did warrants protection.'

'Right.' McEvoy began to sort through the folders, tossing some onto the floor.

This way he reduced the collection to nine.

'I want you to read through these and tell me if you think they need to have a squad car parked outside their homes,' he said. 'A couple of them are individuals I'd like to see locked up, but most are along the same lines as the O'Neills – just lads and lasses who enjoy making their own batch of 'shine. Not really serious distillers at all.'

'We'll give them a look-over,' Tessa said. 'But if they're similar to that poor family from last night, I think we need to offer them protection.'

'Read through them and let me know,' the vice detective said and left them to their work.

The trio set up a kind of production line, passing each file along as they finished, and within the space of an hour had completed the exercise. McEvoy had, of course, been right: there were only two among the potential victims who had either the skill or capacity to produce on a semi-professional level, and they were nowhere near as versatile or as prodigious as Joe Connolly.

Tessa noticed that no one called Elias or with a history of

terrorist activity was among the group. Noel's contact had obviously managed to stay under McEvoy's radar.

Or perhaps the detective didn't consider him because, as Noel had said, he didn't really produce much liquor himself.

Or there was always the chance McEvoy was getting paid off to ignore Two-Toe's activities, or that if he wasn't being included in the protection detail, perhaps he was a big enough operation to have his own security. She decided to visit the topic with McEvoy later.

'We have to assume whoever's behind the disappearance and the deaths is being careful,' she said to her two partners. 'Thorough. Making sure there's no one who could possibly present a threat to their operation.'

'It still seems clumsy to me,' Maggie said. 'There has to be something else going on.'

'Until we know what it is, we protect these people,' Tessa said. 'Let's go and tell Jeremiah we're good to go.'

They went out to the squad room. Pavlov, his tail wagging, trotted over and nuzzled the vice detective's leg.

'Oh, hello, fella,' McEvoy said, reaching down and scratching the little dog's ears.

'We think you should assign protection to each of the nine,' Tessa said.

'You know we're a small force,' McEvoy said. 'It'll put us under serious pressure.'

'Give us a couple of days,' Tessa said. 'With a bit of luck, we'll be able to find out what's really going on, and you can pull your people off protection duty. But for now, we don't need a bloodbath, so let's make sure there are units on each of these people until we know the threat has either gone or been neutralised.'

'I just hope no one decides to rob the post office,' McEvoy said ruefully.

26

Maggie and Pavlov went to the hospital after breakfast to continue their work with Ash, while Danny interviewed more of the Connollys' neighbours and Tessa tried to find something to link the missing parents with the O'Neills, something more than a shared interest in making liquor.

McEvoy set her up with a desk in the corner of the squad room, and she got to work.

Tessa wasn't particularly technologically minded, but she knew how to use a laptop, and while she personally wasn't a fan of social media, she knew almost everyone else was. It followed, then, that when attempting to establish whether or not a relationship existed between two individuals, their social-media pages were probably the best place to begin.

It didn't take her long to learn that Joe Connolly and Tony O'Neill did know one another and shared quite a few interests. Both of their Facebook pages featured a lot of references to local sporting fixtures, particularly hurling and football, as well as various posts about country-music artists they both enjoyed.

Tessa noticed that Tony commented on just about everything Joe posted and shared about three quarters of his posts (all of the music ones). Joe was less eager, and in fairness wasn't a regular Facebook user, but the interactions between the two men showed they were definitely familiar with one another and exhibited an open friendliness.

Instagram told another side of the story. Joe was much more active on this platform and shared lots of images, reels and posts about home distilling and home brewing – Tessa reckoned he did so as a cover. If he was ever arrested for producing some bottles, he could point to the page and show he was an enthusiastic amateur.

Once again, Tony seemed to be a major follower, liking and commenting on each post. Once again, Joe didn't return the favour with the same vigour but was certainly active on the other man's page too.

Tony didn't seem to use Twitter very often, and Joe not at all, and while Tessa knew TikTok existed, she wasn't sure what it really was so didn't even bother to look. She figured she had enough anyway. The two men were obviously online friends, and she had a feeling a trawl of all the comments across both pages would probably reveal references to real-life encounters. They lived in the same county, after all.

Tessa got some tea, found some digestive biscuits in a cupboard in the kitchen and brought a couple back to her desk.

Then, starting with Facebook, she went back two years, and began to read each and every post, first on Joe Connolly's page, and then on Tony O'Neill's, scribbling in a notebook the dates and details of anything she felt illuminated the nature of their relationship, taking screenshots of any comments that struck her as important. When she was finished with Facebook, she did the same on Instagram.

Two hours later, she'd filled five pages in her notebook, taken thirty screenshots, consumed six mugs of tea, had a crick in her neck and was none the wiser.

Monaghan was keeping its secrets close.

In frustration she picked up her phone.

'Noel, I want to meet Two-Toes now.'

27

Danny worked backwards from where he'd finished off his interviews the previous day, moving further and further away from the Connolly homestead, stopping at each house he encountered.

He learned nothing more than he had the previous day: the Connollys were a close couple who adored their daughter, kept a profitable and well-run tillage farm and operated a respected and popular side trade as distillers. They went out of their way to employ only local people whenever they needed extra hands on both the legal and illegal sides of their enterprises, and it seemed to Danny this was a very wise move, as no one seemed willing to entertain the idea that anything they did had a less-than-honourable motive.

The Connollys were local Monaghan royalty, and not a person he met would hear a bad word said about them.

At 2.15 p.m. he was coming out of the home of a single mother named Katie who told him that, without the semi-regular employment she got from the Connollys, she would have been hard-pressed to put food on the table, when he spotted someone leaning against the bonnet of his Golf.

'Can I help you?' the giant detective asked.

The person using his vehicle as a bench stood up when he saw Danny approach and extended a hand. The individual was perhaps sixty and dressed in an expensive-looking black pinstriped suit. His hair looked to be recently cut and was arranged in a wavy comb-over, covering what Danny assumed was a bald pate.

'I wanted to introduce meself,' the man said in a broad Monaghan accent, that Danny, who'd been speaking to locals now for two days, had a suspicion was slightly exaggerated. 'I'm Mogue Kearney.'

'Hello,' Danny said and introduced himself.

'I trust everyone hereabouts is being cooperative?' the man continued.

'Each person I've spoken to has been happy to talk to me,' Danny said.

'And are we any closer to knowin' what happened to Joe and Daisy?'

Danny smiled. He'd been expecting this line of questioning. 'We're following a line of inquiry.'

'And what might that be?'

'I'm not at liberty to discuss it,' Danny said. 'I'm sorry, but who are you?'

'I've already told you. I'm Mogue Kearney.'

'And what's your interest in the case?'

'I'm just a man who likes to keep his finger on the pulse of what's happening locally.'

'Do you know the Connollys?'

'Oh, I do. I surely do. Lovely people. A charming couple.'

'Do you know of any reason why they might have had to leave their farm in a hurry?'

'I do not. Other than to say life can take all kinds of funny turns. Don't they always say we're one stroke of bad luck away from bein' bankrupt and homeless?'

Danny thought about that. 'Are you saying they were in financial difficulty?'

'Oh now, I wouldn't be in a position to make any judgements on that score. That wouldn't be neighbourly, would it?'

Danny moved towards his car. 'Mr Kearney, I thank you for your time. Is there somewhere I can find you if I wanted to ask you any more questions?'

The man took a step forward. As he did, as if by pre-arranged signal, a black Mercedes Kompressor pulled out of a gateway just up the road and cruised slowly towards them.

'Everyone in Monaghan knows where to fine ould Mogue. And sure, I have a feelin' you'll be onto the Google the moment I'm gone, and then you'll have my address and phone number in three seconds flat.'

'Wouldn't it be easier to just tell me?'

'Sure, then you'd have to write it down in your little notebook. I would say this is actually a lot easier.'

The Merc pulled alongside, and Danny saw there was a dark-haired man with a well-defined jawline behind the wheel. He didn't look at the detective, keeping his eyes straight ahead.

'If you keep your finger on the pulse,' Danny said, 'I bet you know all about the O'Neill family too.'

'Terrible business,' Mogue Kearney said, opening the rear-passenger-side door and climbing in.

'Do you have any thoughts on who might have borne them ill will?'

'Tony kept himself to himself. Liked his music. Liked his football. Liked a drink. Just the same as any of us really.'

'So just a quiet guy who minded his own business,' Danny said.

'Well,' Mogue Kearney said, grinning suddenly, 'I wouldn't say *that*. Oh no, I wouldn't say that at all.'

And then he closed the door, and the Merc pulled away and within seconds was gone up the country lane, leaving only

the scent of exhaust fumes and the strange man's awful
aftershave.

28

Noel Randall was nervous.

'Can you, just for a moment, try to imagine the conversation I had to have with this guy to explain why I was bringing a police detective to visit?'

They were in Tessa's Capri, parked outside a large barn that stood on its own in a field of waste ground on the Monaghan side of Castleblayney, near the Armagh border. It was mid-afternoon and the shadows were getting that long look they got as the sun sank lower, and the ever-present Monaghan wind had taken on an urgent, discordant moan as it whispered its way across the low countryside.

'I have no doubt you came up with a convincing story.'

'That's the problem – I didn't!' Noel spluttered, sounding truly horrified with himself. 'I panicked and told him the truth: you and I were in a care home together and you're investigating the disappearance of the Connollys and want to know about the 'shine business locally.'

'Well at least we won't need to try and remember a compli-cated cover story,' Tessa said. 'That's a positive, surely.'

'Let's just go in and get this done!' Noel said despondently.

He led her to a metal door around the side of the huge building and rapped on it smartly three times. There was no response for what felt like an age, and then they could hear echoing footsteps drawing closer, and the door was opened a crack and a blue eye could be seen peering out.

'What?'

The voice was light, almost feminine.

'Noel Randall to see Elias.'

'Does he know you're coming?'

'Would anyone call to see Elias out of the blue?' Noel retorted irritably. 'Go and tell him I'm here, will you?'

The eye disappeared and the footsteps echoed again, going away this time.

'Are you sure you made an appointment?' Tessa asked.

'Don't you start!'

They waited, the light continuing to dim and the wind growing more urgent. Tessa noticed the grass hereabouts seemed to have a greyish tinge, as if there was something unhealthy about the land. She wrapped her coat more tightly about herself and turned back to the door as they heard the gate-keeper approach again.

The door opened fully this time, revealing a slender young man who might have been twenty-one but could easily have been younger.

'Come in,' he said, standing back and making urgent motions with his hand. Tessa couldn't help but notice their doorman was missing a finger on his left hand. Noel had obviously not been overstating Elias's predilection for digital amputation.

The door was closed behind them and locked, the youngster producing a set of keys from the pocket of oversized jeans. Nothing more was said, but he set off down a long corridor, and Tessa and Noel followed.

The walkway opened up into a large room that had been

divided into cubicles, most of which were empty, but Tessa counted five people at workstations, tapping away on laptops, some with headsets on, speaking quietly into microphones.

Sitting behind a desk at the top of the room was a hugely obese man with a surprisingly handsome face, the aquiline nose and porcelain skin at odds with the vast bulk of his body. He had long grey hair tied back in a ponytail, and he looked up at Tessa and Noel with piercing eyes as they arrived with their young guide.

'So you're the copper my friend Noel says is like family to him,' he said, his accent telling Tessa he was from somewhere close to Donegal.

'I'm Tessa Burns. Noel has been good enough to effect an introduction.'

'I don't know if that makes him brave or foolhardy,' the big man said.

He stood up and, using a blackthorn walking stick as support, came around the desk, his hand extended.

'I'm Elias Hicks.'

'Thank you for agreeing to see me.'

'I don't know what you think I can do for you, but I owe Noel here a favour, so let's sit down and have a chat. This makes us clear by the way, Noel.'

'Understood, Elias.'

'Come on,' the obese man said, shuffling towards a door to their left. 'I'm a busy man. Quentin, keep an eye on the shop.'

The slender youth nodded and perched on the edge of his superior's desk, surveying the room as if he expected one of the workers to suddenly run amok.

Elias led them to a small room which had another desk but also a couch and a large armchair, into which he sank with a moan of relief. 'Whaddaya want to know?'

'Do you have any thoughts on what might have happened to the Connollys?'

'You get right to the point, don't you?'

Tessa shrugged. 'You're a busy man. I don't want to waste your time.'

'Am I a suspect?'

'A few names have come up so far in the investigation, but yours hasn't been one of them. That said, with the Connollys gone, I hear you'll become the biggest figure in the illegal booze trade this side of the border.'

'You're a brave woman coming here throwing about accusations like that.'

The threat was clear in the man's voice, and Tessa noted a dark hue passing over his pale eyes.

'I'm not accusing anyone,' she said genially. 'I'm simply stating how it looks. Noel tells me you're someone who knows what's going on in Monaghan in a way no one else does, so I thought your opinion might be worth hearing. I'd like to be educated.'

'I don't see myself as being on the same playing field as the Connollys,' Elias said. 'I am, to use an old-fashioned term, a smuggler. People want certain products they can't get their hands on through legal means, I source those things for them. Or maybe they desire something that is available but at a price that's unattractive, or there are limits on the amount they can buy, restrictions. I get it for them at a lower price and in greater bulk. That, Ms Burns, is what I do, and I'm very successful at it.'

'Bravo,' Tessa said.

'I'm going to ignore the sarcasm in your tone,' the huge man said. 'Joe and Daisy were specialist producers. What made them such a focus of attention was that Joe was able to create copies of popular spirits to a high quality – he could even improve on them – to order. I'm sure you know their plan to initiate a line of fancy drinks for the European market. Everyone in the know was talking about it.'

'So what went wrong?'

'Joe and Daisy were involved with some very dangerous and very... irritable people. In situations like that, lots of things can go wrong. Partnerships can sour. When that occurs, I'm afraid people get hurt. It's the cost of doing business.'

'You're aware of the parties involved?'

'As you say, I keep a weather eye on things in Monaghan.'

'The Donegans and the Shiggins crew?'

'Pffft,' Elias scoffed. 'You're not keepin' up with the news at all, Ms Garda. There were a few others in the mix too.'

Tessa sat forward, interested. 'Who?'

'What's in this for me?'

'I'd owe you one.'

'You already do. I thought that was understood.'

'I'd owe you a big one.'

'Hmmmm. I need you to know, I will collect.'

'I would expect no less.'

'Okay. I know... knew... someone who was close to Joe Connolly. What he told me was that Joe and his missus were keen to get out from under the influence of their families. They wanted to be able to call the shots themselves without having to constantly consult with their respective parents.'

'But hadn't their folks been bankrolling their operation?'

'They had. They were the... um... the seed investors. But from what I was told, word got out about what they were planning. The profitability of the concept was obvious, and Drumlin Spirits was approached by several other interested parties, all of whom were more than happy to buy the Donegans and the Shigginses out.'

Tessa was perplexed. 'Is that even possible? Does criminal enterprise work that way? Can you just negotiate a takeover purely based on the financial side of it?'

'The fact you're here answers your question,' Elias said. 'I'd say someone wasn't happy about being pushed out. Or maybe one of the new faces decided to take a more aggressive negotiating approach. Abduct the talent and hold them until their gangster mammies and daddies were prepared to back down. It's not exactly a new tactic. People have been doing it since the medieval period.'

'Who else was involved?'

'That my source didn't know. He had Joe's ear but not all the way.'

'You keep talking about this source in the past tense.'

'He is, alas, no longer with us.'

'What happened to him?'

'He recently met an untimely end.'

'Tony O'Neill,' Tessa said.

'One and the same.'

'Why kill him, and an even bigger question, why murder his wife and child?'

'He was friends with Joe, as I said. Did some distilling himself.'

'He wasn't all that good at it, according to Detective McEvoy.'

'Jeremiah would know,' Elias said, winking.

'What's that supposed to mean?'

'Ah, Jerry likes a drop of the cratur himself from time to time. By which I mean for breakfast, if he can get it.'

'I see,' Tessa said. 'And you make sure he has a bottle to hand should he need one.'

'I'm a generous man.'

'I'm getting that impression,' Tessa said.

What Elias was saying didn't mean Jeremiah McEvoy was in his pocket exactly, but it definitely suggested a weakness in the detective's character. One that could be exploited by others, if they were so inclined. Tessa decided there and then to keep a closer eye on McEvoy.

'Why were the O'Neills murdered?' she asked.

'I genuinely don't know. I only heard about it this morning.

If I had to guess, I'd say Tony annoyed the wrong person and it came back to bite him. He had a habit of making claims he couldn't back up. Inflating his abilities, if you know what I mean. He was a man whose abilities didn't match his ambition. I know Joe Connolly trusted him, but I always felt that was a mistake. I'd bet Tony told someone he'd do something and then couldn't deliver. As to the wife and child... it happens. I don't personally like carrying on that way, but this is a vicious business.'

Tessa sighed and ran her hand through her hair. She'd had three hours' sleep the previous night and reckoned she would need a lot of caffeine to stay sharp until she made it to bed that night.

'If you wanted to find out who the other interested parties were on the Connolly takeover, who would you ask?'

Elias pursed his lips. 'You're gonna owe me a *big* favour. If I get a reputation for talkin' to the coppers, I could be finished.'

'I won't mention you if I don't have to.'

'The man you're gonna need to talk to won't give you the time of day if I don't vouch for you.'

'Give me a name. I'll chase it up myself.'

Elias tutted. 'It doesn't work that way. If you're half the cop Noel says you are, you ought to know that.'

Tessa held the big man's gaze. 'One child is in hospital and so scared she's barely saying a word. Another has been murdered, along with her parents, and if the Connollys are dead too, we're looking at five homicides. I could haul you into the station right now, arrest you as an accessory after the fact. Hold you until you decide to give me the name.'

Elias didn't look away. 'I could push a button on the underside of my desk which would bring four lads with guns in here, who would restrain the pair of you while I sliced off your fingers, one at a time, with a pair of secateurs.'

'They wouldn't make it through the door,' Tessa said and in an unhurried motion took her gun out from under her jacket.

'Well, that scared the living daylights out of you, didn't it?' Elias said and laughed merrily. 'You are one tough lady. Noel, she's a ticket. I'm enjoying this visit.'

Tessa tried not to look bemused. 'Are you going to give me the name?'

Elias took a mobile phone from the pocket of his cardigan and pulled up a number.

'I'll go one better. But remember, one hand washes the other, Tessa Burns. And I collect on my debts.'

29

Maggie and Ash were playing draughts while Pavlov and Bunny watched closely.

'I don't remember much about what happened the day my mam and dad went missing,' the little girl said as she took two of Maggie's pieces – Ash was on red, Maggie on black. 'I think there was a lot of shoutin', and maybe somebody was screamin', but I'm not sure that wasn't me. I know I ran across the fields, because I can remember my pyjamas was all wet from the grass, but the next thing I know, I was being found by that guard.'

'Garda O'Connor,' Maggie said.

'I was bad scared of him.'

'He's a nice man really,' Maggie said. 'He can just seem a bit gruff is all.'

'The woman guard was nice. I liked her.'

'I don't think I met her.'

'I wish I could remember more. I've thunk and thunk, and I just can't.'

'That's okay,' Maggie said, moving one of her pieces forward. 'Anything you can recall, even from the days before, would be a help.'

'There was lots of people callin' to our house, I remember that,' Ash said. 'Always men comin' and going.'

'Can you remember anything about them?'

'There was a man who talked funny. Like he was from a different country.'

'Okay,' Maggie said. 'That helps a lot. Can you try and talk like he did for me?'

The little girl thought for a second, and then said, in an accent that sounded to Maggie to be a cross between Punjabi and Yorkshire: *'We'll make a deal, Mr Connolly. You'll like working with us, I promise you this.'*

Maggie listened without interruption and tried to keep her expression serious, but then Ash started to giggle, and they both creased up.

If anyone heard us, they'd think we were callous and cold-hearted, the family liaison officer thought, *laughing away when this child's parents could be dead or being tortured or hiding in terror for their lives. They don't understand the pain behind the giggles. You can't until you've been there yourself. Until you've experienced this kind of loss and uncertainty.*

'I don't know if that's really it,' the little girl said. 'But it's as close as I can do.'

'I bet it's a very good impression,' Maggie said. 'What about the others? Were they all Irish?'

'Yes. I think so.'

'Do you remember anything unusual about any of them?'

'There was one I really didn't like.'

'Tell me about him.'

'He was an old man. Like, I think he may be a hundred years old.'

'Very old then?'

Ash nodded. 'He was always lookin' to talk to my dad. I remember him sayin': "Joe, you gots to cook us up somethin' real special. Somethin' no one else has done before." I remember Dad would always say: "Everythin' I does is special," but this old guy, he didn't seem to think that was true.'

'Do you remember what your dad called him?'

'No. I used to leave when he came in. Go to my room and play or go outside. He smelled *real* bad. I never wanted to be around him.'

Maggie took three of Ash's pieces in one move, and the girl cried out in mock annoyance.

'Hey! I'm gonna get you for that!'

'I think you have to crown my piece first, Ash!'

'Did you see that, Pavlov? She distracted me and when I wasn't lookin' – she stole three of my counters!'

The dog whined sympathetically.

Maggie laughed. 'Hey, remember who feeds you, Pav!'

Just then the door to the room opened, and a man in a white coat came in, a stethoscope slung around his neck. His head was lowered as he read from a clipboard, but even without getting a good look at his face, Maggie knew she hadn't seen him before. She thought this was unusual, as she'd met most of the doctors who were treating Ash, but reasoned she'd only been there about twenty-four hours, and there were probably several shifts that ran parallel across the week.

'I'm Dr Ellis,' he said. 'Might I have a look at this young lady?'

Maggie reversed her chair away from the bed to give him room, but he said: 'Can I ask you to be so good as to move outside for a few moments please?'

Maggie glanced at Ash and saw that the child had frozen. She wondered if it was just a reaction to a strange man (she'd just admitted to being frightened of Garda O'Connor), but something about the fixed way the child was staring at the newcomer made her a little uneasy.

'Might I ask why?' Maggie said. 'I'm here as a Garda liaison at present, as Aisling's parents are currently... unable to be around.'

'I'm sorry,' the man said, and the whole time he was speaking, his head was still lowered. 'There's nothing here indicating you're in loco parentis. I need to examine Aisling, and I prefer to protect patient confidentiality. This is my job, and my legal and ethical responsibility.'

Maggie angled her chair so she could get a better look at the man, and as she drew a little closer, she caught a scent of tobacco from him, and sweat, and saw there was dirt under his fingernails.

'It's also my legal and ethical responsibility to protect Ash,' she said, feeling her body relax as she prepared herself for swift action. 'Ash, would you like me to stay while Dr Ellis examines you?'

'Yes please,' the child said.

'There, you have your patient's consent,' Maggie said. 'I'm staying. If you're unhappy with this, might I suggest you contact the hospital's chief medical officer? They'll confirm for you that I'm acting fully within my remit as Ash's liaison.'

The man sighed and, leaning over, placed his clipboard on the windowsill. As he did, Maggie could see his face fully for the first time. There was something not right about it: it was too smooth, as if it had been crudely moulded out of playdough. There was a nose, and a ridge for the eyebrows, and a gap for the mouth, but the lines and crevices that create character and define an individual's look were completely absent. Even the hair didn't look real, and Maggie wondered if it might be a wig – it seemed to sit on the man's head rather than grow out of it.

'Okay,' he said, reaching inside his white coat.

Maggie didn't wait to see what he was reaching for. With her left hand, she hit the alarm button on her chair. The result was instantaneous, the room filling with a piercing whistle. If the man was hurt by it, he gave no sign. Luckily, Maggie knew never to rely on the alarm alone as a deterrent, and at the same time she was operating it with her left hand, she was whipping out the baton with her right. Using her elbow on the chair's joystick, she shunted it forward and, now within range, drove the base of the baton sharply into the man's larynx, while at the same time smashing him in the groin with the handle of her chair.

She couldn't see what was happening behind her, but she knew Pavlov had taken up a protective position in front of Ash, and if she failed and the man got past her, the dog would fight to the death to protect the child. She hoped it wouldn't come to that, but it was some comfort to know there was a contingency plan if it did.

The two blows should have disabled the imposter, but to Maggie's horror, he seemed undeterred and lunged at her, making to grab her by the throat. She swung the baton across his left cheekbone, leaving a red welt, then again across his right, and, shocked, he took a step back.

That was the advantage she'd been waiting for. Rather than retreating, she pushed forward, putting the chair into a rapid acceleration, executing a hard swerve and crushing the man's right foot with her right front wheel.

He gasped in pain, swearing loudly, and she silenced him by smashing the baton with all her strength into his mouth. There was a crunching sound, and she knew she'd taken out some of his teeth.

She reversed off the mangled foot, feeling the back of the chair collide with Ash's bed. Glancing quickly back at the child, she saw she was still covering her ears, and realised the alarm continued to sound. She deactivated it, and as she did so, the door flew open and a nurse rushed in, a tall, elegant African woman named Patience.

'Is everyone okay in here?' Patience asked, and then she saw the battered and bloodied visage of the man who'd claimed to be a doctor.

'What's going on?' she asked, the horror raw in her voice.

The injured man spat blood and fragments of tooth at Maggie and drew a handgun from inside his jacket. He said something, but his mouth was too shredded to work properly.

'Patience, get down!' Maggie said and, tossing the baton into her lap, blasted pepper spray into the interloper's face.

He screamed, loud and full-throated, as the stinging substance aggravated the open wounds about his face and mouth, and in his agony and panic squeezed off a shot that thudded into the wall right beside the door.

'Drop the gun!' Maggie shouted. 'I don't want to hurt you anymore, but if you don't drop, it you give me no choice!'

Instead of complying, the man, blinded, swung his weapon in the direction of her voice.

'You fucking *moron!*' she said and, tossing the can of mace into her left hand, grabbed the baton again and brought it down hard across the wrist of his gun hand once, then twice. The second blow caused his hand to go limp, and the gun dropped to the floor.

'Now stand down!' Maggie shouted, but before she'd even finished the command he was on her, screaming wordlessly and clawing at whatever he could get his hands on, seemingly beyond reason.

She tried to push him off, but the exertion of the fight had already exhausted her.

'Ash,' she said, turning her head away from him so the child could see her face. 'Run!'

The girl nodded and, grabbing Bunny, scooted down the bed. Patience, who seemed frozen to the spot, came back to her senses, took the child by the arm and disappeared into the hall-way. Maggie felt hands closing on her throat and knew the battle was reaching its conclusion.

As her windpipe was crushed closed, she heard a snarl, and then something thudded into them both. She heard a growling and felt a shuddering and shaking, and then the man who was choking her screamed again, and she realised Pavlov, her beloved friend, had come to her rescue.

Whatever the dog was doing, he distracted the man enough that he released his grip for a moment, and Maggie let herself go limp and slid out of the chair and onto the floor. She lay there for a moment, her head swimming, and waited for her vision to clear. Somewhere above her, Pavlov barked and raged, his ferocity telling her he was unharmed, ready to go another ten rounds if the fight called for it.

Shaking her head to dispel the dizziness, she saw what she'd gone to the floor to find: the man's handgun.

Maggie technically held the rank of detective sergeant, and detectives in the Irish police force were entitled to carry sidearms. Due to her cerebral palsy, however, Maggie chose not to exercise this option – her condition meant she sometimes experienced muscle spasms, and these made shooting a weapon potentially hazardous, as she might lose control and tighten her finger on the trigger involuntarily. And as a family liaison officer, her duties rarely called for the use of a gun anyway.

But that didn't mean she didn't know how to use one.

Grabbing the weapon, she used what strength she had in her legs to shove herself backwards, away from her attacker, and then, holding the weapon two-handed, she aimed it up at him. She couldn't see Pavlov, and the man seemed to be lunging around, trying to grab him, though unsuccessfully – the dog was clearly ducking and dodging out of the way. She could see from where she was lying, however, that one of the man's ears was missing its upper part. She assumed her dog was responsible.

'Hey!' she cried.

The man stopped and spun, his eyes still blurry from the mace.

'I am a member of the Garda Síochána, and I am placing you under arrest. Cease and desist any further aggression, and your wounds will be treated and you will be given a chance to recover and granted access to legal counsel.'

The man seemed to ponder this for a second.

'Do we have a deal?' Maggie asked, hoping he would say yes because she thought her arms were about to give out from holding the gun – she was drenched in sweat and afraid she was going to pass out.

She was aware of voices outside the door, and called: 'No one come in here! It's not safe!'

And as she did, the man made to throw himself on her, and she fired.

The shot hit him in the middle of the chest, and he staggered back, landing against Ash's bedside locker before sliding down it, coming to rest in a half-seated position on the floor.

'Now what did you have to go and do that for?' Maggie said in temper.

Pavlov jumped down and came to her, and, her dog in her arms, Maggie closed her eyes and let unconsciousness take her for a while.

30

The first thing Maggie saw when she came round was Ash's face peering down at her, Pavlov's furry one close beside it.

'Maggie?' the little girl said tremulously. 'Are you okay? Did the bad man hurt you?'

Maggie smiled tiredly and held out her arms, which felt like they weighed a hundred pounds, and the child came to her and hugged her tightly.

'I hear you got in a scuffle,' a voice she recognised said, and Maggie realised she was in a private room in the hospital, and Tessa and Danny were there too.

It was Tessa who'd just spoken.

'Yeah, well, what can I say. My mam didn't raise a shrinking violet.'

'Can't take you anywhere, can we?' Danny said and reached over to squeeze Maggie's hand. 'Ash has refused to leave your side. She's been very worried.'

'I'm okay,' Maggie said, stroking the little girl's hair. 'He didn't hurt me. It's just that, you know how I'm in the wheelchair? Well, it means if I have to do certain things, I get tired faster than other people.'

'And fighting that man made you tired?'

'It did. He was very strong, and he didn't want to stop fighting.'

'He's gone now though, right?'

'Yes. He's gone.'

'Okay then,' Ash said, still holding on to Maggie as if for dear life.

'Ash, the way you looked at him when he came in,' Maggie said. 'It was almost as if you knew him.'

'I don't remember,' the child said.

'You're sure?' Maggie pressed her. 'It was your face when he walked in that made me wary of him.'

'I really don't know, Maggie,' the child said. 'Just that I was scared.'

And wiping her eyes she sat back, scooping up Bunny and cuddling him.

'Are you afraid now, Ash?'

It was Danny who'd asked the question, much to Tessa's surprise.

The little girl nodded.

'Because Maggie is tired and can't protect you if something happens?'

The child nodded again.

'I'm quite a big person, aren't I?' Danny said. 'Look, if I stand right beside the door here, my head is almost as high as the top.'

He did just that, and then went up on his tiptoes and showed her that now he could touch the top part of the door frame with his head.

Ash watched him wide-eyed and then giggled. Danny laughed too, and then Tessa laughed, and Maggie laughed, and Pavlov barked and turned in a circle three times before sitting down again.

'If anyone comes in here to try and hurt you, they'll have to get past me first,' Danny said. 'And Tessa here might not look like much, but she's pretty tough too. And you know, Maggie will be fine again soon. She just needs a rest. So you've got lots of people who care about you and want to look after you.'

The child listened with grave seriousness, and everyone could see her relaxing. Tessa gave the big detective a thumbs up, and he grinned.

Patience stuck her head in. 'Miss Ash, I have a special order of ice cream for you. Chocolate and banana flavour, just as you requested. The special prize for being such a brave girl. How about you come with me and let your friends talk for a bit?'

Ash looked at Tessa, who nodded. 'Danny and I will come and find you shortly.'

'Can Pavlov come too?'

'Well that dog was also very brave,' Patience said. 'Maybe I can find a prize for him as well, if Maggie says it's okay.'

'Oh, I'd be grateful, Patience,' Maggie said. 'He saved my life, so I think he deserves all the prizes he can get.'

Patience winked and clicked her tongue, and Pavlov hopped down, his tail wagging, and followed Ash and the tall nurse out.

'So what the fuck happened?' Tessa asked as soon as the door was closed.

'He was dressed as a doctor,' Maggie said. 'If he'd had better personal hygiene, I might have fallen for it.'

'What can you tell us about him?' Danny wanted to know.

'Irish accent, but not from any region I could tell. He spoke like a newsreader or a radio presenter – what do they call it, a mid-Atlantic accent? He could take one *hell* of a beating and keep coming. And he wasn't going to be taken as a prisoner. He gave me no choice but to shoot him.'

'And he was after Ash?' Tessa asked.

'Yes.'

'Was he here to kill her?'

'I believe so. I mean, I don't see how he could have got her out. My guess is he planned to make it look like he'd given her a sedative. There was an empty syringe in his coat pocket. By the time we worked out she was dead, he'd be long gone.'

'Lucky you were here,' Tessa said.

'There wasn't a single other police officer in the hospital,' Danny said. 'They were all out protecting moonshiners up and down County Monaghan.'

'Which was very convenient,' Tessa agreed.

'You don't think...' Maggie said.

'That the O'Neill family were killed to create a distraction, get us to redirect our resources to leave Ash wide open?' Tessa finished for her.

'It's too awful to even countenance,' Maggie replied, horrified.

'And yet, here we are,' Danny said. 'My guess is they knew you'd be here but figured you wouldn't be much of a threat.'

'A serious miscalculation for the poor fucker currently laid out in the morgue,' Tessa agreed.

At that moment her phone buzzed.

'Tessa Burns,' she answered. 'Yes. That's great. We'll be right down.'

'Who's that?' Maggie wanted to know.

'The medical examiner. She was already here to look at the O'Neills, and she's ready to give your former friend the once-over.'

'I want to come,' Maggie said, trying to sit up and then falling back almost immediately, still weakened by her ordeal.

'Maggie, rest,' Tessa said, going to her friend and placing a kiss on her forehead. 'You saved that child's life today, and from what I saw of yer man, you put up one hell of a scrap to do it.'

'Me and Pavlov,' Maggie said, and then her lower lip started to tremble, and tears sprang to her eyes. 'It was me and Pavlov. I'd not have made it without him.'

'You're one hell of a team, you and Pav,' Tessa said, her own voice filling with emotion. 'It's why I wanted you both on mine.'

'You're a serious badass,' Danny agreed. 'And Pavlov is too.'

'Let us go and see what we've got, and we'll come back and fill you in on everything we learn.'

Maggie nodded, sniffing. 'Okay. I might... I might just take a nap.'

'Good plan,' Tessa said, but her best friend was already asleep.

31

Professor Julia Banks was a short, heavyset woman with a grey bob, and she was already peering at the dead man's facial injuries through a high-powered magnifying glass when they arrived to the morgue.

'He sustained quite a beating,' she said. 'Multiple maxillofacial fractures. And did someone pepper-spray him?'

'Prof, we know what *happened* to him,' Tessa said. 'I want to know who he is.'

'That'll take time,' Julia said.

'I know. Can you tell us anything?'

'Well, he's wearing a wig,' she replied, removing the hairpiece gingerly, 'and not a good one.'

'I'm going to hazard a guess and say that was part of his disguise,' Tessa said. 'Anything else?'

'He's in good shape. Very good muscle tone. It looks to me as if he's had some tattoos removed – I'm seeing signs of laser therapy on his arms and upper torso. But what interests me is his face.'

'I told you, he didn't give Maggie any choice. This guy was trying to kill a child,' Tessa said irritably.

'No, not that – although you know there's going to be an investigation into the degree of force used, don't you?'

'Bring it on,' Tessa said dryly.

'No, it's his skin. I've only ever seen this kind of thing once before.'

'What?' Danny asked.

'This man looks as if he's had multiple cosmetic surgeries. I mean, *a lot*. It's difficult to say what he looked like because of the facial injuries, but I would guess with a fair degree of certainty that he gave the impression his face was made of modelling clay.'

'We can look at the hospital security footage,' Tessa said.

'Yes. Do. This man was... a work in progress.'

'You said you saw something like it once before,' Tessa said.

'I did, yes.'

'Can you tell us who that person was?'

'It was a case from many years ago, in the UK.'

'That doesn't answer my question.'

'The person I'm referring to was an assassin. A man who'd had his appearance altered again and again to hide his identity.'

'Right,' Tessa said, feeling the bottom drop out of her stomach.

'The man was a professional killer,' the professor said. 'I would bet pounds to pence this chap is too.'

Tessa and Danny looked at one another, each pondering the ramifications of this new part of the puzzle.

DAISY CONNOLLY

Something else sat with her in the dark, crouching like a monster on her chest.

It was terror as to the fate of her and Joe's daughter, Aisling.

Daisy had made sure she was hidden, but how could she be sure the men hadn't found her? The reality was, she couldn't. The men had been professionals, hunters who were experts in tracking down human prey. She and her husband were hardly amateurs, and they had, stupidly, allowed themselves to be taken.

Why hadn't they set up safeguards? Security? Lord knows, either of their parents would have loaned them men to watch the perimeters of their land. Daisy begrudgingly admitted it was Joe's arrogance that had been their downfall. He'd come to believe he was so important, no one would dare make a move on him.

He'd been wrong.

And yet, Daisy thought, listening to the deafening silence that hung around her tiny cell, he'd been right too. It was because he was so important the other hoodlums couldn't let him go, couldn't let him strike out alone.

His talent, as well as his arrogance, had been their undoing.

And now she and Joe were here, held against their will, and Aisling was out there somewhere, alone. If they had her, Daisy was sure this fact would be revealed sooner or later. They would use the child as a bargaining tool, a way to get her and Joe to cave. They would threaten to hurt her. Suggest all kinds of violence and horrors would befall the child if she and her husband didn't comply with their wishes.

And Daisy knew, beyond any doubt, that if that happened, she would give the men anything they wanted.

32

Two hours later they were all gathered in Maggie's room again. The sleep had revived her, and the doctors informed her she could leave in the morning. Patience had made up a camp bed for Ash, who refused to be away from the family liaison officer unless it was to eat ice cream, and the child was now sleeping fitfully, Pavlov curled up at her feet and her toy bunny beside her on the pillow.

'Who's the biggest gang involved in all of this?' Tessa asked. 'Who would hire a hitman like the one in the morgue?'

'Wouldn't any of the gangs involved know how to hire someone like that?' Danny wanted to know.

'Why would they though?' Maggie asked. 'Wouldn't the Shiggins crew or the Donegans just do it themselves? Send one of their own people?'

'He mightn't have been hired,' Danny said. 'He might just be a gang member. An enforcer, something like that.'

'I dunno,' Tessa said. 'Would the Donegans or the Shiggins people abduct their own son or daughter and send someone to kill their grandchild? I mean, that's cold.'

'They're all governed by the demands of the business,'

Danny said. 'I don't think they have loyalties that don't serve the financial bottom line.'

'Which brings us back to the fact that one of the gangs is behind all of this,' Tessa said. 'We just don't know which one.'

'We should check the records and see if there's any reference to a hitman bearing the physical description of our recently deceased friend,' Maggie said. 'He's nothing if not distinctive.'

'If he's been having lots of cosmetic surgery, wouldn't that appearance change all the time though?' Tessa said. 'I mean, isn't that the whole point?'

Maggie nodded. 'I suppose it is.'

She sighed, drumming her fingers on her bedspread. 'Did we learn anything else today?'

'Well, I had a conversation with a chap called Mogue Kearney,' Danny said. 'He was waiting for me outside one of my interviews.'

'Who's Mogue Kearney?' Tessa asked.

'He wasn't inclined to tell me, but I googled him afterwards, and he's a Monaghan County councillor and runs a legal firm here in town.'

'What did he want?' Maggie asked.

'I don't know. To let me know he's keeping an eye on us, I think,' Danny said. 'He hinted that the Connollys might have been in some financial difficulties, and that the O'Neills might not have been as innocent of wrong-doing as we've been led to believe.'

'But he wasn't more forthcoming than that?' Tessa asked.

'No. That's all he said.'

'Perhaps we need to speak to him again,' Tessa mused. 'And in the meantime, let's look over the Connollys' financials one more time. It looked to me like they were breaking even, but maybe we've missed something.'

'What about the O'Neills?'

'They've no criminal record,' Tessa said. 'But it certainly seems to me as if Tony was snapping at Joe's heels. I went through their social media today, and at first I thought there was nothing going on other than Tony obviously hero-worshipping Joe a bit.'

'At first?' Maggie prompted.

'Yeah. The more I think about it, the more I believe what I was actually looking at was something quite different. Tony O'Neill was ambitious. He wasn't anywhere near as good as Joe but wanted to be. I'm wondering if that manifested itself in him selling Joe out in some way and then getting murdered himself to keep it all quiet.'

'That's a big leap of logic,' Danny said.

'But not an outlandish one,' Tessa pointed out.

And Danny couldn't argue with her.

PART THREE

FACELESS MEN

33

The following morning Maggie was permitted to leave the hospital, and as she was settling into her wheelchair, Ash's actual doctor, a young Sikh named Badraha Singh, informed her he would be happy for Ash to leave as well. Maggie called the local fostering office of Tusla, the Irish Child and Family Agency, and was informed they wouldn't have a free bed for three days.

'Can she stay here until then?' Maggie asked.

'I'm sure we can make some arrangements,' Dr Singh said. 'But are you going to be able to stay with her? We aren't equipped to be a child-minding service, and we already have a forensic unit taking over the room she'd been using.'

'If you're saying she's fit, I'll take her out with me for the day,' Maggie said. 'I can drop her back later, and if you'd prefer, me and Pavlov can stay with her until the foster carers can take her.'

'I think that would be fine,' the doctor agreed. 'I'll let the registrar know.'

So it was that Maggie, with Aisling Connolly strapped into the back seat of her Focus, her toy bunny held tightly in her arms, arrived out at the farm she had, up until very recently, called home.

Tessa and Danny were there to meet them when they pulled up outside the house, the interminable wind blowing in from across the endless flat countryside a haunting background note.

'Hey, Ash,' Danny said as she climbed down. 'How are you? It's so good to see you out of the hospital.'

'I'm okay,' the girl said, clutching Bunny as if her life depended on it.

'How does it feel being home?' Tessa asked.

'Weird,' Ash said.

'I'll bet it does,' Tessa commiserated.

'Can we go back to the hospital?' the child asked, turning to Maggie. 'I don't wanna be here.'

'We'll go back soon, sweetie, and you know we're going to make sure you're safe,' Maggie said. 'We're going to take turns staying with you – Danny and Tessa here will take a shift, and then me and Pavlov. You're not going to be alone for a moment, I promise.'

'I don't feel safe now!' Ash said, and there were tears in her eyes and a note of anger in her voice.

'Ash,' Maggie said, reaching down and lifting the child up and sitting her on her knee. 'You and me are friends, right?'

The little girl nodded.

'And you know Tessa and Danny are your friends too?'

'And Pavlov.'

'Of course – that goes without saying.'

She looked up into Maggie's face. 'Let's go back to the hospital and play draughts, okay?'

'Ash, I do want to do that with you, and we will, but first we need to do something very important here.'

'What?'

'You know the man who came to the hospital? The one who was pretending to be a doctor?'

'Yeah. The bad man.'

'We think he might have something to do with what happened to your mam and dad.'

Ash looked at Maggie with huge eyes. 'I don't remember that night. I already told you that.'

'Yes, but maybe if you're here, you might remember better. I'll be there with you, and so will Tessa and Danny and Pavlov and Bunny. You'll be safe. And remember, it's only memories. Stuff that happened in the past. They can't hurt you now.'

'I don't want to,' Ash said, close to tears.

'I know you don't, love, and I wouldn't ask if it weren't really important. I need to keep you safe, and we all want to find your mam and dad. The only one who really knows what happened is you, Ash. I know it's really hard and you're scared, but if you could just try, it will help us to protect you and tell us where to start looking for your folks.'

Ash, tears streaming down her face, looked from Maggie to Tessa to Danny.

'Okay,' she said. 'I'll try.'

'You're such a brave girl,' Maggie said. 'And we're all so proud of you.'

And they went into the house, where that night of terror had begun for the Connollys.

34

'Now,' Maggie said, 'I do a lot of work with kids who've had nasty things happen to them. Things that make them afraid. And you know what? A lot of kids – most, in fact – don't remember the bad stuff. It's like their brains tell them it's too scary, and some part of them takes it and puts it in a box deep inside them and hides it.'

They were sitting in the living room. A sheet of plastic had been taped over the mantlepiece and that section of wall, so the bloodstains weren't visible.

'Is that what you think happened to me?' Ash asked.

'I think it did,' Maggie said. 'But you know, there are ways we can get into that box and have a look at those memories. Ways that don't need to be scary.'

The little girl sobbed a couple of times, looking about the room as if something dreadful was about to spring out at her.

'We was in here that night,' she said. 'Me 'n' Mam 'n' Dad.'

'On the night your folks vanished?' Maggie asked.

Ash nodded. 'I'd been s'posed to go an' stay with Grandad and Nanny Connolly that night, but I had a cold so I stayed at home. I was meant to go when I got better.'

'So you weren't meant to be at home on the farm that night?' Tessa asked.

Ash shook her head. 'Dad always read me a bedtime story down here, and then Mam would bring me up and tuck me in. He was just startin' when somethin' happened.'

'What was that, Ash?'

She shook her head.

'Okay. Close your eyes for me.'

The child did as she was asked.

'Now, what story was your dad reading?'

'It was *The Twits*.'

'By Roald Dahl?'

'Yes. It's funny.'

'I love that book,' Maggie said. 'Which part was he reading?'

'The bit about the wormy pasghetti.'

'Oh yes. And how Mr Twit ate it anyway?'

The child nodded.

'So he's reading that. Where are you sitting?'

'On the couch. He sits at the end near the fire, against the arm of the couch, and I snuggle into him, and he has his arm around me.'

'Okay, that sounds nice. He's reading to you about how Mrs Twit puts worms in Mr Twit's spaghetti Bolognese. Does he get all the way through that chapter?'

'Nearly. Mrs Twit is laughing, telling Mr Twit they was really big worms he ett and then...'

The child paused, her eyes scrunched shut as she concentrated.

'There was a bangin' on the door.'

'Someone knocking?' Maggie asked.

'Not knockin'. It was like they was kickin' the door or hittin' it with something.'

'What happened?'

'Dad said to Mam: "Go into the larder and lock the door."

And then he went out to the hallway, and Mam took me and we ran into the pantry, just off the kitchen, and she did as he said.'

'She locked you both in?'

Ash nodded.

'What happened then?'

The child, breathing heavily now, shook her head. 'I don't know. I was scairt, because I knew my mammy was. I could see she was real scairt.'

'Maybe if we go in there, it might help you remember?' Maggie suggested.

The girl opened her eyes. 'Okay.'

The larder was a long, narrow room, one wall lined with shelves, the other with cupboards, all containing food: cans, jars of pasta, rice and grains, and some paraphernalia of brewing and distilling – there was one shelf full of various sizes of Kilner jars and Maggie saw a large box labelled 'brewer's yeast'.

'You come in here with your mam,' Maggie said when Pavlov had trotted in behind them and was sniffing about in the corners.

'Yeah. She shutted and locked the door.'

Maggie nodded at Danny, who was closest, and the detective closed the door and turned the key in it.

'What do you remember next?'

'Mam was cryin',' Ash said. 'I could see she was tryin' not to, but I could still see the tears comin' down her cheeks. I said: "Are you okay, Mam?" and she nodded and tried to smile, but I could see she wasn't.'

'Could you hear what was happening outside? With your dad?'

'There was shouting. Voices shouting.'

'Men or women?'

'Men. Voices... I think one was that man who was pretendin' to be a doctor. There was others too, but I ain't heard them before nor since.'

'Did you hear what they were saying?'

'They kept sayin': "Hand it over to us. Give us the list. We want the list. We had a deal."'

'The list?' Maggie said. 'Do you know what that means?'

The child shook her head.

'You never heard your mam or dad mention it before?'

'No. I don't know what it means.'

'Okay. So they're shouting about this list, and you and your mam are here, in the larder.'

'There was bangin' and crashin'. I could hear my dad calling out. Like... like they was hurting him.'

'What did that sound like?'

'Like... he din't say ow or nothing like that. But he was making noises – like "ah" and "oh", and it sounded like he was bein' pushed or thrown down on the ground.'

'I understand,' Maggie said. 'I know what you mean.'

'We was in here, and we waited, and then we heard footsteps outside and someone was tryin' to get in. And then a voice said: "We know you're in there, Mrs Connolly. If you don't come out we'll..."'

Ash choked all of a sudden, and they had to wait while she cried bitterly.

'You are so brave,' Maggie said, holding her tight on her knee. 'Such a courageous little girl.'

'He said: "If you don't come out, we'll beat your husband to death."'

'What did your mam do?'

Ash hopped down from Maggie's knee and went over to the wall that was lined with cupboards. She opened the one nearest the door, reached inside and felt around for a few moments, and then they all heard a click, and the whole panel swung open, revealing a space behind, little more than a narrow cupboard itself.

'She didn't say anythin', but I knew she wanted me to get in.

So I did. Before she closed the door she said: "Wait until I or your dad comes to get you, but if we don't, wait until there are no more sounds of people, then sneak out, and go and hide in the container in the north field. Someone will come to find you." And then she closed the door and left me.'

'Did you hear any more after that?'

'There was more shouting. More banging. I could hear Mam crying and I think I heard my dad crying too, even though I don't know 'cause I never heard that before. It seemed to go on for a long, long time, but then I thought I heard the front door open and close, and then there was no more noise at all. So I waited. And I waited, and then I got hungry so I came out. And there wasn't anyone here. So I made myself a sandwich and I did as Mam had told me, and I ran to the container on the north field and I stayed in there until those police found me.'

'Can you remember anything else?'

'That's all,' Ash said.

'You didn't see the people who were here?'

'I only heard them.'

'Could you guess how many there were?'

'I think I heard three voices.'

'Men or women?'

'All men.'

'Did they have accents, or were they all Irish, like the fake doctor?'

Ash nodded. 'All Irish. Maggie, I'm tired,' she said suddenly. 'Can we go back to the hospital now?'

'Yes, sweetie, we can,' Maggie said. 'You've done so well.'

The child climbed back up into her lap and was unconscious almost immediately.

'I'll take her back,' the family liaison officer said to Tessa and Danny. 'After that, she may not wake again today at all.'

'She's earned the sleep,' Tessa said.

'More than,' Maggie said and made for her Focus.

35

When Maggie, Pavlov and Ash were gone, Tessa and Danny struck out for the container where the girl had been found. Neither of them had seen it, and Tessa suggested it might not do any harm to see where the child had survived for almost thirty hours on her own before the police had stumbled upon her.

'What are you thinking?' Tessa asked the big detective as they trudged through the fields.

'It seems Joe and Daisy were taken,' Danny said. 'Either dead or alive.'

'Agreed.'

'Definitely the same people who tried to kill Ash.'

'I also concur.'

'They were looking for information. This list...'

'A list of what though?'

'Suppliers? Customers? Potential investors?'

'Any and all of the above,' Tessa said. 'I don't know either.'

'You know what I'm thinking though?' Danny said.

'Go on.'

'If they didn't give up the information, Joe and Daisy might still be alive.'

'I was thinking the same thing.'

'And maybe the guy Maggie shot wasn't trying to kill Ash. I think he might have been planning on taking her after all.'

'To use as leverage,' Tessa said.

'Exactly.'

'This changes everything.'

'I know.'

The copse behind which the shipping container was situated loomed ahead of them.

They were about to walk around and have a look inside when Danny froze, holding up his hand to stop Tessa.

'There's someone up ahead of us,' he said, just above a whisper.

'Where?'

'They're walking away from us, headed north, about two hundred yards.'

Tessa, who'd been a little behind her partner, came up beside him and looked in the direction he'd indicated. Sure enough, there, still visible in the distance, was the figure of a man. If Danny hadn't pointed him out, Tessa thought she probably would have missed him, because he was dressed in green and brown hues – not quite camouflage but clearly meant to blend in.

'Could be nothing,' Tessa said. 'Just someone out for a walk.'

'Everyone hereabouts knows what happened on this property,' Danny said.

'So it might easily be a nosy neighbour.'

'I'd like to check it out all the same.'

'How are you going to do that?'

'Catch up with them and ask them.'

Tessa looked at Danny and then at the figure, growing smaller and smaller as he moved away. 'Be my guest. I'll be scoping out the container.'

'Won't be long.'

He shrugged off his jacket and handed it to her, then took off at a sprint across the field. Tessa watched him go, wondering how someone of his immense size could put on such a burst of speed with seemingly no effort at all.

She watched him race across the rough ground of the field in pursuit of the possible intruder, and then ducked behind the copse and into the shipping container to try and better understand the terror Aisling Connolly had experienced.

36

Danny felt the initial exertion of putting his huge frame into a burst of such powerful propulsion, but as he took in air, he felt his blood and muscles becoming oxygenated, and the movement became freer as his joints loosened up, and then, as if he was somehow slipping the shackles of the bulky body he'd been gifted, he was at one with himself and the earth beneath him, and all was well with the world.

Ahead, he could see the figure drawing closer and closer. There was something familiar about them, something he couldn't put his finger on but which put him on his guard.

Not wanting to alert his quarry to his approach until it was completely unavoidable, he veered to the left, giving himself more distance to cover but hoping it would give him the element of surprise, for a little while at least.

Drawing closer again, he was able to discern more about the interloper: they were tall and thin. He could make out long hair. A rough leather jacket. And then he knew where he'd seen them before: this was one of the men who'd been in the hospital car park. One of the ones who'd harassed that woman and her child.

Could he just be, as Tessa had suggested, having a look at the scene of a notorious local crime? Was he just out for a stroll? Or was this too much of a coincidence?

Danny didn't believe in coincidences. In the world of policing, they gave you nothing to work with. He pushed harder, increasing his speed.

He was about fifteen metres from the man when the sound of his feet pounding off the earth gave him away.

'Stop – police!' he called, albeit breathlessly, but the man didn't comply, instead taking off at a sprint himself.

Danny doubled his efforts and within twenty seconds had closed the gap by half.

I've got him! he thought. *He's out of condition. Won't be long now.*

Another ten seconds and he was close enough to launch himself at the man and wrap his arms about the skinny legs, bringing him to the ground.

'All I wanted to do was talk to you,' he said, panting and sweating from the run. 'Now get up.'

He stood and offered his hand, but instead of taking it, the fallen man rolled over and delivered a crushing kick to Danny's testicles. The detective didn't see it coming and caught the boot fully into his groin. He doubled over, fought the wave of agony and then pitched over onto his side, trying not to throw up.

He sensed rather than heard the man making good his escape.

It was ten minutes before he was able to get up and make his way back to Tessa.

37

Tessa was sitting on the ground outside the shipping container, arms wrapped around her knees, when he came upon her, walking stiffly and still feeling more than a little nauseous.

'Well?' she asked, though he could tell she knew his mission hadn't been a success.

'He got the drop on me,' Danny said, the words little more than a mumble.

'Did he now?'

'He did.'

'What happened?'

He told her.

'You're an interesting contradiction, Daniel Murphy,' she said, springing upright with apparently no physical effort.

'How so?'

'You'll beat a man to a pulp at the drop of a hat, and there sometimes seems to be a barely suppressed rage bubbling away just below the surface. Yet in this instance, that guy had the chance to kick you in the nuts because you were leaning in, offering to help him up like a gent. Which was a courtesy he clearly didn't deserve.'

'Are you making fun of me?'

'Nope. Just making an observation. You're a good man, Danny. We just need to sand some of the edges off, and you need to decide what kind of a cop you want to be.'

'I already know.'

'Tell me then.'

'I want to be a good cop.'

'That doesn't mean anything.'

'Of course it does. You're a good cop. Maggie is a good cop.'

'And we do the job completely differently. The question is about how you approach the challenges you meet every day. You want to do your best, but so far you haven't worked out how to do that without harming yourself in the process. That's what we need to work on.'

'How do I learn that?'

'Experience is a big part of it. But also watching how other people handle things.'

They were walking back towards the house, slower now, as Danny was still a bit tender.

'So how would you have dealt with what just happened?'

'You saw how I addressed it.'

'But you didn't respond to it at all!'

'I did, just differently to you.'

'I don't get it.'

'That guy was too far away to make a pursuit on foot over this kind of terrain worthwhile. By the time you caught him, as we saw, you weren't physically together enough to restrain him. So he got away.'

'But you let me do it anyway.'

'I wasn't completely sure of your fitness levels. I thought it was possible you might be able to achieve it, although I thought it unlikely. I wanted to see.'

'You were testing me.'

'I think you were testing yourself, Danny. I just allowed you to do it.'

'Very kind of you. So you would have just let him go?'

'Not quite. We saw him walking away from us, towards the boundary of the Connolly land.'

'I know. I was there.'

'Don't get petulant, Danny. If he was here because he's part of the abduction of Joe and Daisy, or is one of the other competitors in the liquor distribution deal, what could have brought him to this field?'

The big detective thought about that. 'The container.'

'Bingo. So I went and had a look in there to see if it had been interfered with in any way. O'Connor told us it had been left intact as a still, nothing really out of place. If that weren't still the case, I'd know he'd been there.'

'And?'

'The place has been trashed. Completely turned over. I would say that whoever he works for didn't know the container existed until recently, and they sent him to search it for whatever it is they're looking for. This list.'

'He was one of the guys we saw in the hospital car park,' Danny said. 'So we have to assume he was there to see what kind of security there was around Ash.'

'My thoughts exactly,' Tessa said. 'You'd best get back there in case Maggie needs some backup. I've called McEvoy to send forensics out to brush the container for prints and swab for DNA. And I have a visit to make.'

'You do?'

'I do. My new friend Elias Two-Toes called while you were having your cross-country run. He's made an introduction for me with a man who, he tells me, taught Joe Connolly all he knows about distilling.'

'How will that help us?' Danny asked.

'Apparently, this is a man Joe trusted more than anyone

else,' Tessa said. 'So if there's a person in Monaghan who knows what he and his wife were planning, this is it.'

'But will he tell you? You're not exactly like any other Gardai I've known, but that doesn't make you any less of a guard. I feel the people I've spoken to here are always respectful and polite, but most of them are only telling me a fraction of what they know or suspect. They're still locked into that old-school thing of not wanting to look like informants.'

'You're probably right,' Tessa replied. 'But this is our job, Danny. We keep talking to people and asking questions until we find out what we need to know. That's all there is.'

'Even if we get kicked in the testicles for our trouble?'

'Even then.'

38

Elias texted Tessa an address, an area called Tedavnet, that Google maps showed her was really just an area of countryside with a couple of villages in the middle that were more the meetings of roads than concentrated human settlements. The satnav capacity of the Google Maps app more or less gave out as she drove deeper into the Monaghan countryside, constantly buffering as coverage phased in and out.

It was also, Tessa noted, an address not among the nine McEvoy had identified may need protection. She was beginning to wonder about the vice detective's critical faculties. And to seriously doubt his loyalties.

In fact, she had a feeling a conversation was going to take place between her and the detective before very long.

The trip to Tedavnet was when Tessa learned an eccentric and deeply irritating fact about Monaghan's road signage: the local authority saw fit to always point you in the direction of one of the county's 130 lakes, clearly harbouring a deep sense of pride for the many bodies of water. Towns and villages, however, were often ignored, and didn't seem to garner a mention.

Why this was, Tessa was unable to fathom. Finally, completely lost, she pulled up at a little pub that seemed to appear out of nowhere. It was a small, whitewashed, single-storey building with the word **PUB** printed in block capitals above the door.

Inside was much as Tessa had expected. The floor was bare flagstones, the walls whitewashed and decorated with ancient advertisements for various beers and spirits the detective had never heard of. Just inside the door was a short bar that had only Guinness and Smithwick's on tap. Behind that were shelves made of rough wood that held an array of bottles, most of which she didn't recognise. There were five tables, each of which had three chairs arranged about them. The barman (at least, Tessa assumed that was his role) was small, almost dwarfish, with arms that appeared too short for his body. Dressed in a shirt and tie that Tessa reckoned must have been specially tailored to fit, he was perched on a high stool, reading the local paper. The only other denizen of the bar was a man in an Aran jumper and woolly cap, who was supping a large bottle of stout and a glass of whiskey.

'I'm looking for Oisín Kelly's place,' Tessa said, although no one even turned to look at her when she walked in.

'What do you want with Oisín?' the barman said without raising his eyes from his newspaper.

'I need to talk to him. Elias Two-Toes called ahead to tell him I was coming.'

The little man smiled to himself at that. 'Did you call him that to his face?'

'I was advised not to.'

The barman closed his paper and folded it carefully, then turned to gaze at the detective. She saw he was probably in his late sixties, maybe even older. His face was wreathed in lines and wrinkles.

'Joe Connolly is a very good friend of mine,' he said. 'Closest thing to a son I'm ever going to have.'

'I'm trying to find him,' Tessa said. 'Him and his wife.'

The little man hopped down from his stool and said to the elderly drinker: 'Pat, I'm steppin' out with this young lady. Watch the place for me, will you?'

'Aye, I will,' the old man said, and that seemed to be sufficient.

'Right, let's go.'

And he headed out the front door.

Tessa followed. 'Are you him? Oisín Kelly?'

'Of course I am. Isn't it obvious?'

The small barman was heading around the side of the bar at a fair clip, and Tessa had to run to keep up. She caught up with him as he was dragging a pile of dead branches from over what looked to be a manhole cover. Grabbing a handle in the middle of the round disc, he pulled, and the whole thing lifted, revealing darkness beneath.

'Down you go,' he said to Tessa.

'I'm not going down there!' she said, feeling a wave of claustrophobia wash over her. Tessa was afraid of very little, but enclosed spaces made her hyperventilate and sweat bullets.

'It's completely safe,' her host informed her. 'It opens up once you're in there, I swear. I'll go first.'

He did just that, climbing into the hole and disappearing below.

'You'd better not be bullshitting me,' Tessa warned as she felt about with her foot, found the top rung of a ladder and went into the darkness.

39

Oisín wasn't lying.

Once Tessa had descended five rungs and had a terrible moment of claustrophobia as the initial tube closed in just centimetres from her face, she felt space opening below her.

'If you feel about to your right, you'll find a light switch,' Oisín called down to her, and she did, and suddenly the panoply below her was awash with pale electric light, and she saw she was making her way down a metal ladder to a vast underground distillery. 'Go down and I'll be right with you.'

The cellar stretched into the distance, so far Tessa couldn't see the end, which disappeared into darkness.

'This place was built by the Baron of Rossmore back in the nineteenth century,' Oisín said as he came down to her side. 'It was originally used to store potatoes, grain and turnips.'

'And it's now home to a very different crop,' Tessa said.

Her diminutive companion looked up at her tetchily. 'Am I gonna get any trouble from you?' he asked.

'Not if you can help me.'

'What do you want to know?'

'Where to look for Joe,' Tessa said. 'He's missing and I haven't a clue where to even begin searching.'

'I wish to God I could help you, but I can't. All Joe and I ever talked about was the art. He never wanted to talk about anything else much.'

'The art of distilling?'

'It's the only one he really cared about. He was a genius, was Joe. Had the gift. The touch. He could make a glass of something fit for the Lord himself if you gave him an empty jar, some water, a fistful of popping corn and some sugar.'

'Is that all it takes?'

'Let me show you,' Oisín said.

He walked her over to a large metal bin that looked to be full of grain of some kind.

'You want to make whiskey, first off, you'll need a base, and whiskey is by definition a grain-based spirit. You've got options: corn, rye, wheat or barley, or you can blend multiple grains. It doesn't really make a difference in terms of creation – you'll end up with liquor, but you should understand that each grain has a distinguishable taste. For the sake of argument, let's just assume you want to use corn.'

'Is that what Joe mostly uses?'

'He uses lots of different things, and he doesn't just make whiskey. But this is how I got him started.'

'So he came to you to learn?'

'Yeah. He was still based in Limerick back then. Wanted to learn and heard I was the best. So I took him in, showed him the ropes.'

'It's not an exact science, is it?'

'That it is not. You have to develop an instinct for it. And that's what Joe has.'

He pointed to a pipette that was drip-drip-dripping a clear fluid into a glass jar. 'That's your liquor! It's just basic science, the whole process, but you have to have the instinct to make the flavours shine.'

'So this is moonshine,' Tessa said.

'Well... if you want good, old-fashioned poitín, then yes. It's a clear liquid and traditionally isn't aged. If you want to call your fresh new batch of alcohol real whiskey then you need to let it age in a barrel first. Like these ones.'

He showed her a stack of wooden barrels, all piled on top of each other, taps protruding from their bases to release the contents.

'The alcohol absorbs the qualities of the wood, so you'll get notes of oak, cedar or other things that come directly from the wood itself. You can leave it in as long as you want, but if you're making your own small batch, you'll probably want to try it sooner than later, right?'

'How long are we talking?'

'Oh, ideally no less than three years.'

'Seriously?'

He laughed. 'You can have your whiskey out of the barrel in three months, particularly if it's a small batch in a small barrel. It'll be more than drinkable.'

'So the entire process, from start to finish, would have you with a batch of saleable whiskey in the space of four months?'

'Ah yeah. Sounds about right.'

'This is what you taught Joe?'

'This is the basics. We looked at many more complex techniques, different types of drinks, different ways of speeding up and slowing down the process. He was a gifted student.'

'So I've been told. A pity he didn't use his gifts for a purpose that wasn't so likely to get him in trouble.'

The small man shrugged. 'He was talking about getting out, you know.'

Tessa gave her host a quizzical look. 'Getting out? Of the distilling business?'

'Oh, I don't think he would ever want to get out of that. No, I mean the criminal side of things. He knew being involved with gangsters, particularly when the money gets *really* big, that shortens your life expectancy. So he wanted to get himself and his family out.'

'It seems to me, with respect, that he was only getting deeper in. He was developing a huge project and looking for investors... this was going to cement his position as a criminal, not obliterate it.'

'He told me he had a plan.'

'Did he say what that was?'

'He told me he didn't want to show anyone until it was done. He's like that, is Joe. Proud, like.'

Tessa thought about that. 'When was the last time you spoke to him?'

'The afternoon of the day he and Daisy vanished.'

'Does "the list" mean anything to you?'

Oisín scratched his chin. 'A shopping list? List of ingredients? A guest list to a meeting or a party?'

Tessa nodded, but she'd already thought of all those, and none brought her any closer to finding the Connollys.

'Did he say anything that gave you cause to worry about him?'

Oisín thought for a moment. 'In the days before he disappeared, Joe was under a lot of stress,' he said. 'I was beginning to be quite concerned about him.'

'Why?'

'He was saying strange things. Stuff that didn't make sense – or didn't back then. In hindsight, I can see he wasn't being paranoid.'

'What did he say?'

'He... he believed he was being watched.'

'Did he say by whom?'

'He did.'

'And?'

'Joe told me his farm was being stalked by... by faceless men. He said he was followed everywhere he went by men with no faces.'

And for a moment, Tessa thought perhaps she was going to pass out.

It was 10.30 p.m., and Danny was sitting in one of the uncomfortable hospital chairs reading *My Dark Places* by James Ellroy. Maggie and Ash had switched beds since the family liaison officer had been given a clean bill of health, and Maggie was now asleep on the camp bed, with Pavlov on the floor at her head, while the child took the hospital bed proper.

Danny was engrossed in the book. It told the story of crime novelist James Ellroy's attempts to solve his mother's murder, which had happened when he was ten years old. The death had, understandably, had a huge impact on Ellroy, sending him into alcohol and drug addiction, and almost certainly pushing what was already an outsider personality even further into introversion.

Danny understood that better than most.

The big cop didn't have many memories of his parents. He'd been barely four years old when their car had collided with a juggernaut on the N11, the main road from Rosslare Harbour in the south-east of Ireland to Dublin.

No one had told him much about the circumstances of the accident, despite his asking every adult he encountered, but as soon as he'd joined the Gardai, he'd looked up the report and learned his father had been almost twice the legal blood-alcohol limit. He had, in other words, been driving drunk.

Danny had sat in the squad room in Bray, the old file spread out on the desk in front of him, and felt a shocking surge of anger. He had, ever since his parents' death, harboured hatred towards the man driving the juggernaut. Surely, Danny had thought, it had to be this individual's negligence that had resulted in his parents' demise.

Then he'd learned that his father's intoxication had been the catalyst that had altered the trajectory of his young life.

He'd fought hard not to despise his father. To try and understand he hadn't killed himself and Danny's mother on purpose. But it was difficult. And it impacted Danny's ability to form relationships in all kinds of ways.

He found it hard to trust people, taking no one at their word until they'd proven repeatedly that they would do as they said. He was painstakingly truthful and upfront, sometimes to the point of being hurtful – he never sugar-coated bad news, choosing instead to deliver the full truth just as it was rather than leave out the harsher details. As far as he was concerned, that only led to pain further down the line.

His superiors in the Gardai learned quite early in his career that Danny Murphy wasn't the person to send when a family needed to be told that a loved one had died due to some misfortune. His skills lay elsewhere.

Despite finally finding a loving foster family, the losses Danny experienced in his formative years had made him wary of long-term relationships. He'd had girlfriends but none that lasted more than a few weeks. Danny simply didn't see the point in putting in the effort to sustain such interactions. Most people, he reasoned, were going to let you down anyway. Why try to postpone the rejection?

Far better to just get it over with.

Ellroy's book explored how being touched by a crime had shaped the author's life, mostly for the worse, and led him to write crime novels. Danny could identify with that: his own loss had certainly impacted on him negatively, and it had resulted in him becoming a police officer.

He turned the page to begin a new chapter when a small voice piped up: 'Hello, Danny.'

He looked up to see that Ash was awake, watching him sleepily.

'Hello, Ash.'

'Watcha readin'?'

'A book about a man whose mammy was killed when he was little.'

'Oh.'

'When he grew up, he became a very famous writer, and he tried to find out what happened to her.'

'He find out?'

'I don't know yet. I'm only this far in.' He showed her.

'It a good book?'

'I like it, yes.'

'I miss my mammy. My daddy too. He worked a lot, so I din't see him as much. So I think I miss my mammy more.'

She stopped and looked confused. 'Is that a bad thing to say? Would my daddy be mad at me? Or sad?'

'I don't think so,' Danny said. 'It seems pretty normal to me. My mam and dad died when I was younger than you. I miss my mam more too.'

'Oh. Your mam and dad is dead?'

'Yes.'

'You sad 'bout that?'

'Yes. Of course I am.'

'Still? Even though you big now?'

'Yes.'

'You cry still?'

Danny thought about that. 'I do still get very, very strong feelings. Sometimes they're sad. Sometimes angry. I think I get them because I'm still upset over what happened to my mam and dad.'

Ash sat up in bed. Pavlov, sensing she was awake, jumped up and lapped at her face a couple of times before settling down beside her.

'If your mam and dad was dead, who minded you?'

'I was placed in foster care. Do you know what that means?'

'Yeah. Maggie says I be goin' to a foster family in a coupla days.'

Danny nodded. 'Yes, I believe so.'

'What was it like? Was they good to you?'

'I was with three different families. Mostly they were good people.'

'How come you was with three? You not like it with two of 'em?'

'It... it just didn't work out.'

'Grown-ups say that when they don't wanna tell kids stuff.'

'You're right,' Danny said. 'I'm sorry. One of them, the mam got sick. The second family were too old and didn't want a young, noisy kid. The others were lovely, and I still call them Mam and Dad.'

'I don't think I can call no one else Mam and Dad except my real mam and dad.'

'I hope you won't have to. We're trying really hard to find them.'

'What if... what if they dead?'

'I really don't think they are.'

'That the truth?'

'I don't tell lies,' Danny said.

Ash looked at him. It was a hard, deep look for such a small child. Danny felt as if her eyes were penetrating his soul.

'You don't tell lies,' she said. 'Most grown-ups do, but you don't.'

Satisfied, she snuggled back down again. 'I'm gonna sleep now.'

'Okay, Ash.'

She closed her eyes but then opened them again. 'D'you like ice cream?'

That puzzled him. 'Yes. I like ice cream very much.'

'There's a ice cream shop near the Diamond, here in town. Want to go with me there tomorrow?'

Despite himself, Danny felt a warmth inside. 'Yes,' he said. 'I would like to do that.'

'Okay,' Ash replied, closing her eyes and throwing an arm about Pavlov. 'See you in the morning.'

She was asleep in moments.

Danny put his book aside and watched the sleeping child, the little dog nestled beside her and the remarkable woman on the camp bed below them. He remembered the conversations he'd had with Tessa, all of which were rooted in her seeing value in him he couldn't see in himself.

And for the first time, he thought maybe she might be right.

How did I end up here, in this place with these people? he wondered. *How did I get this lucky?*

41

They all met for breakfast in the hospital canteen. Ash was spending some time with a social worker in advance of her move to the foster family, so they availed themselves of her absence to have a meeting about the case.

'Men with no faces,' Maggie said. 'Isn't that what you said about the person who killed your parents?'

'It has to be a coincidence,' Tessa replied.

'Coincidences aren't useful,' Danny piped up around a mouthful of bacon.

'I know they're not, but they do happen sometimes,' Tessa said, spreading jam on a piece of scone.

'What do you think it means?' Maggie asked.

'Could be they were like the guy you took down? His face was kind of featureless, wasn't it?'

'The prof said it was because of lots of plastic surgery,' Danny reminded them. 'Could we be dealing with a group of assassins?'

'I thought that shit only happened in video games,' Tessa grumbled.

'If it's true, Ash is still at serious risk,' Maggie said.

'We have to work under the assumption it's a real threat,' Tessa said. 'She can't be left alone. At least one of us needs to be around the whole time.'

'Have we had any results from the prof's medical examination of the man who tried to take her?' Danny asked. 'Do we know who he is?'

'DNA and dental came back blank,' Tessa replied. 'If you think about it, this guy's hardly going to put himself through all those cosmetic surgeries, only to let his DNA be held on the system.'

'So we're no better off,' Maggie said.

'The prof found evidence of multiple laser tattoo removals, from all over his body,' Tessa said.

'It's not unusual for Special Forces guys to get tats in different places they've served. I saw it when I was in the army,' Danny agreed.

'They had to have them removed to preserve anonymity,' Tessa finished for him.

'What about the guy you saw out at the Connolly farm?' Maggie asked, causing Danny to flush in embarrassment at the memory. 'Did forensics find anything on him?'

'He didn't leave any prints in the shipping container,' Tessa said. 'The only thing of interest that was picked up was some odd plant fibres.'

'Odd how?' Danny asked.

'These were very small particles from a kind of reed. I don't remember the scientific name. I wrote it down, so don't worry. But it's a kind of sedge.'

'Why is that unusual?' Maggie asked. 'Those fields have lots of reeds in them.'

'Yes, but not of this type,' Tessa said. 'This one only grows near water.'

'Isn't there a stream on the property?' Danny suggested.

'You're not listening to me,' Tessa said. 'This type of reed does not grow on the Connolly land. It will only be found near deep water. So beside lakes and that.'

'Well, that gives us something to go on,' Maggie said. 'He spends time near a lake, this guy.'

'Yeah,' Tessa replied. 'There are 130 of the fucking things in County Monaghan alone. That'll be easy to narrow down.'

'We've got him cornered,' Maggie said dolefully.

42

When breakfast was over, Maggie went with the social worker to meet Ash's prospective foster carers, and Tessa went to the police station to comb the archives to see if she could find anything that might give them some clue as to the identity of the men who'd haunted the Connollys and tried to take Ash too.

Danny said he would make good on his promise and take the little girl for an ice cream.

The parlour Ash was referring to was not actually on the Diamond, as she'd suggested, but was still in the town centre on Old Cross Square. It was, charmingly, called Smooch Ice Cream.

'See, you can have a ice cream burger,' the child explained to Danny, pointing to a picture of one on a poster in the window. 'I ain't never had one, but my dad likes them. He'd have a cup of coffee with it, and he said it was his weekly treat.'

'You came here every week?' Danny asked.

'Yeah. It was somethin' him 'n' me always did.'

The detective nodded. No wonder she'd asked him to take her. She must have been craving something familiar amid all this strangeness.

'So if you don't want that, you can have a ice-cream cup, which is like a takeout coffee cup, only with ice cream in it instead of coffee, and they put your fav'rite sweets and stuff in too.'

'Okay,' Danny said, listening carefully.

'Or you can just have a ordinary ice cream, like a 99. Or a milkshake. Or a special cup with Ferrero Rochet or Oreos in it.'

'There's a lot of ice creams to choose from,' Danny agreed.

'I always gets a ice cream sundae with chocolate sauce on it.'

'I just had breakfast, so maybe I'll stick with a cup of coffee.'

Ash looked at him aghast. 'You *gots* to have ice cream. You just *gots* to.'

Danny realised he'd made a giant faux pas and did his best to correct it immediately. Clearly the fact both parties were eating ice cream was an important part of the weekly ritual.

'You know, those milkshakes look better than a coffee. I think I'll opt for one of them.'

'They're powerful nice,' Ash said. 'I had one once, but it was so delicious I drunk it too fast and I got a headache. My dad made me drink a cup of warm water, and that made it better.'

'I'll be careful.'

'What flavour you want?'

Danny, who mostly lived on a diet of high protein and low carb, devoid of fat and sugar where possible, looked at the menu, which listed an absurd number of flavours and toppings, some of which he didn't even recognise as food items.

'Is vanilla an option?' he asked, very unsure of himself.

'You don't even want chocolate?'

'What are your favourite flavours?'

'I likes chocolate and banana. Like a banoffee pie, kind of.'

'Can I get that then?'

'In a milkshake?'

'Would it work?'

'Oh yeah. I think that would be real nice. Or even better, you like peanut butter?'

'I think so. I haven't had it in a while.'

'Peanut butter and banana is *really* good. How about that?'

'Yes. I think that would be quite nice.'

'Cool. Let's order.'

To Danny's dismay, the shake was enormous, but he faked an expression of delight, and when Ash had her chocolate sundae, they took a seat at a table on the pavement just outside the store's front window.

'Mmmmm,' Ash said, tucking in. 'Isn't it good?'

Danny took a slurp from his straw, and yes, the concoction was delicious. It was thick and unctuous, and the peanut butter gave it a slight crunchy texture, and the bananas, which had been real fruit, not a flavoured syrup, made him feel like there might be some healthy properties to the drink, even if they were minimal.

'It's very tasty,' he said, grinning at her.

'I knew you'd like it,' the girl said proudly. 'I knows my ice cream. You know the way my daddy is real good at making different types of drinks? When I get big, I think I'm gonna make ice cream. Lots and lots of different kinds.'

'That sounds like fun.'

At that moment, a grin spread across Ash's face, and she stood up and waved. The detective followed her gaze and saw she was trying to catch the attention of a young woman who was chaining a bike to a railing at St Diarmuid's church across the square.

'Who's that?' he asked.

'That's Lola. She used to help Dad.'

'Really? What did she do?'

'Her job was to fill the bottles.'

Danny nodded. 'Did she help him a lot?'

'Oh yeah. She worked for him all the time.'

Danny took his phone from where it was sitting on the table and took a quick photo of the woman.

Then they continued with their ice cream eating.

Later, the big detective had to admit he'd had a wonderful time.

43

After they'd finished their ice creams, Danny and his young friend called to the police station to say hello to Tessa.

'It's good to see you, because I'm about ready to go stir-crazy,' she informed them. 'There's a playground just across the road. Why don't you and me go and have a wander over that far. Danny here can work off his milkshake by going through some more files to see if he can't find our gangster.'

Danny thought Tessa might be getting the better end of the deal but knew he'd had an easy run of it that morning and agreed.

He had no more success than his colleague and was sitting back in the chair stretching when McEvoy wandered in.

'How goes the trawl through the organised crime archives?' the vice detective asked.

'Not very well. Oh, could you take a look at this person and tell me if you know her?'

Danny pulled up the photo he'd taken of the woman Ash had called Lola and passed it over.

'Lola Sherlock.'

'Ash says she worked for Joe.'

'I didn't know that, but it doesn't surprise me. Her husband is Barry Sherlock, currently serving a five-year stretch in the Joy for being a drugs courier. Too fucking dumb to do anything that required more ability.'

'Who did he work for?'

'I don't think he was affiliated with anyone in particular when he went down. Leastways, he wouldn't admit to being. He worked for whoever paid him.'

'Street-level thug then.'

'He was bad. Violent. Dumb as a plank. Used to beat the crap out of Lola. Fucked anything that had a hole in it.'

'What about her?'

'Lola? I always thought she was a nice kid, to be honest. Smart, for sure. Had potential. Pity Barry got his claws into her. She might have amounted to something.'

'She could still, surely.'

'You're more optimistic than me, mate.'

'Do you have an address for her?'

'She's in the system. Get it yourself.'

Danny did.

The visit changed everything they thought they knew about the case.

44

Lola Sherlock lived in an apartment in a four-storey building on Canal Street.

She opened the door to Danny's ring but left the chain on, peering out at him warily.

'May I come in and have a few words with you, Mrs Sherlock?' the detective asked, holding out his ID so she could read it.

'I ain't got no time,' she said. 'I have to go to work.'

'I won't keep you very long.'

She eyed him with unveiled irritation but released the chain and stepped back to permit him inside.

'You home is very nice,' Danny said, and he wasn't just being polite.

The apartment had been decorated in a clean, minimalist style, complete with furniture the detective was pretty sure hadn't come from IKEA and a TV that took up an entire wall and had long, beautifully designed speakers on each side.

'Thank you,' Lola replied. 'What do you want?'

'You worked for Joe Connolly.'

The woman stared at him but didn't answer.

She looked to be about thirty with a slim, athletic frame and was dressed in the uniform of a housekeeper from one of the local hotels. She had big brown eyes and dark skin, her black hair worn long but tied into a neat ponytail.

'You aren't in trouble,' Danny said. 'My colleagues and I are trying to find Joe and Daisy, so we're asking anyone who might have information that could help.'

'I don't know nothin'. I worked for him, yeah. He was a good boss, paid me well, treated his people nice. That's all I can say.'

'You know he's missing.'

The woman nodded. 'He's dead.'

Danny felt cold fingers walking down his spine. This was the first time anyone had suggested so absolutely that the Connollys had been killed.

'You can't be certain,' he said. 'All we know for sure is that Joe and his wife are missing.'

'I know. We all know. He's dead.'

'How do you know?'

Lola shook her head. 'I've said too much. I'd better go to work now.'

'Lola, did you see me in town earlier?'

The woman wrapped her arms around herself as if she was cold but nodded.

'You saw I was with Aisling Connolly?'

'Ash. You was with Ash.'

'Do you like Ash?'

She nodded. 'She's a nice kid. Polite. Always friendly.'

'I like her too. Someone tried to take her from the hospital a couple of days ago. If my friend hadn't been there, he surely would have too. Do you want something bad to happen to that little girl?'

Lola shook her head vigorously.

'If her parents are dead, all I can do is try to protect her. And I can do that best if I know what I'm protecting her from.'

The woman gazed at Danny for a moment then looked about her as if she thought something awful might be hiding in the clean, sparsely furnished room.

'Strígòil,' she said. 'Joe Connolly, he made a bad enemy. The Strígòil were sent to kill him. When the Strígòil come, they don't just kill you. They kill your wife. Your child. Your dog if you have a dog. This is how they are. You can't stop them – they keep going until the job is finished.'

Danny listened intently. 'The people who came for Joe, they're called Strígòil?' he asked. 'That's their family name? The name of their gang?'

'There's three of them,' Lola said, counting it out on her fingers to make sure he understood. 'One, two, three. Three men. They call themselves that name. These men, they're like the Strígòil in the stories. They come but leave no sign, no way to know they were there. It's like they... vanish. Vanish into air. Or they turn to birds and fly away.'

Danny spoke to her gravely. 'If it was these Strígòil who were sent, they're looking for a new member of their group. My friend Maggie killed one. So they're not quite as mysterious as they'd have you believe.'

Lola looked at him aghast. 'Your friend did this?'

'She did. She's pretty tough.'

'She a soldier?'

Danny thought about that. 'Yes, I suppose she is.'

'I have to go to work,' Lola said.

'Is there anything else you can tell me?' Danny asked. 'Anything. Even if you aren't sure it's important, I'd still like to know.'

The dark-eyed woman looked exasperated, as if she wanted to say something but felt she couldn't.

'You speak to Mogue Kearney,' she said. 'Talk to him.'

Danny couldn't hide his surprise. 'The county councillor?'

'You go talk to him. Ask him about the Professor.'

'The Professor?' Danny asked, making sure he'd heard correctly.

'Yes. Ask him to tell you about the Professor.'

'Okay. I will.'

'I'm going to work now,' Lola said.

The conversation was over.

That afternoon Ash went to meet the family who'd be taking her in on a temporary basis (at least, everyone hoped it would be only over the short term), and Tessa arranged for a police detail to park outside in case of emergency.

She, Danny, Maggie and Pavlov met in the bar of their hotel for a brief gathering to take stock.

'Here's what we've got,' Tessa said. 'Joe and Daisy had formed a plan to export a line of specialist booze to hot under-ground European drinking clubs. The endeavour had been funded by their gangster parents and a Ukrainian collective, but word leaked out and some other powerful groups wanted in on the deal.'

'Which, according to our sources, was an idea the Connollys were looking favourably upon,' Maggie said, 'as they wanted to cut the parental apron strings.'

'We don't know who these other interested parties were, or how many there were,' Tessa went on, 'but we have some new information now. According to Oisín, Joe really wanted to get out of the illegal side of the business and go straight. And he had a plan to do it. We don't know what that was, but we do know that in the days before he was abducted, Joe believed he was being followed by what he called "faceless men".'

'And Ash was attacked by a man whose features had been all but removed through plastic surgery,' Danny said.

'We now know from Ash that while Joe and Daisy were being abducted, the men who broke into his home repeatedly asked for a list,' Tessa continued. 'And the distillery the local police found beneath the barn, as well as the one in the shipping container, were both turned over, as if someone was looking for something.'

'And we have the scruffy-looking guys in the hospital car park, as well as on the Connolly land,' Danny said. 'They had Irish accents, but they're obviously involved in this somehow.'

'We also have the murder of the O'Neill family,' Maggie said. 'Tessa, you told us that Elias Two-Toes believed Tony was in over his head in something too. And we know he and Joe were friends. Can we draw the conclusion they were mixed up in the same thing?'

'There's something about Tony's posts on Joe's social media that jars with me,' Tessa said. 'I just don't feel the affection rings true.'

'Mogue Kearney, when I spoke to him, suggested Tony wasn't good at minding his own business,' Danny said. 'And speaking of Mogue...'

'Indeed,' Tessa said. 'We learned a lot more today due to a chance encounter Ash had while out having ice cream.'

'Lola Sherlock worked for Joe,' Danny took up the story, 'and is convinced he and Daisy are dead, murdered by a trio – now a double act – of assassins she calls the Strígòil. She says they're named after some kind of ghouls or goblins from Irish lore and have a fearsome reputation. Their MO is to wipe out not just their mark but his entire family, after which they disappear, leaving not a trace.'

'Which fits what we're seeing here,' Tessa added.

'She also says we should go and talk to Mogue Kearney,' Danny said. 'She didn't tell me why, but she seemed certain he knows a lot about the Connollys and what happened to them, and while we're there, we should ask him about someone called the Professor.'

'Is it just me,' Tessa asked, 'that feels the more information we get, the less we seem to know?'

Just then her phone buzzed.

'Yes, Tessa Burns.'

She listened for a moment.

'When?'

Shook her head.

'Okay, thanks. We'll be right out.'

The other two looked at her expectantly.

'Oisín Kelly was found dead this morning.'

The distiller lived a hundred yards up the road from the pub he ran. Situated on a bend in the road, his cottage was a traditional thatched, single-storeyed building, with a pretty flower bed out front and a small herb garden to the side.

Inside, it was full of antique furniture, watercolour paintings and, in the small living room, a collection of old folk albums on vinyl. Oisín had a beautiful stereo system, with an old-fashioned turntable and vintage box speakers. While Tessa could see the place had been well kept and was scrupulously clean, Oisín's home was upside down, with chairs lying on their side, records out of their sleeves and strewn about, cushions torn apart and their stuffing exposed.

McEvoy was there with the usual group of uniforms and forensics.

'The place, as you can see, has been turned over,' he said.

The small distiller was lying on his face on the living-room floor.

'Do we have a cause of death?' Tessa asked.

'One shot to the chest, one to the head with a small-bore weapon. Probably a .22.'

'Same as the others.'

'Yeah. Poor Oisín – he was worked over pretty good first though.'

'They were looking for something,' Maggie said.

'Did you look in his distillery?' Tessa asked.

'You know where it is?' McEvoy asked.

Tessa nodded and led them all to the pile of scrub behind the pub, only to find it already tossed aside and the manhole cover open. They all stood, gazing at the black hole that led to the subterranean levels.

'They could still be down there,' Danny said.

'Or they could be well gone,' McEvoy replied.

'You go down first then,' Tessa said, and there was no humour in her voice.

'Well, they might be...' McEvoy said and then closed his mouth quickly when Danny gave him a hard look.

They drew their weapons, and Tessa called down: 'Police! If anyone is there, be warned, we are coming down and we are armed.'

Her voice could be heard echoing about the subterranean space.

They all strained their ears for even the slightest movement: the wind blowing through the manhole cover created a wash of sound. Below it a steady drip-drip-drip could be heard. And nothing else.

'If someone's down there, I'm giving you one more chance to identify yourself,' Tessa called.

They waited, nerves a-jangle. Tessa realised she was actually holding her breath.

After twenty seconds had ground by, she shook her head.

'I'll go first,' she said and, gritting her teeth against the claustrophobia, began to descend the ladder, followed by Danny and then McEvoy.

By the time she was halfway down, Tessa knew the place had been trashed, just as Oisín's home had been.

'It's like they're looking for something,' she called up to Danny.

'We have to assume they are,' the big cop agreed. 'They must have thought Oisín had the list.'

Tessa reached below-ground level and turned in a full circle, surveying the devastation.

'So why wasn't the O'Neills' place trashed too then? Why did they kill that family but not turn the place over?'

Danny came to stand beside her. 'They obviously knew they *didn't* have it.'

'So why kill them then?'

Danny shook his head. 'I assumed it was to draw resources away from protecting Ash, but in truth have no idea. Come on – let's make sure no one is hiding down here among the rubble.'

They spread out, searching the area systematically, guns held in front of them in defence. It took them six minutes to confirm the former underground grain store was empty of anyone but them. Only then could they truly take in the scale of destruction.

The distillery was in ruins.

The still had been punctured, probably using a sledgehammer; glass jars smashed; vats of base mix tipped over and left to congeal on the stone floor.

Papers, boxes, packages of brewer's yeast, bags of sugar – all were strewn about the area with wild abandon.

'Fucking hell,' McEvoy said as he put his gun back in its holster. 'There's nothing left.'

'Oisín was Joe's mentor,' Tessa said. 'They probably thought if he was going to leave this list with anyone, it would be him.'

'Do you think he did?' Danny asked.

'I would say from the ferocity that was used to destroy his life's work that if he did, Oisín didn't tell.'

'Whatever it is, this list is claiming a lot of lives,' McEvoy said.

'And it might not be done yet,' Tessa agreed.

46

Tessa and Danny went to pay a visit to Mogue Kearney, and Maggie remained in the bar of the hotel and used the computer console on her wheelchair to research the Strígòil.

In Irish mythology, Strígòil were troubled spirits that had risen from the grave. They were said to be able to transform into an animal, become invisible and gain vitality from the blood of their victims. Unlike modern ideas of vampires, however, Strígòil weren't believed to look like humans but were misshapen, terrifying-looking creatures. In fact, Maggie learned, the word *stréach*, the root of their name, was the Irish word for 'scream'.

Appropriate, she thought.

One of the aspects of the Strígòil myth that interested Maggie was that the creatures were supposed to have a profound hunger for children – in fact, many stories suggested they killed parents only as a way to access the children those unfortunates were trying to protect.

She found an 1865 article by the folklorist William Smith that described the Strígòil as nocturnal creatures that preyed on infants. Smith reported a tradition in which, upon the birth of a child, a person should toss a stone behind them and call out 'this into the mouth of the Strígòil!' – a spell of protection, apparently.

And so the stories went on.

In 1932, a parish priest in Gragaugh, a townland in County Tipperary, called for the body of a man he'd recently buried to be dug up, asserting he'd seen the undead corpse of the man walking about the graveyard in the dark hours of the night. When the coffin was opened, the priest intoned a decade of the rosary while one local man held the corpse down and another hammered an ash rod through the dead man's heart.

The man, whose name was never given in the police report, was believed to have become a Strígòil, a ghoul that hungered for the souls of the living. After he was buried once again, the priest reported no more disturbances.

Having gone toe to toe with one of the Strígòil Lola had made reference to, Maggie knew that man, at least, had not been a supernatural creature. He'd bled when he was cut (and when he'd had half his ear bitten off by a tenacious dog), he'd felt pain and, in the end, a shot from a very traditional nine-millimetre Glock had taken his life.

Tessa and Danny's trawl of the files had come up blank, but with the name Strígòil to work with, she logged onto the organised crime database of the National Bureau of Criminal Investigation.

And got a hit almost immediately.

The Strígòil in this context were a freelance group of killers who worked primarily for international gangs. They had a fearsome reputation. As Lola had indicated, their modus operandi was to wipe out the entire family of their victims. If the Strígòil were sent to kill you, they wouldn't relent until your entire line was wiped out.

And they never left fingerprints, there was no DNA on record for any member of the group, and no witnesses had ever come forward to speak of having encountered them. Neither were there any photographs, police-artist sketches or even verbal descriptions of the killers, and no one who'd come face to face with them had survived, so all information on the file was based on rumour and conjecture.

But one facet of their identity repeatedly showed up in reports about them, so much so it was now accepted as fact.

The Strígòil were Irish, probably ex-Special Forces who'd been deployed all across Europe while they were serving.

There were three gangs they were reputed to work for most regularly, though only one dealt in the export of illegal liquor. They were the Moores, a local mob that was run from a betting office in Finglas.

Perhaps it was time one or more of the Burns Unit made a trip back to Dublin.

PART FOUR

HIGHWAYMEN

47

Mogue Kearney had offices on Mill Street, just off Church Square.

A severe-looking receptionist, who seemed unimpressed by their police credentials, told them to sit while she established whether her employer had time to see them.

'Tell him we can always bring him to the station and talk to him there,' Tessa said, smiling warmly.

'Please have a seat,' the woman repeated, making no attempt to keep the distaste from her voice. 'I will inform you if Mr Kearney has a few moments.'

They did as she suggested.

'Why does it feel like we've no authority here?' Danny asked Tessa.

'Mogue is a local politician and, according to his website, has been practising law in these parts for close to forty years,' Tessa said. 'Hereabouts, *he* is the one people will look to for leadership and protection.'

'Why?'

'You didn't grow up in a small rural town,' Tessa said. 'Things are different here. Someone like Mogue Kearney has power because he assumes it. It's been that way since the Stone Age.'

'And our positions as Gardai mean nothing?'

'They don't mean as much, no. We're also close to the border with the North. People around here are wary of what we represent. It's all tangled up in the history of the place, the oppression people experienced, the role the police took during the Land Wars and the brutality of the Black and Tans and the Auxiliaries.'

'None of which has anything to do with us,' Danny said, sounding annoyed. 'That's ancient history and has no bearing on the role of the police force now.'

'History isn't dead, Danny. It influences everything we do. You'd do well to remember that.'

'Mr Kearney will see you now,' the steely-eyed receptionist said.

Tessa and Danny stood, and she led them down a short hallway, up some stairs and knocked on a heavy oak door.

'Come in, come in,' a voice called.

The woman opened the door and stood aside while the two detectives entered the room, closing the door behind them.

Mogue Kearney remained seated, smiling up at the two detectives from behind a desk covered in leather-bound legal volumes and many stacks of files. The wall behind him was dominated by a black-and-white photograph, taken at the end of the nineteenth century, of a family being evicted from their land by the bailiffs. The people in the sepia-toned image, separated from Tessa and Danny by a gulf of more than a century, looked miserable, half-starved and devoid of hope.

Tessa wondered if this was the tone Mogue Kearney wanted to set for people visiting his office for the first time: *abandon hope all ye who enter here.*

'D'ye like the photo?' the lawyer asked.

He was wearing a blue-and-red pinstripe today, and his

comb-over was held in place by product so heavy it made his hair look like it was made of plaster of Paris. The aftershave he was wearing, which Tessa thought smelled as if it had been concocted by Joe Conolly or one of his associates, pervaded the entire room.

'It's very... vivid,' Tessa said. 'Was it taken locally?'

'Just outside Emyvale, in the year of our Lord 1895.'

'It's an... an interesting choice as far as a piece of art goes,' Tessa said.

'It's not art,' Mogue Kearney said. 'It's real life. It's the world we live in. Okay, so it was taken nearly 130 years ago, but the scene you're lookin' at could have happened only last week. Poor people bein' victimised by the rich.'

'And you want to redress the balance?' Tessa asked.

'It's what my life has been about. Mogue stands for the small man. Always has done.'

'Well, I think we'd both like to sit, if that's okay,' Tessa said.

'By all means,' the lawyer said, motioning towards two wooden chairs arranged in front of his desk. 'What can I do for you both? How are you getting on with the Connolly case?'

'That's why we're here, as it happens,' Tessa said.

'I'd assumed as much.'

'Your name has come up as part of our investigations.'

'Has it now? Well I shouldn't be surprised by that. Everyone around Monaghan knows old Mogue.'

'You told Detective Murphy you know Joe and Daisy. The O'Neills too.'

'I know everyone.'

'How well do you know Joe and Daisy?'

'Ah sure, I know Joe distils a fine bottle of poitín. I'd be lying if I didn't admit I've sampled some of his handiwork myself from time to time. Very pleasing it was too.'

'He's probably the biggest producer of illegal alcohol in the county,' Danny said. 'He employs a lot of people, and according to what we've been told, he was in the process of expanding his business even further. You told me you like to keep your nose to the ground or your finger on the pulse or something like that. What do you know about what he was planning?'

'As far as I'm aware, he's only a small-time operator,' Kearney said. 'You have to understand, the finest poitín has been produced in County Monaghan since the Celts rode across the plains in their chariots. Nobody makes a big fuss about it, and the Gardai have always taken a... well, an *indulgent* view of the whole thing. I wouldn't be surprised to learn that what happened to Joe and Daisy had nothing to do with the poitín business at all.'

'What do you think was the cause of their disappearance then?' Tessa asked.

'It's common knowledge both Joe and Daisy have connections with some very dangerous people. I don't like to be the fella to start rumours, but isn't it far more likely that this is all to do with something from their past? Something they were involved in long before they came to Monaghan?'

'Our investigation doesn't indicate that,' Tessa said.

'Well, that's my belief. And I've been practising both law and politics for a long time around here. I would say my opinion is pretty valuable.'

'How about you indulge us for a moment? Let's say, for the sake of argument, that Joe Connolly's a big producer, and had hit on a business model and a product line that was attracting a lot of attention.'

'It's a fiction, a fairy story,' Kearney replied. 'But I'll play your game.'

'In terms of outside interests, who do you think might be inclined to want to muscle in on Joe's success?'

'His success as a poitín-maker?'

'Poitín and other spirits, yes.'

Kearney made a dismissive wave. 'You're dreamin'. I

promise you that Joe and Daisy have met a nasty end as a result of somethin' dodgy they were involved in long before they came to my county to live.'

'You told me you thought they might be in financial trouble,' Danny said.

'I stand by that. I'd say whatever trouble they're in, money's at the back of it.'

'Have you heard any conjecture locally about the Connollys wanting to go straight? To leave criminality behind them?'

Kearney allowed an expression of deep shock to cross his face for just a second before he hid his surprise with a scornful scowl. 'I don't think such a drastic alteration in the Connollys' lifestyle was on the cards, no.'

'And the O'Neills?' Tessa asked.

'Tony was always gettin' in strife. He had a habit of runnin' his mouth off. People found him hard company so he didn't have a lot of friends. Sad really.'

'You don't see his and his family's deaths as being connected to the disappearance of the Connollys?'

'Why would I? Are you saying it is?'

Tessa suddenly stood. Danny did the same.

'Thank you for your time,' she said. 'We'll be in touch if we need to know anything else.'

'I'll be here,' Mogue Kearney said. 'I'm always here.'

Tessa had just opened the door when she stopped, looking back at the lawyer. 'What do you know about the Professor, Mr Kearney?'

The pinstripe-suited man visibly blanched this time – and stayed that way. His mouth dropped open, and then closed and then opened again, but no sounds came out.

Finally he said: 'I don't know what you're talkin' about!'

'Really?' Tessa said. 'You're sure about that?'

'I'm a very busy man,' Kearney said. 'I bid you both good day.'

Tessa nodded at their host and stepped out, closing the door behind her and Danny.

'He knows about the Professor,' Danny said.

'He so does,' Tessa agreed.

They didn't say goodbye to the receptionist.

DAISY CONNOLLY

It was evening on the sixth day after she'd been taken. She'd been in the dark now for thirty-six hours.

Sleep was becoming less of a problem, as she found herself drifting into a faint with alarming regularity.

There was an intercom attached to the wall beside her ear, and she pressed the 'talk' button with a trembling blue finger.

'Hello,' she said, and she could barely recognise her own voice. 'I... I need help. I'm not well. I can't feel my legs very well anymore and... if I could please have something to eat. Anything.'

There was a long pause at the other end, then a burst of static.

'Hello, Miss Daisy,' the voice of the man who was responsible for her and Joe's captivity purred. 'I would, of course, love to oblige you by providing you with sustenance. Nothing would make me happier. But before we can sit down to a nice bit of something to eat, you know what I need.'

In that moment, down in the dark and the cold, she almost gave in. She came close to it. But then she remembered when she and her husband had been in the boot of the car of the men who'd taken them from their home, travelling through the night to this hellish place. Joe had hissed to her: 'If we give them what they want, we're dead. Whatever happens, we can't tell them anything. We can't crumble. We have to stay strong.'

Gathering what resolve she had left, Daisy said: 'All I want it something to eat. It's so cold down here. I need... I need the calories to keep warm.'

'And I would be so happy to provide you with those important nutrients. But you have to do something for me first.'

Daisy sobbed and closed her eyes.

The only positive she had was that she was sure that, if they had Ash, they'd have used the child to make her and Joe give in.

Somehow, against all hope, their daughter had evaded capture.

Daisy would have to take whatever solace she could from that.

Tessa's phone rang as they emerged from Mogue Kearney's office building.

'Hey, Maggie. All okay? I'm putting you on speaker so Danny can hear.'

'Hi, Danny.'

'Hello, Maggie.'

'The Strígòil are on the OC database. The only Irish-based gang that deals in illegal liquor I can find who they work for are the Moores.'

'I know them,' Danny said. 'I've had some dealings with the head of their organisation here. A man called Teddy Moore.'

'Are you and he on good terms?' Tessa asked.

'Why would I be on good terms with a vicious gangster?'

Tessa shrugged. 'I dunno. People aren't all just one thing.'

'Most of the time, I think they are,' Danny said.

'Agree to disagree,' Tessa replied. 'So this Teddy bloke may have Joe and Daisy?'

'That's my take on it, yes,' Maggie said. 'He could be worth a visit.'

'They work out of a bookie's office in Finglas,' Danny said.

'Fancy a road trip?' Tessa asked.

Danny didn't answer though, because he was looking across the street at a group of men standing in the doorway of a newsagents. They were laughing loudly and raucously. As Tessa turned to look at them, she saw one of the men pass a pouch of rolling tobacco to one of his fellows who, rather than create a cigarette, took a wad of the stuff out and packed it into his mouth to chew. The three loud individuals were dressed in a mix-and-match of clothes, all of which were dirty and worn, and they all had long, untidy hair and beards.

'Hey!' Danny called and, without discussing it with Tessa, began to cross the square.

'I tell you what, why don't we go and talk to these guys?' she said, mostly to herself, and followed in his wake.

The group saw Danny coming and stepped out of the doorway, forming a loose line, their laughter falling quiet and looks of dull annoyance settling over their faces.

'Excuse me,' Danny said, approaching the one in the middle. 'You and me have some unfinished business.'

The man he was addressing was about the same height as Danny but probably four stones lighter. He neither moved nor spoke as Danny stood, glowering, in front of him.

'I'm talking to you,' Danny said, an edge coming to his voice. 'I could have you on assaulting a police officer. Give me one reason why I shouldn't.'

'I don't know what you're talkin' about,' the skinny man said.

Tessa had come alongside her partner now, and she looked at the group closely. They were all lean, their clothes hanging off them, and each of them stank to high heaven of unwashed humanity. The guy on the left had a bruise on one cheek, and the guy on the right had only one eye, the other one just a red hole in his face.

'You and I... ran into each other yesterday out on the

Connolly farm,' Danny said. 'You took off before we had a chance to finish our discussion.'

'I think I'd remember meetin' a big lad like you,' the scruffy man said and spat a stream of brown tobacco juice onto the pavement – and all over Danny's shoes.

'How about we finish our conversation at the police station?' Danny said, and Tessa could hear an edge to his voice now that she didn't like.

'Me and my friends are quite happy here,' the thin man said, and there was an edge to his voice too. 'I think we'd like to stay and enjoy the sunshine.'

'The mistake you're making,' Danny said, 'is that I would get a kick out of forcing you to come with me.'

The thin man, his eyes still on Danny, slid his right hand into the pocket of his long coat. Danny, who was eyeballing him, didn't see it, but Tessa did. She stepped in between the two men, the top of her head only coming to Danny's chin.

'I think what Detective Murphy is trying to say to you is that we would very much appreciate the chance to ask you a few questions. If you could spare some time.'

'We don't ever have time for the fuckin' guards,' the guy with the bruise on his cheek said. 'Now we was just mindin' our own business here, and this guy started harrassin' us. I reckon a judge might not look too kindly on your treatment of three innocent citizens. Just because we look a bit... a bit wild doesn't justify interferin' with us. Profilin' is what I'd call that.'

'I don't care about those other two,' Danny said, and he took a step closer, pushing Tessa forward in front of him. 'But I *will* finish what I started with you.'

'I think I'll be the one to finish things,' the skinny man said, and Tessa sensed him coiling to strike, and on instinct she grasped his right hand before it cleared his pocket.

'What the fuck is goin' on here, eh?'

The voice came from behind them, but Tessa recognised it as belonging to Jeremiah McEvoy.

'Are you shower of gobshites causin' trouble again?' He walked right past Danny and Tessa and right up to the middle man, getting nose to nose with him. 'Run along now before I fuckin' lock you up for makin' the town look untidy.'

Tessa pulled the man's hand from his pocket, keeping a tight hold of the wrist. He had his fingers closed in a fist and, prising them open, she found a red-handled Swiss Army knife, all the blades still folded within. Knowing she'd have a task passing that off as a concealed weapon, she pushed the man away.

'These gentlemen have been hanging around the hospital when Ash was there, and we spotted this man out on the Connolly land,' she said to McEvoy.

'They're always lurking around the hospital car park,' the detective said. 'They're barred out of most of the shops and cafés in town, so they go into the lobby and use the vending machines to get coffees and teas. Every now and again the hospital authorities run them, but they always come back. As to the Connolly land, my guess would be they knew the place is empty and were scoping it out to see what they could rob.'

'I take offence at that,' the lead one said.

'Ah, fuck off, Peter. Fuck right off now before I lose patience with you.'

The three men did just that, the tall one giving Danny a last, seething look.

'Who are those people?' Danny asked, virtually trembling with anger when they were gone.

'They're the Moynihans, a bunch of ne'er-do-wells and hippies who spend their time giving me and the other guys at the station a pain in our arse,' McEvoy said. 'They're always starting fights. A big guy like you, they'd see it as a challenge. Let them go. They're just bored and looking for a row is all.'

'You don't think they might be involved in the Connolly disappearance?' Tessa asked.

'Them?' McEvoy said, scratching his head. 'No. They'll steal the lead off the roof of their house if they think no one is watching it. But they wouldn't be organised enough to kidnap a dog if you left it tied up outside the shop when you went in to buy a Cornetto. Forget about them. They're not who you're looking for.'

'You're sure of that?' Tessa asked, getting up close to McEvoy. 'Because I'm getting a *very* bad feeling about them.'

'I'm sure,' McEvoy said through clenched teeth.

And the vice detective stalked off, leaving Tessa and Danny standing where they were.

49

Tessa and Danny decided to make the trip to visit the head of the Moores the following morning.

'Can we take my car?' Danny asked as they walked out of the hotel together.

'I don't mind. Sure,' Tessa said.

'Good. I'd prefer to drive.'

'I'll have you know I'm an excellent driver. I took advanced courses in the army, and I've done all the Garda evasive-driving training.'

'I don't doubt you can drive,' the big detective said.

'What's the problem then?'

They were at Danny's Golf GTI at this stage, a black hatch-back with red trim. He operated the central locking and they both got in.

'I've been in your car for short trips,' he said.

'Yes. And?'

'The first thing you do when you get in is put on your seat belt.'

'Of course. As you've just done.'

'Then you check your mirrors. The one in front of you and both wings.'

'Standard driving practice.'

'You turn on the ignition, and once that happens, your phone connects to the stereo in your Ford Capri via Bluetooth. Your car's vintage in all ways except for the stereo system, which is utterly twenty-first century.'

'I enjoy listening to music while I drive,' Tessa said.

'Exactly. And *that* is why I don't want to do the trip to Dublin in your car. Etiquette dictates the person who's driving picks the music. And I don't enjoy your taste in tunes.'

'What? Seriously? How could you not like my music?'

'Tessa, I didn't even know what to call your music. I had to google it.'

'I like rock!'

'Specifically, you like eighties and early nineties heavy metal. I found an article that called it *mullet music*.'

'Now I take *serious* offence at that. Danny, this is the good stuff! Guns N' Roses. AC/DC. Metallica. Van Halen. A bit of Def Leppard. What's not to like about that?'

Danny looked at her blankly. 'I would say just about everything.'

Tessa didn't know how to respond. 'What do you listen to then?'

'I usually have Lyric FM on. The classical music station.'

'Tell me you're joking!'

Danny switched on the engine, and the sounds of Yo-Yo Ma performing Bach's Cello Suite No. 1 in G Major immediately resonated from the Golf's speakers.

'No!' Tessa moaned.

It was going to be a long drive.

50

Maggie, Pavlov and Ash were in the North Road Community Centre, a two-minute walk from the police station. The community centre was a single-storeyed building that consisted of a wide entrance lobby which held a reception desk and a waiting area with chairs. Three doors led off this, one which opened onto a very well-equipped playroom, where Maggie, Ash and Pavlov were that morning. The second brought you to a hall that was used for bingo, AA meetings and by groups like the local youth club. The third led to the toilets.

Maggie wanted to spend some time with Ash that morning addressing the fact that the child would be moving to a new foster family over the next couple of days. Ash was extremely resistant to the imminent move, and Maggie was determined to make the transition as easy as possible.

Which was presenting her with some problems, as Ash was determined not to make the move at all.

'I ain't goin'.'

'You have to, Ash.'

'I wants to stay in the hospital and hang out with you until Tessa finds my mam and dad.'

'You can't do that. I wish you could, but hospitals are for sick people, and you're not sick. This family, the Mythens, have said you can stay with them for a while, and it's the best option we have.'

Ash put on a mighty pout and turned so her back was to Maggie.

'I said I ain't goin'! You tole me you'd *always* listen to me and hear what I had to say, and now you ain't listenin' at all!'

'I can hear you're scared and unhappy.'

'I ain't scared!'

'I think you are.'

'I'm *mad* is what I am! I don't wanna move in with no stupid ass family! I don't know them an' they don't know me, and I don't wanna do it! Do you hear me? *I don't wanna do it!*'

This outburst culminated in the little girl throwing herself down on the ground and crying bitterly, deep, body-wracking sobs that seemed to come from a place of bottomless grief. Maggie did something she rarely did and pushed herself out of the chair and, painstakingly, got down on the floor beside the child and placed a hand on her back, patting her gently so Aisling knew she was there.

They stayed that way for a long while, until the child's weeping diminished somewhat. When it had, Maggie asked her: 'What are you afraid of, Ash? Maybe if we talk about it, I can help you be less scared.'

'I dunno,' Ash said haltingly, the recent bout of crying causing her to hiccough slightly as she tried to speak. 'I s'pose it's cause they're strangers.'

'You've met them though,' the family liaison officer reminded her. 'So they're not *really* strangers. And you seemed to get on really well. They're a nice family, aren't they?'

'Yeah, but they already gots kids. Two of 'em. Why they want me to come and live there too?'

'I think they're just good people who want to help kids who need to be somewhere safe for a while.'

'Yeah but... how do I know I'll be safe there? Is that mam tough like you?'

Maggie put her arm around the child and squeezed. Here it was. She knew this was the root of the little girl's anxiety. And she had to be honest. If she wasn't, their relationship could be irreparably damaged.

'I don't know,' she admitted. 'I do know she'll do everything she can to protect you though.'

'Yeah, but what if more bad men come? She don't look to me like she'd be able to fight them like you did.'

'Would you have looked at me before a few days ago and thought I'd be able to?'

'No,' Ash admitted. 'Prob'ly not.'

'There you go then. You can't judge people until you've spent some time with them.'

'That dad ain't nowhere near as big as Danny.'

'Most people aren't as big as Danny.'

'I know that.'

'Mr Mythen – Glen – wants you to be happy while you're with his family. He told me he's very happy you're going to be spending some time with them. He's a really good guy.'

'You and Danny still be around though, right?'

'Yes. Me and Danny and Tessa and Pavlov won't be going anywhere until we find out what happened to your mam and dad. But in the meantime, I need you to stay with the Mythens and try to be brave. Can you do that?'

'I'll try.'

They lay side by side on the floor in silence for a bit. Then Ash said: 'Danny's real nice though, ain't he?'

'He is. I know he likes you a lot.'

'Seems a bit... sort of sad sometimes.'

'Do you think?'

'Yeah. I think he liked goin' for ice cream with me. Maybe him and me can do that again sometime soon.'

'I bet he'd love to. Right, now you've decided that, how about we practise what you're going to say on your first day with the Mythen family?'

They used dolls from the toy house to represent Maggie's new foster parents, and they were so engrossed in their game, they didn't notice that things had gone deathly quiet out in the community centre's lobby.

51

Albinoni's Adagio in G Minor was playing as Danny drove the Golf through Carrickmacross.

'Can we put on, like, a top-forty station?' Tessa asked.

'I don't think the top forty exists anymore,' Danny said. 'It's all downloads and streaming now.'

'Okay. Is there a download chart show?'

'Probably.'

'Can we put that on?'

'No.'

'Please?'

'My car, my rules.'

'But, Danny!'

'You should have thought of that before you let me drive.'

They passed through the town and were out on country roads again. Tessa leaned forward and turned the volume down slightly.

'You said you've dealt with this Teddy bloke before.'

'I did. One of his crew thought he'd extend the boundaries of his drug-dealing territory as far as Bray. I arrested the kid – he was, in fact, just eighteen. He made bail, and Teddy was in court with the lawyer. He paid the bond, and I was with the lad in the waiting area when he came to take him.'

'What did you make of him?'

'Teddy is... I think you'd probably call him charismatic. He dresses well and he speaks well, and I got the impression the kid looked up to him. But he's not a nice man. He looks like a banker or someone who sells upmarket cars. But that's not who he is. He's a killer. It's a good idea to remember that when you're speaking to him.'

'I'll keep that in mind,' Tessa said. 'Now, are you sure we can't listen to something else, just for half an hour?'

'I believe I've made myself clear on that point,' Danny said, but Tessa could hear the humour in his voice now.

And that was when a Range Rover drove out of a gateway at top speed, colliding with the driver's side of Danny's car and running them off the road.

52

'It's okay to tell your new foster family you feel scared,' Maggie said to Ash.

The little girl considered this. 'Won't that hurt their feelings though? I don't wanna do that. It be better they like me and not think I'm a mean kid.'

'I promise you they won't think that,' Maggie said. 'Feeling a bit weird about going to live in a new place is normal. I expect they'd think there was something wrong with you if you didn't.'

Ash looked at the woman who'd been her closest friend since the night the bad men had come to her home. Maggie's body was rail thin, but her face was warm and friendly. Today she was dressed in blue canvas trousers and a loose-fitting black top that had strings to close it up at the neck. Ash had been fascinated by Maggie's chair when she'd first met her: it wasn't like any wheelchair she'd ever seen. It looked more like something from a science-fiction show, all buttons and extra bits to make it a sort of superhero chair.

And Ash had come to think of Maggie as a superhero. After seeing how she'd stood up to the man who'd come to try and hurt her, there was no tougher person on earth as far as the little girl was concerned. She trusted the woman implicitly.

'You and Pavlov and Danny and Tessa still come and see me though, right?' she asked – she knew she'd asked this before, but it was a point she wanted to be absolutely certain of.

'Try and stop us. You and me will continue to spend time together every day until we find your mam and dad.'

Ash felt something clench inside her when Maggie mentioned her parents. 'You think they okay?'

'Tessa and Danny and I believe your folks are alive, Ash, if that's what you're asking.'

'No. I know that. Danny told me. You think they *okay* though? Like, is those bad men treatin' 'em okay?'

'That I can't answer,' Maggie admitted. 'We have to be positive. Believe they're going to be all right. Worrying they're not won't help them or you.'

At that moment, Pavlov sat up straight, his ears and tail pointed at the ceiling. He snarled once, and then jumped from the beanbag and ran to the door, sniffing at the crack underneath it.

'What is it, Pav?' Maggie asked.

The dog looked at her and barked once.

'Ash, get behind me,' the woman said, and as she did, the door opened and a man walked right in.

He was dressed head to foot in black, his face covered in a woollen balaclava that revealed only a thin slash of a mouth and dark eyes.

Maggie whipped open her baton, but the man, without breaking stride, pointed what looked like a remote control at her and pressed a button. A wire flew from the device he was holding, and something stuck in Maggie's chest. There was a buzzing sound and she went rigid, her skinny legs shooting out straight in front of her and her arms locking, the baton still clenched tightly in her fist.

This seemed to go on forever, but then the man released the button and Maggie slumped back down in her chair.

'Pav,' she said, her voice little more than a whisper. 'Get help.'

The dog shot out the door immediately, and the man pressed his button again, and Maggie's words were turned into a gurgling wail.

Ash, knowing her friend, superpowers or not, couldn't help her now, turned and ran.

53

The impact of the Range Rover colliding with Danny's Golf was shocking.

It felt to Tessa as if she'd been punched by a giant fist. The car, which had been travelling at eighty kilometres per hour, was pushed off the wheels on the driver's side, doing a kind of side-wheelie before skidding, swerving and then flipping onto its side, tumbling twice before landing on its roof in the ditch on the opposite side of the road.

Tessa experienced all of this from inside the vehicle, and it was much as she imagined going through the spin cycle in a washing machine might be. As the car went into its series of rolls she thought: *If this is how it comes to an end, it'll be a stupid fucking way to go out.*

Those were her last thoughts before she blacked out for a second, coming back to consciousness with a start to find herself hanging upside down, still strapped into her seat. Nausea overwhelmed her, and she thought she might be sick, but she fought the feeling, taking deep breaths, relieved to discover as she did that there was no smell of leaking petrol, just damp earth and vegetation.

The airbags had been activated but had deflated and were hanging limply from the dashboard and steering-wheel, respectively.

Looking to her right, she saw that Danny was unconscious. The door on his side was crushed inwards, and she was worried her partner might need to be cut out. The glass from both the windscreen and the driver's-side window had exploded, and blood was running from several cuts on the big man's face.

'Danny, talk to me, mate,' she called, reaching over and squeezing her friend's shoulder gently. 'Come back to me.'

There was no movement.

Placing her hand on his barrel-like chest, she could feel the rise and fall of his breath. He was alive at least.

Looking past Danny, she could just make out the front grille and headlights of the vehicle that had hit them. And as she watched, the midsection of a black-clad person passed in front of it and began to walk towards the immobile Golf.

Tessa could see the person was carrying a gun.

'Shit,' she said, taking her own from under her arm. 'Danny, wake the fuck up *now!*'

The big detective remained unconscious.

Tessa, still suspended upside down, trapped in her partner's car, directed her gun at the window and waited.

54

Ash, who'd been standing behind Maggie's chair, ran to the back of the playroom in her attempt to get away from the bad man.

Her first thought was to climb out the window, but it was closed and there was no time – he would have her before she even got it open. The only option she could see was a closet. She didn't know if she could lock it from the inside – in fact she doubted she could – but she thought there might be somewhere to hide inside anyway, maybe a small space to squeeze into.

Pulling open the door, she saw the space was filled with rolled mats, an old doll's house, some child-sized furniture and a plastic slide that was about the right size for a toddler. Getting inside and pulling the door behind her, she squeezed between and around all of this stuff, managing to get to the very back of the cupboard. Once there, she huddled down, trying to make herself as small as possible.

She had barely done this when the door was flung open. The bad man paused for a moment, obviously puzzled that his prey had somehow apparently disappeared, but then he began to grab items one at a time and throw them aside.

Ash felt panic rising.

Suddenly she realised she was cold, as if a breeze was blowing up the back of her T-shirt. She felt behind her and realised there actually was. Her fingers touched some kind of grille – an air vent. She managed to get a firm grip of it and pulled, and to her surprise it came away from the wall. Lying down flat, she was able to squirm inside, her feet disappearing into the narrow space just as the bad man hauled the baby slide out, her last piece of concealment.

Ash was in a square tunnel just big enough to house her. If she put her arms ahead of her and pressed them against the walls of the duct, she could drag herself forward a little bit at a time. Fresh air was coming from up ahead, and she prayed this meant an exit to the outside world.

'Aisling,' she heard the bad man say. 'Please come out. I'm here to take you to your mam and dad. Don't you want to see them? They miss you very much.'

Ash stopped dead. Could he be telling the truth?

She believed he knew where her parents were, but would someone who'd hurt Maggie really be there just to reunite her with her mam and dad?

'Please. I'm your friend, Aisling. I want to help you.'

Ash still didn't move. She wanted so much to trust him.

'Please, Aisling. If you don't come out, I'll be very sad. Your parents will be sad too.'

If you don't come out.

The words echoed in Ash's head, reverberating like the toll of a church bell. She'd heard those words before and she suddenly realised they'd been said by this voice.

If you don't come out, the voice had said the first time she'd heard it, when she and her mother had been hiding in the larder, *we'll beat your husband to death.*

It was the same man.

Her mother had given in to his demands the last time, and that hadn't ended well.

She wouldn't make the same mistake.

Taking a deep breath, she gripped the walls and slowly dragged herself towards the source of the breeze.

55

Tessa tried to ignore the pounding of blood rushing to her head and concentrate on the clear and present danger.

'I am a member of the Garda Síochána,' she called out. 'I am informing you that I am armed and I will use extreme force if you do not stand down.'

Through the shattered and warped window, she saw the figure pause.

'I'm giving you the chance to get in your vehicle and drive away,' Tessa said. 'I'm not in a position to come after you right now, but I tell you this and I fucking mean it: come one step closer and I will shoot.'

The figure didn't move.

'Right, I'm counting to three,' Tessa said. 'If I get that far, it's on your head.'

She waited a beat. Still no movement.

'One.'

The figure remained frozen, gun still in hand.

'Two.'

No change.

'Three.'

The individual did move, but from what Tessa could see, it was to sink into a crouch, probably to get a better position to fire on her.

Fuck it, I warned the idiot, Tessa thought, and, sighting down the barrel, she pulled the trigger.

To her horror, her gun only clicked.

For the first time in her career, both in the army and in the police force, Tessa's weapon had misfired.

56

Detective McEvoy was at his desk, about to enjoy an apple Danish and a black coffee when he felt something tugging at the leg of his jeans.

There was a time when such an experience would have scared the crap out of him – he would have assumed it was a rat or something verminous that had decided to make the old Monaghan police station its home. Since the trio he thought of as the Burns Unit had come to work in Monaghan, however, he'd become accustomed to a different way of life.

Taking a bite of his pastry, he looked below his desk to see the black-and-white mongrel Maggie Doolan insisted on taking everywhere with her.

'What do you want, Pavlov?' he asked.

The animal barked at him and skittered a couple of feet towards the door.

'I'm on my coffee break,' he said. 'Whatever it is, it can wait.'

The dog barked again.

'Where's Maggie?' McEvoy asked, irritated now.

He knew Tessa and Danny were on their way to Dublin so

reckoned Maggie must be busy with the Connolly kid, meaning the dog was obviously looking for attention.

'Okay, dog,' he said, sitting back up and picking up his cup of coffee. 'You are not my problem. Run along and find your mistress. I have more important things to do.'

The vice detective was about to take a large slurp of coffee when the fucking mutt rushed forward and nipped him on the ankle.

'Ow! I don't believe you just did that!'

Pavlov yipped shrilly and to McEvoy's extreme annoyance dodged in and bit him again.

'Right! Now you're fucking for it!'

He jumped up, grabbing a newspaper from his desk and rolling it into a makeshift baton, then charged after the dog, which took off at speed, shooting through the squad room and out through the lobby.

Detective Jeremiah McEvoy didn't know it, but he was being led to the community centre.

57

Tessa felt her heart sink as her Sig clicked once and then a second time.

That's it, she thought. *We're done.*

In the world that existed outside the bubble of the ruined Golf, she heard laughter.

'You didn't maintain your weapon,' a voice said, speaking in an accent that was Irish but gave away no sense of which part of the country its owner originated from. 'That's a very dumb mistake.'

Trying to remain calm, Tessa jacked the bullet out of the Sig's chamber and released the magazine, reaching to her belt and trying to get her spare out of the pouch she kept there. Suspended as she was, the position was awkward, and she was still struggling when a hand holding a Glock 17 was thrust through the window.

'You're going to pay for your mistake right now,' the voice said.

Tessa stopped struggling with the pouch. There was no longer any point.

'Get it over with,' she said.

At that moment, Danny Murphy's hand shot out, grabbing the black-clad man by the throat. In a display of remarkable strength and speed, he dragged their attacker off his feet, delivering a crushing headbutt (Tessa winced at the dull, popping sound of bone colliding with bone) that rendered the man immediately unconscious.

Letting the assassin go, Danny allowed the prone man to fall. He came to rest on the ceiling of the Golf. Tessa saw his face was obscured by a balaclava.

'Danny,' she said, reaching over and grabbing her partner's hand. 'Are you okay?'

'I think I'm going to live. My head hurts.'

'I hurt all over.'

'Could you ring for assistance?' Danny asked. 'I don't think we're going to get out of here unaided.'

'I was just thinking the same thing,' Tessa said.

And she rooted about for her phone.

58

Ash edged her way along the air duct, pressing her fingers into the sides of the tunnel and forcing herself forward. Despite the breeze, it was close and stuffy in the narrow space, and her T-shirt was stuck to her back with sweat.

As she painstakingly crept towards what she hoped was a way out, she could feel the man outside banging, crashing and thumping against the inside of the cupboard, trying to break through to her. The entire wall shook, and, peering back, she saw the metal buckle and cave in slightly just at her feet.

He was coming! Terror threatened to overwhelm her, but Ash pushed it deep down and tried to drag herself forward even faster.

'Aisling, it would be easier if you came back out,' she heard him call. 'I'm getting annoyed, and you don't want me to be angry, I promise you that. I wanted to be your friend, but you're making it very hard.'

There was another thump, and the metallic tube that was the air duct buckled and actually broke. Ash froze for a second, and as she did so, a hand exploded through the gap and grabbed her by the ankle.

The child screamed shrilly and kicked with all her strength, furiously pinwheeling her legs in an attempt to break from the grip the disembodied hand had her in. She could hear muffled grunting from the other side of the wall.

Getting as firm a grasp on the sides of the duct as she could, Ash jerked her leg towards herself, her heart thumping in her chest, hair stuck to her forehead with perspiration. At her first attempt, the leg remained firmly trapped, and the fingers if anything tightened their grip.

Gasping and fighting the panic rising in her like a tidal wave, Ash gathered her strength, and the next time accompanied the pull for freedom with an attack of her own, slamming the heel of her trainer hard down on the joint where the thumb met the hand. She did it once, then twice, and on the third time, with what she assumed was a swear, the grip loosened just enough for her to slide her leg loose, and with as much speed as she could muster, she skittered back deeper into the pipe.

The hand disappeared.

'You can run, but you can't hide,' the man called, and with a roar, the metal just above the hole he'd made was forced in, buckled and then burst open. 'I'll drag you out of there like the rat you are!'

Weeping in fear, Ash squirmed away from the advancing danger.

But she knew she wasn't going fast enough.

Jeremiah McEvoy charged into the lobby of the North Road Community Centre, chasing after Maggie's delinquent mutt, but immediately stopped dead in his tracks.

The centre's receptionist, a blonde woman in her early thirties named Grainne, was incapacitated, lying on the floor, bleeding from a head wound. Pavlov had stopped at the open door of the playroom, and through it McEvoy could see Maggie Doolan, slumped in her wheelchair, either unconscious or dead.

The vice detective pulled his gun from its holster. He could hear a banging sound coming from the playroom – it seemed to be emanating from what he took to be a cupboard at the very far end of the room.

'This is Detective Inspector Jeremiah McEvoy,' he called out. 'I am requesting you identify yourself.'

The banging stopped abruptly.

'I'm coming in,' McEvoy said, but he'd scarcely taken a step before a black-clad figure sprang from the cupboard and opened fire on him, getting off three shots, one of which was so close, the detective felt the heat of it.

McEvoy dropped to the ground as the shooter ducked back into the cover of the storage unit. He was afraid to return fire for fear of hitting Maggie, whose chair was dead centre between him and the shooter. He was counting on her not being dead. Jeremiah McEvoy suddenly realised he really didn't want her to be dead.

'Pavlov,' he hissed. 'Pav!'

The dog, who was, regardless of gunfire, still standing in the doorway, looked over at him.

'Help Maggie!' he said, unsure how much the animal understood or if he only followed specific commands. 'You need to wake Maggie up.'

The dog looked at his beloved friend, then back at McEvoy, and then in a single bound jumped into the family liaison officer's lap, licking her face vigorously with his rough tongue. The gunman fired again, the bullets whizzing over the vice detective's head.

McEvoy made to grab his mobile phone to call for backup, only to realise he'd left it in the station in his hurry to punish Pavlov for his wilful behaviour.

I'm not catching a break today, he thought and looked about to see if there was a landline. He suddenly remembered there was one behind the reception desk, which was only yards from where he was but might as well have been in Timbuktu for all the good it did him.

'Jeremiah?'

Looking up, he saw Maggie had regained consciousness. She seemed groggy but was sitting up straight and looking around her.

'Get out of there!' he said. 'You're in the line of fire.'

He saw realisation dawning on her face, and without another word, she set the chair in motion. As she did, the man stepped out of the cupboard, his weapon raised, and McEvoy shot him, hitting him in the chest and knocking him backwards into the wall, where he remained for a moment as if suspended, before tumbling forward onto his face.

'Fucking hell,' McEvoy said, slumping forward onto the ground himself, worn out from the fear and anxiety of it all.

'Where's Ash?' Maggie asked urgently. 'Did he get Ash?'

'I haven't seen her,' McEvoy said. 'Your dog brought me here so that guy could shoot at me!'

'I sent Pavlov to get help.'

'Yer man was bangin' about in the cupboard.'

Maggie swung her chair around and whizzed over to the closet. McEvoy hauled himself up and followed her. The contents of the storage space had all been removed and were scattered hither and thither about the floor outside, and the two police officers could see what they both took to be an open air vent. The wall all around it had been smashed inwards, the plasterboard kicked in from where the dead man had obviously been trying to create an access point.

'She's in the air duct,' Maggie said. 'Ash, it's Maggie! Are you okay?'

'I'm stuck,' a little voice called out. 'I'm at the end and I can't get the grate off.'

'Just wait there – we're coming,' Maggie said.

They followed the wall of the centre around, checking each vent until they found the right one. Maggie nearly wept with relief when she saw the child's face, smeared with grime from her passage along the pipe, peering out at her.

'I'm gonna have to kick it in,' McEvoy said.

'Can you move back just a little bit?' Maggie asked.

'I think so.'

Ash's face receded into darkness, and McEvoy delivered first one, then two kicks to the grille. It stove in at the first and broke at the second. The detective got to his knees and pulled the piece away.

'Here – take my hand, love.'

Reaching inside, he felt about until Ash grabbed his open hand, and then in one triumphant heave, he dragged her outside into the air and light.

McEvoy sprawled on his back, the child lying on his chest, both exhausted from the fear and exertion.

'Is the bad man gone?' Ash asked.

'I sincerely hope so,' McEvoy muttered.

Pavlov hopped from Maggie's lap and nuzzled the detective's bristled cheek.

'You're forgiven,' McEvoy said, accepting the gesture. 'And you made your point. Next time, I'll just come right away.'

59

As it happened, a passing motorist had already called the emergency services, and paramedics and the fire service arrived on the scene while Tessa was still making her call.

Danny informed them he and Tessa were police officers, and that the unconscious man below them was responsible for the collision, which was part of an attempt to kill them. A fireman called Francis, who lived up to every stereotype in the book about members of his profession, cut Tessa's seat belt and caught her as she fell, gently lifting her from the car.

'Detective, I should warn you that you're likely to pass out when I turn you the right way up,' Francis said.

'Call me Tessa.'

'Tessa, you're going to pass out when I stand you upright. Gravity is going to make the blood rush from your head fairly quickly, and there's every possibility you'll faint.'

'Well, no time like the present.'

'You ready?'

'As I'll ever be.'

It felt as if the entire world had gone topsy-turvy. The horizon twirled, then tipped, then spun, then seemed to condense into a tiny point of blackness, and Tessa drifted in it for a while. Then suddenly she was back.

She was being held upright by an absurdly handsome fireman, her head was thumping with pain and her mouth felt like it was lined with three-day-old newspaper. But she was alive, and Danny was alive, if still trapped in his car.

'You okay now?' Francis asked.

'Yeah. Just let me cuff this guy.'

She pulled a pair of handcuffs from another pouch in her belt and restrained the hands of the unconscious assassin before pulling off his balaclava. Casting about the ceiling that was now the floor of Danny's Golf, she found the man's Glock and pocketed it.

'We've called the Gardai and they should be here any minute,' Francis said.

'Good. Thank you. Now would you help get my friend out?'

'Of course, Detective.'

'Tessa.'

'Of course, Tessa.'

As she'd suspected, Danny had to be cut out of the vehicle, but when he was out and the medics examined him, they informed her that, other than bruised ribs and a cut on his cheek that needed stitches, he was none the worse for wear.

The same couldn't be said about his car, however.

'My Golf,' he said mournfully.

'You should have let me take my car,' Tessa said, patting him on the shoulder as they watched his damaged Volkswagen being winched onto a recovery lorry.

'I probably should've,' the big detective said. 'If I had done, though, the car would be a write off and we'd both be dead, as I'm assuming it doesn't have airbags.'

'That's true,' Tessa said. 'And you know another good thing about what just happened?'

'Judging from the look of the man you knocked out, we can

be pretty sure we've captured one of the Strígòil alive and can now question him about the Connollys and the O'Neills?'

'The only good thing other than that.'

Danny looked down at his partner. 'No. I don't know what that is.'

'Will I tell you?'

'Please.'

'Okay. You know when that Range Rover smashed into us and we started to roll?'

'Of course.'

'Well when that happened, the damn classical music switched itself off.'

Danny sighed deeply and shook his head.

'Too soon?' Tessa asked.

'Too soon,' Danny agreed.

60

Tessa called Dawn Wilson, who advised her to have the assassin brought to the Mater Hospital in Dublin, where she would have some members of Tessa's old unit waiting to stand guard while he was treated for any injuries he may have sustained.

'He's probably got a concussion at least,' the commissioner said. 'I can imagine Daniel's head would make quite an impression.'

'He's still out, boss,' Tessa said. 'But I'm not sure if he's faking it or not.'

'Keep him cuffed and make sure someone has a gun on him at all times.'

'Oh, Danny is keeping a close eye on him as we speak.'

'Once he's given the all-clear, we'll have him taken to Harcourt Street for a bit of a chat.'

'Sounds like a plan,' Tessa agreed.

'Have you heard from Maggie?'

'No, boss. I was just about to ring her.'

'Do. You're not the only one who's had some drama.'

Maggie was her usual self-effacing self, but she filled Tessa in on what had happened.

'Fucking hell,' Tessa said when she was finished. 'He tased you, the bastard.'

'Well I did mace his brother and knock out quite a few of his teeth. And I followed it up by shooting him dead, so...'

'True. Thank God for Jeremiah.'

'He held up his end, that's for sure,' Maggie said.

'And young Ash had already escaped?'

'Got into an air vent and followed it to the back of the community centre. If she'd been able to knock the vent out at that end, she'd have been home free.'

'She is one awesome little girl.'

'She really is. It's lucky she was so fast moving. When we went to have a look at the closet, our deceased friend had been trying to kick a hole in the wall to get in at her. If Jeremiah hadn't arrived when he did, he'd probably have succeeded.'

'Well we've had our own altercation with the last one of the Strígòil crew,' Tessa said, and told Maggie about her and Danny's ordeal. 'Our guy is just like the other one – his face is like a piece of marble the sculptor hasn't started working on yet.'

'Our was too. Yours is still alive?'

'Yup.'

'Danny hasn't gone and given him brain damage or anything, has he?'

'No way to tell. Yer man is still out for the count.'

'We'll just have to hope. I know Danny was only trying to save your lives and all of that, but it would be really good if we could get some kind of information from this guy.'

'We'll do our best.'

'I know you will.'

'Okay. Take it easy,' Tessa said. 'Try not to get killed before we get back there.'

'I can't promise anything. It's getting harder and harder to avoid these days.'

'I'll give you that. See you soon.'
'Count on it.'

61

The Strígòil regained consciousness on the trip to Dublin but remained stoically silent, even when one of the paramedics offered him some water or a paracetamol for his head.

'You might be glad of it,' Danny, who was accompanying him in the ambulance, said.

The man just glowered at him.

The detective shrugged. 'Have it your own way.'

A clean bill of health was promptly given in the hospital, and by 6.30 p.m., they were in Harcourt Street.

The interview room was small and square. The walls and ceiling had been painted magnolia at some point years ago but were now stained and faded, with all kinds of graffiti written and scratched into them by the many people who'd passed through there. A two-way mirror covered one wall, so those involved in the case who weren't interviewing could view proceedings, and a metal table with a Formica top sat in the room's centre. An old cassette recorder was embedded in its surface but hadn't been used in more than a decade, replaced by a digital video camera that hung from a harness on the wall.

Tessa and Danny sat on one side of the table, the Strígòil on the other, his cuffs now attached to a chain that was padlocked to a loop affixed to the middle of the table.

'We have you on the attempted murder of two police offi-cers,' Tessa said. 'Now, I'm sure some lawyer will try to make a case that you never had any intention of running into us, that the whole thing was just a great big misunderstanding, but I have to tell you, the fact you stuck a Glock through our window does suggest less than honourable intentions.'

The man said nothing.

'This would go easier if you were prepared to talk to us,' Tessa said. 'We're not after you really. You'll serve some time, but what we really want is to know who paid you to come for the Connollys. For Ash. Play ball with us and you could be out and up to your old shenanigans in a year.'

He only glared at them, still refusing to utter a single word.

'Okay, we're going to give you some time to think,' Tessa said. 'Come on, Danny.'

They stood up, leaving the man where he was.

Dawn Wilson, dressed in a grey trouser suit, her red hair hanging loose about her shoulders, was in the observation area, leaning on the desk that housed the controls for the camera and microphones in the interview room. Beside her, dwarfed by the commissioner's height, was a short, skinny man in a thigh-length leather jacket, grey canvas shirt and black jeans. His dark hair was long and had patches of grey in it, and a scar curled down his cheek and across his upper lip.

'Guys, this is Luca Bodahn. He's an undercover officer with the Organised Crime Unit and I thought he might be able to help with some aspects of this case.'

'Any helpful thoughts?' Tessa asked Bodahn, shaking his hand.

'I've heard of the Strígòil but I've never come across one of them before,' the vice detective said. 'Frankly, I never expected

I would. There are more than a few who think they're an urban myth among the criminal classes.'

'Well they're not,' Danny said.

'Clearly.'

'From what I know of these guys, he won't talk. My guess is he'll wait in complete silence until his lawyer shows up.'

'Did you say you were here to help?' Tessa asked, looking at the man with disdain.

'I'm a realist,' Bodahn said. 'If you've got any bargaining chips at all, I'd use them now. Once he lawyers up, it'll be too late.'

'No time like the present, I suppose,' Tessa said and pushed open the door to the interview room again.

The assassin watched her carefully as she strode over to him and sat down once more.

'Let's cut the crap,' she said.

He sat up a little straighter at the steel in her voice.

'We have the list,' she lied. 'We've got it.'

A look of horror spread across the assassin's face, just for a second, but it was quickly replaced by a grin.

'Without the Professor,' he said, 'it's useless.'

Tessa knew she had him on the ropes. She decided to push her advantage.

'Who says we need the Professor? How do you know we don't have someone equally as... skilled?'

'Okay,' the Strígòil said. 'Let's say I believe you. If you have it, no one else does, so the race is over. My job is done.'

He sat back, looking at her languidly.

'Where *is* the Professor?' Tessa asked, thinking she had nothing to lose.

'Far, far out of your reach.'

'That seems a bit vague, as answers go.'

The killer gave a loud guffaw. 'This conversation is over. I want to see my lawyer now.'

'He's on his way.'

The Strígòil narrowed his eyes at Tessa, and his thin lips curled into a smile. 'You dream of a man like me, don't you?' he asked, his voice a guttural whisper. 'A man with no face?'

Tessa remained where she was for a moment then stood and walked out, closing the door carefully behind her.

It took five minutes for her hands to stop shaking.

62

The Strígòil was taken to a cell, and Tessa, Danny, Dawn and Bodahn made the short walk to Captain America's, a diner on Grafton Street, to get something to eat and talk things over.

Captain America's, which had been operating since the 1970s and claimed to be the restaurant that brought the burger and other American culinary staples to Ireland, was situated at the top of the pedestrianised street and up a flight of stairs. Inside, it was all dark wood and low lighting, and to Tessa's delight, Thin Lizzy's 'Don't Believe a Word' was playing over the stereo system.

'I always thought this would be a comic-book themed place,' Bodahn said as he slid into the booth they'd been led to by their waitress.

'You'd think, but no,' Dawn said. 'They've got a few posters of Cap up, all right, but it's mostly just Americana themed – cars, Hollywood and rock 'n' roll. I don't know if they pay Marvel anything for the use of the name, but this has been a Dublin landmark for years.'

They ordered.

'So what do we know that we didn't know before?' Dawn asked, sipping from her glass of Coke.

'I was surprised to hear mention of the Professor,' Bodahn said.

'You've had dealings with him?' Tessa asked.

'No, but I've heard of him. I used to be with the drugs squad, and the Professor was sort of an urban legend for the guys I worked with. They say he's a French chemist who made his name by cooking some crazy-addictive crystal meth, that he could make heroin pure enough it doesn't impact on the user's health for a lot longer than usual, which keeps your customers addicted but alive. I also heard he could grow marijuana that got you stoned but doesn't have that weird, cat-piss smell, so is more easily smuggled.'

Their food arrived, and they paused while the correct plates were put in front of the right people.

'So this Professor is someone gangs would be falling over themselves to employ,' Dawn said, taking a bite of her chicken burger.

'He is – or so I believe,' Bodahn said, putting salt on his steak and baked potato. 'I've heard he demands huge money upfront before he'll even consider taking on a commission.'

'Well whoever has the Connollys seems to have acquired his services,' Danny said, dipping some chicken from his Caesar salad into its dressing, which he'd asked for on the side. 'Is he easily contacted? I would imagine he'd have to operate some kind of vetting system before he'd agree to meet potential employers.'

'The last I heard he was supposed to be holed up some-where in France, working for one of those alt-right biker crews that are selling dope to fund the revolution,' Bodahn said. 'But the short answer is I don't know. You're probably right, but how it all works is beyond me.'

'We have an infamous, virtually legendary drug producer,'

Dawn said, 'and a mysterious list that only he'll know what to do with.'

'Has to be some kind of formula for cooking dope,' Danny said. 'We think this deal is just about sending specially made booze into European clubs, but why not narcotics too?'

'Joe's devoted his talents to distilling alcohol,' Tessa said. 'His mentor told me he thinks of it as an art form. I can't see him being drawn to cooking dope. And anyway, according to the late Oisín, he wanted to go straight!'

'What if he wasn't being given a choice?' Danny suggested.

'Why do they need the Professor then?' Bodahn asked.

'What if Joe, with his degree in chemical engineering,' Tessa said, thinking aloud, 'was forced to come up with the recipe for some kind of special drug, but then he refused to make it? They've brought in the Professor to do it, but Joe's hidden the recipe, this "list", because he knows once they have it, they'll kill him.'

They were all quiet.

Tessa had joined the dots, creating a narrative that worked with the information they had.

'If your mysterious Professor has come to the Emerald Isle,' Tessa said to Bohdan as she had some of her linguini, 'let's hope we can extend his stay.'

'You'll have to find him first,' Bodahn said. 'And unless you're more astute than I am, nothing our strange-looking friend said this evening brought me any closer to working out where he might be.'

'Tomorrow, Danny and I are going to pay Teddy Moore a visit,' Tessa said. 'While we're there, we can ask him.'

'You are?' Bodahn said, clearly not believing her.

'Yup.'

'You're serious?'

'As a heart attack.'

'Tread carefully. The man is a snake.'

'Then Danny and I are mongooses,' Tessa said. 'Mongeese? What's the plural? Dawn, you're the commissioner. You should know these things.'

'Mongi?'

'That makes no sense,' Danny said.

'You people don't make sense,' Bodahn said, shaking his head wearily.

'No, but we're a lot of fun,' Tessa said, grinning.

63

The town centre of Finglas, a suburb to the north-west of Dublin City, overlooked the valley of the River Tolka.

'I can see why Teddy would want to run his business from here,' Danny said. 'It's like being in the country while still being in the city.'

'I bet you'd pay for the privilege,' Tessa replied.

'Still. Nice though.'

Across the street from where they parked the unmarked Ford was a small betting office, about the size of an old-fashioned newsagents, its façade painted in sky blue, the words 'Winning Ticket Betting' written in white on the sign above the door.

'This the place?' Tessa asked.

'Yes.'

'And he's usually here?'

'So I'm told.'

'Let's go and say hi then.'

Inside, the bookies was small and cluttered. An island in the centre of the shop floor held pencils and betting slips, and a counter ran along each wall, stools at intermittent points for the customers to sit while they lost their money. In one corner was a small booth with a glass window, behind which a girl took the bets and paid out winnings when called upon to do so.

The place was full to capacity when they went in, the throng of men (for the denizens of the shop were all male) glued to two television screens, one of which was showing greyhound racing, the other a football game.

Among them, reading a newspaper, was a square-shaped man in an expensive-looking grey suit with an open-necked blue silk shirt. Tessa noted he had well-manicured hands, and his hair was perfectly coiffed and full, like a newsreader.

She looked at Danny, who nodded, and the pair approached the man.

'Teddy Moore?'

He looked up at her with very sharp blue eyes. 'I am Teddy, yes. Who are you?'

'I'm DI Tessa Burns,' Tessa said, holding up her ID. 'This is DS Danny Murphy. We'd like to have a few words with you.'

The man sighed and closed his paper.

'Everyone out,' he said in a voice that remained quiet but could somehow be heard above the sounds of the televisions.

The announcement was met with some murmurings of annoyance, and the man spoke again, with a sharper tone this time: 'I said everyone out! Now!'

That seemed to cause the men to scatter like skittles, and within seconds the shop was empty but for the girl in her booth, who pulled down a screen and disappeared.

'What do you want, Detectives?'

'Mr Moore,' Tessa said, 'normally we would do a little dance where I ask you if you know a couple named Joe and Daisy Connolly, and you say you don't, and I give you examples of witnesses who saw you in their company, and then you say something like: "Oh, that Joe and Daisy Connolly", and we dance around a bit more until I come right out and ask you if you kidnapped them, and where you're holding them.'

'I am familiar with the process, yes.'

'We currently have the last living member of the Strígòil in custody,' Tessa said, 'You've probably noted that Detective Murphy and myself have sustained a few knocks recently. Well, your man gave it a good try, but he failed in his attempt to kill us and stop our investigation. His two brothers failed too, in their bids to kidnap or kill Ash Connolly – we don't know which they wanted to do – and to kill our colleague Maggie Doolan. Both assassins are dead, but our one is in a cell. I have a feeling he'll talk, sooner or later, and tell us you hired him. Why not save yourself some hardship and just tell us where the Connollys are.'

Moore shrugged. 'I knew they'd disappeared, but I had nothing to do with it.'

'You were involved in this project they were developing.'

'I was at the beginning. But others tried to come on board. They called a meeting, and there were representatives from nine groups there. I've remained in this business as long as I have because I'm careful. Too many parties in on a deal means too many mouths likely to get loose-lipped. So I took my people out.'

'When was this?'

'About three weeks ago. There was also a... rumour circulating that Joe was in the process of creating something really special but that he intended to try and sell it to a legitimate distributor for mass production. That made me very uncomfortable.'

'A rumour?' Tessa asked. 'Might I ask where this titbit of information originated?'

'Some friend of Joe's, I believe. I didn't like it at all. If you want to succeed in this game, you can have a legitimate business as a cover, like this betting office, but that can't be your main earner – it can't be a flagship project. You'll draw too much attention on yourself, and then you've got people like the Revenue, and the Criminal Assets Bureau and all sort of others crawling all over you.'

'Unless Joe wasn't planning on staying in the crime game over the long term,' Tessa suggested.

'Exactly. Which would have meant an investment wasted. The Connollys were getting too big for their boots. If I'd stayed involved in the initiative, I think I would have to have dealt with them sooner or later. Joe was beginning to believe his own hype, and as for Daisy – she thought she was Don Corleone, moving all the pieces around on her board. I'm not surprised things went south. The Connollys have been forced to learn a hard lesson. I imagine they're still alive, but I doubt they're very comfortable.'

'How come you're so confident they're alive?' Tessa wanted to know.

'Because they have something everyone involved in that profit-sharing deal wanted. This special product.'

'And what was that?' Tessa asked.

Moore grinned and waggled his finger at her. 'Nope. You'll have to ask the Professor about that.'

Danny, who'd been silent this whole time, suddenly lunged forward and grabbed Moore by the scruff of the neck, lifting him off his stool and slamming him into the wall.

'Where do we find the Professor?' he asked, and Tessa could see he was shaking. 'Where are the Connollys? There's a little girl who's been through hell and just wants her parents back, and I am *damned* if I'm going back to her empty-handed. Now start talking or I'll start breaking things off you!'

'Stand down, Detective!' Tessa said, placing a hand on Danny's shoulder.

Moore was staring the big man dead in the eye.

'Do you think pain holds any secrets for me?' he asked, his

voice completely calm and steady. 'You can do your worst. It won't serve you other than to give you some exercise, which might help you burn off this anger you're carrying.'

'*I said stand down, Detective,*' Tessa said again, and this time Danny seemed to snap out of it and released his grip on the mobster.

'Okay,' she said, trying to keep her own temper in check now. 'Let's go. Thank you for your time, Mr Moore.'

They were almost at the door when he said: 'I'm a grandfather. I don't like the idea that someone would harm a child. I know the Strígòil's reputation for killing little ones. I was loathe to work with them in the past, and when I did, at the insistence of my business partners, I insisted always that on any jobs I commissioned, no children were to be killed. There's no honour in that. I reached a point where I put my foot down and stopped employing them altogether. I had no stomach for it.'

'Help us then,' Tessa said, looking back at him.

Moore looked at his shoes for a moment, then said: 'I will tell you one thing, though believe me, following where this clue might lead will only bring *you* pain.'

'Say what you have to so I can get my friend out of here,' Tessa said.

'I've already told you, in the end there were many parties competing to go into partnership with the Connollys. One group, whom I'd never encountered before, seemed to be very much at the rear of the pack – I won't pretend I even saw them as contenders. But as things progressed, I started to understand they might be more of a threat than I had at first supposed. I saw ambition in them, ambition and a kind of... ferocity.'

'You're saying they were dangerous, even by your standards,' Tessa said.

'They didn't seem to care about anything except coming out on top of the deal,' Moore said. 'If I'd been prepared to kill everyone else at the table, or even worse, threaten to torture their children, I could have won, but then, how would I hold my head up when I go to play with my grandson?'

'I didn't know you had such moral standards,' Tessa said.

'Everyone must have some rules,' Moore retorted. 'But these men didn't. If I were trying to find Joe and Daisy, I might look to this group.'

'Who are they?' Tessa asked.

'Joe referred to them as the Moynihans,' Moore said. 'And they are in fact neighbours of the Connollys. You'll find them on an island in the middle of a lake in County Monaghan.'

'A lake,' Tessa said, almost to herself. 'Fucking particles of sedge. It was right in front of me this whole time.'

'These people are unpredictable,' Moore said. 'If I were you, I would be extremely careful.'

He paused, as if thinking, then said: 'Or don't. Quite honestly, I don't care. I don't like sharing information, even about competitors I don't respect, with the police.'

'Why tell us then?' Tessa asked as she opened the door and pushed Danny out.

'Maybe I think it would be interesting to see what you and the Moynihans make of one another,' Teddy said. 'Especially your angry friend. Now get out of my betting office.'

They did.

Tessa didn't speak to Danny all the way back to Harcourt Street.

The big detective didn't seem to notice. He just stared out the window in silent contemplation.

64

They reported back to Dawn, and she told them not to waste time. 'Get your arses back to Monaghan and see if this intelligence is worth anything.'

'Yes, boss.'

'Go! Take the Ford.'

'Okay.'

'Danny, I have the motor pool working on your Golf. Tessa, that lad Jimmy you put forward for a position has proven to be a real genius with vehicles, and he tells me it's not as big a job as you might have imagined. It should be good as new within a week.'

'I... I appreciate that, boss. Thank you.'

'Least I could do. I know how silly you boys can get about your vehicles.'

'Not just the boys, boss,' Tessa piped up.

'Oh, I know you're another motorhead,' Dawn said, throwing her eyes up to heaven. 'Yours is an old Capri, so I hear.'

'My most prized possession.'

'Well, don't let me keep you from it. Report back if I can help at this end.'

'We will. Thanks, Commissioner.'

The drive back to Monaghan Town was just as silent as the one from Finglas to Harcourt Street. Tessa made a point of synching her phone up with the Ford's stereo and played her 'mullet music' at full volume for the entire drive. Her partner didn't complain once, even when she sang along (very discordantly) to Black Sabbath's 'Paranoid'. Which was something most people Tessa had shared a car with took great offence at.

By two that afternoon they were gathered in the conference room of the police station. Garda O'Connor and Cadet Mooney, the two uniformed officers who'd found Ash in the shipping container and who'd been first on the scene, joined them.

'The Moynihans,' McEvoy said. 'You're feckin' serious?'

'Yes,' Tessa said. 'The same people you told me and Danny were just a bunch of harmless ne'er-do-wells. Remember that?'

'I've never had cause to see them as any different!'

'Do you think them capable of something like this?' Maggie asked.

The vice detective shook his head. 'Maggie, we've both been doin' this work for a lot of years. One thing it teaches is that anyone is capable of almost anythin' if they're desperate enough.'

'According to Teddy Moore, the Moynihans were desperate to win a controlling stake in this deal,' Tessa said. 'So I think you've just answered the question, Jeremiah.'

'What can you tell us about them?' Maggie asked.

'They're kind of a family,' McEvoy said. 'I don't know how

close the familial bonds are, but every man on the island claims the name "Moynihan" as his surname. Maybe that's part of some kind of rite of passage. Certainly the community looks to be fluid – there are always people coming and going.'

'Which island are we talking about?' Tessa asked.

'There's a piece of land, about a square acre in size, in the middle of White Lake, near Ballybay,' McEvoy said. 'They all live out there.'

'Paddy Dorney mentioned a "man from the island" right back at the beginning of our investigation,' Maggie said. 'And only a couple of days ago, forensics came back with plant particles from a reed that's only found in or around lakes, particles they discovered in the shipping container on the Connolly land that someone recently turned over. The combination of these two things didn't set any alarm bells ringing for you? I mean, this couple are missing now for *a week* and you're still not joining the dots – dots only you can see, might I add!'

'Don't you start givin' me a hard time, Maggie Doolan. I put myself at risk for you yesterday, so I did!'

'Which is your fucking job, Jeremiah,' Tessa said tightly. 'Any one of us would do the same for you. Not because we particularly like you, but because you're a brother officer *and that's what we fucking do!*'

'Like, we had case conferences and talked about Monaghan being landlocked and how a man from an island seemed an impossibility,' Maggie said, really annoyed. 'They were hanging around outside the hospital when Ash was in there and you dismissed it! Now we're being told they're the most likely suspects, and in fact the place Joe and Daisy are most probably being held is an island you knew about, populated by people you've had dealings with, and it never occurred to you this might be where we should look?'

'These lads have been arrested for bar fights,' McEvoy said. 'Once or twice one of them has been caught driving while under the influence. There was one incident of a knife attack, and I will admit there's an undercurrent of violence in their community, but you have to understand, these people are reclusive – they hardly ever come out of the lake. One Moynihan or other has owned the island for generations. It doesn't even have a name anyone can remember, and it seems that's the way they want it.'

'They also want to be a controlling party to an illegal alcohol smuggling and distribution business,' Tessa said, 'very likely, we now believe, with the extra incentive of selling drugs or something worse to an international client base. They may have spent generations hiding out in the middle of the lake, but it seems they're ready to rejoin society.'

'Who's in charge out on the island?' Maggie asked. 'Is there any hope we can reason with them?'

'The current patriarch is a man named Diarmuid Moynihan,' McEvoy said. 'He's in his seventies and as bitter, misogynistic and unpleasant a man as you could hope to meet.'

'That's a no then,' Tessa said.

'Well...' McEvoy said, looking distinctly uncomfortable.

'What?' they all said in unison.

'Mogue Kearney represents their legal interests.'

'You have got to be kidding me,' Tessa said.

'I wish I was.'

'Come on,' Tessa said to McEvoy. 'You and me are going to go and have a chat with Mogue.'

DAISY CONNOLLY

According to the digital watch, it was night on the seventh day she'd been in the darkness.

Water was seeping in from outside, and Daisy was lying in several inches of it now, adding to her misery quite profoundly. She drifted from a nightmare in which Ash was being chased by a huge creature that had only shadows where its face should have been, waking with a start as the intercom crackled into life.

'How do I find you this fine evening, Miss Daisy?'

It was the man called Diarmuid. The one who was behind their abduction, imprisonment and torment.

'Please,' she said. 'Please let me out of here.'

'Now, my dear,' Diarmuid said. 'You know I would dearly love to do so. And please remember, you have the power to end all this unpleasantness in an instant. Say the word, and I can have you released.'

She screwed her eyes tight shut and tried to stop her teeth from chattering.

'Let... let me out and we can... we can talk about it.'

Diarmuid laughed, the sound alien and harsh in the confined space where Daisy was being held.

'Oh, you must believe me to be very stupid indeed. Do you really believe I'm that gullible?'

'I... I'm not trying to manipulate you,' Daisy said urgently. 'Let Joe and me out, and maybe we can reach... an agreement.'

'Hmmm. I'd like to think we could. But you see, your husband just told me to, and I quote, go and fuck myself. Now, that doesn't sound to me very much as if he wants to reach a compromise.'

'Joe... Joe gets angry. He's a creative person. You... you know what people like that are like.'

'I do, I do. And, Miss Daisy, I am sympathetic to the artistic spirit, truly I am. I like to think I hold some of that creative impulse inside myself. But you see, that doesn't help us, does it?'

'If you let us both out, I could try to talk to him.'

'Perhaps. Perhaps. But what can you yourself offer me, Miss Daisy? Can you offer me the skills and information I require? Can you take your husband's place? What is your skillset?'

Daisy fought to get her mind working. To try and grasp any chance to escape from her current grim circumstances. Could she bargain with this man? Reach an agreement? Offer him something, anything that might get her closer to a way out?

'I was involved in every aspect of the business. I know all of it.'

'You do?'

'Yes. If you were just prepared to sit and talk to me, I might be able to tell you anything you wanted.'

'That's not what I've been told,' Diarmuid said. 'I've been reliably informed you were just the business and marketing side of the enterprise.'

Daisy felt panic building. She was losing her grasp on the conversation.

'Yes, that was what I had responsibility for, but I worked alongside Joe from the very beginning.'

'I think you're pulling my leg.'

'I'm not!'

There was a long pause. In the freezing darkness, it seemed to stretch out interminably. Daisy was sure Diarmuid was gone – then his voice came in a low drawl.

'I might just let your husband out long enough to cut off a part of him, a part he'll miss a good deal. We can see if that helps to make him, and maybe you too, a bit more open to working with me. What do you think of that, Miss Daisy?'

'Please don't do that,' Daisy said, fighting back tears. 'Please don't hurt him.'

'I might. But then again I mightn't.'

Daisy couldn't hold back the crying then. Over gulping sobs she heard: 'Perhaps I'll just leave you there for another night, and we can revisit things in the morning.'

And the intercom fell silent.

Daisy lay in the cold, sodden darkness and wept.

65

'He doesn't have a criminal record at all, you know,' McEvoy said as he and Tessa walked briskly towards Mogue Kearney's offices.

'Who doesn't?'

'Diarmuid Moynihan. Not a single offence.'

Tessa stopped and glared at the vice detective. 'Have they paid you off, Jeremiah?'

'What?' The man looked appalled; genuinely hurt.

Tessa almost felt bad, but she was too annoyed. It seemed to her, in that moment, that she was surrounded by incompetent men, and she was about sick of it.

'I went and talked to Elias Two-Toes,' she said. 'He told me he sends you a crate of 'shine every now and then to keep you in pick-me-ups, and in turn you look the other way when you stumble across any of his people or products in the course of your daily work.'

'And you believed him?'

'I'll be honest and say I wasn't sure,' Tessa said. 'I wondered if he was trying to play a mind game with me, have me doubt my people. He hinted you're an alcoholic, see, and I kept an eye on you, but I've seen nothing since coming to Monaghan to back that up. Burned out? Yeah, absolutely. Cynical as all fuck? Once again, a big yes from me. A lazy bollix who's putting in his time waiting for retirement so he can cash in on his pension? Hell, yeah. But an alcoholic? No. I wasn't convinced.'

'Jesus, thanks for the vote of confidence.'

'You're welcome. See, Jeremiah, despite a series of mistakes and what I can only describe as lazy policing, I was under the apprehension you were still a pretty good cop. Yesterday, you saved my best friend's life, and I was convinced, when she told me, that I'd been right. When your back was against the wall and you had to act, you did the right thing. You stepped up.'

'Of course I did!' McEvoy said, and there was pain in his voice. 'I like Maggie. I like all of you annoying busybodies from Dublin. I didn't at first, but you've won me over.'

'As you did me. And the others. But this, Jeremiah. *This.* The second Danny mentioned a man from the island, the Moynihans should have been your first thought. Even if it wasn't, that combined with the plant particles from the sedge, which only grows on the shores of lakes... come on! Two plus two, Jeremiah.'

The detective raised his hands in supplication. 'Yeah. I dropped the ball. You got me.'

'You wouldn't drop a ball of this magnitude,' Tessa said. 'So I'm asking you one more time: are the Moynihans paying you off?'

'No. They are not.'

'So what the fuck is going on?'

McEvoy looked about him, checking to ensure there was no one nearby. 'If I tell you, you have to promise not to say a single word to anyone, right? I am going to talk to the sarge, but in my own time.'

'I'm promising nothing until I know what it is,' Tessa said.

'You're not going to draw me into a vow that binds me to something that'll leave shit all over me too.'

'Tessa, for fuck's sake, will you just ease up for a second?'

'Give me a reason to.'

'I've got early-onset Alzheimer's.'

Tessa heard the words, but they didn't register for a moment. She hadn't known what to expect, but it was absolutely not this.

After a moment of just staring at the detective, she shook her head in disbelief. 'Are you sure?'

'Yes. My father was barely sixty-five when we had to put him into a nursing home. He didn't know who he was or where he was. It was heartbreaking to see. When we all looked back on it, he'd been showing signs for quite a while that he was going downhill.'

'Jeremiah... I'm so sorry.'

'It seems to be hereditary. I'm fifty-seven. For the past few years, I've noticed myself forgetting things. I've got into trouble with my bills, just plain forgotten to ensure there was cash in the account. I'll miss meetings at work, and when I'm reminded of them, I will have no, and I mean *no*, recollection I was ever told about them. I started putting alarms on my phone, but that was no good. I'd forget they'd gone off. Or I'd forget what they were for, and the few words I'd write to flash on the screen with the alarm would mean nothing to me. Even if I'd look at the note an hour later and know exactly what it meant, at the time it would all just look like gibberish.'

'There's nothing the doctors can do?'

'Not really. I've seen an occupational therapist and I'm doing everything she tells me, but it's getting progressively worse – and fast. Tessa, I don't remember you saying anything about a plant that only grows near lakes. I've no memory of that. I'm sorry if it sounds like a stupid excuse, but I don't. And I know Maggie said you told me about the Moynihans hanging around outside the hospital, but I don't remember that either.'

'It's okay, Jeremiah,' Tessa said. 'We got there in the end, didn't we? I will forever be grateful to you for saving Maggie and Ash's lives. You deserve a fucking medal for that alone.'

'I'd already requested light duty,' McEvoy said. 'I was never supposed to be anything more than a helping hand to your team. Show you around and that.'

'You're too good a cop though,' Tessa said, putting her hand on the detective's arm. 'You had to help when you saw we needed it.'

'I'm going to tell the sarge. I've just been waiting for... for the right time.'

'When you're ready,' Tessa said.

'You won't tell the others?'

'It's not my story to tell.'

'Thank you.'

She shook off his thanks.

'I've done nothing,' she said. 'Let's go and see if Mogue Kearney can't help us negotiate with the Moynihans.'

66

'Detectives, I'm shocked that I have to remind you that any dealings I have with the Moynihans are protected under legal privilege.'

'All we want to do is speak to Diarmuid Moynihan,' Tessa said. 'Can you call him and ask him to come in and talk to us?'

'Mr Moynihan doesn't own a phone.'

'How do you communicate with him then?'

'He comes to see me if he wants to discuss something.'

'Don't you ever have to send him documents to look over?'

'He looks at any legal papers here in the office.'

'And if a legal matter arises in the meantime?'

'There's a mailbox on the shores of White Lake where I can leave letters for him. It's checked by one of his people every second week or so.'

'That often?' Tessa said.

'It's a system that works.'

'Mr Kearney, if I find out you're bullshitting me, I will make it my mission to see you lose your licence to practice,' Tessa said with a friendly smile.

'You won't be the first and you won't be the last,' Mogue Kearney said. 'Take your shot, Detective.'

'Don't underestimate me,' Tessa said. 'People have before. Some even lived to regret it.'

And with that, she and McEvoy stalked out.

67

Later that night, Danny was lying on his bed in the Westenra Arms when there was a knock on the door.

'Who is it?' he asked, picking up his shirt from the chair at the end of the bed.

'Room service,' came Tessa's voice.

'I didn't order room service.'

There was nothing for a beat, then: 'Well it's outside your fucking door with a bottle of whiskey and two glasses, so open up and let me in!'

He did, and his partner pushed her way inside.

'Put that shirt on,' she said as she put the glass and a bottle of Black & White Scotch down on the table. 'We need to talk, and while I have no feelings for you other than a currently annoyed level of friendship, your fucking pecs are distracting. You look like the side of Mount Everest.'

'Sorry, boss.'

'Are you being snotty with me now?'

'No. I... I forgot.'

'Sit down and have a drink.'

She poured a measure into each glass, immediately swallowing the contents of hers before pouring another, which she took a sip from before putting it back on the table while Danny buttoned the aforementioned shirt.

'I'm not a big whiskey drinker,' he said.

'I don't care. You're having a drink with me while we talk.'

The shirt mostly fastened, Danny sat opposite and she pushed the glass over to him. He sipped, grimaced.

'Can I have a mixer?'

'Get a drop of water.'

He got up and went into the bathroom, adding a splash of water to the Scotch. He looked at the colour of the drink, deemed it too dark and added more.

'Now sit down and let's you and me have a serious discussion.'

Danny did as he was bid.

'Tomorrow morning, you, me and O'Connor are going into a situation where it's highly likely we're going to come up against serious aggression. I need to know you're not going to lose it.'

'I held it together fine during the attack on the car,' he said, feeling his colour rising.

'I'll give you that. But this is going to be worse. We might find Joe and Daisy dead, or in any kind of condition. Can you take that and not go apeshit on me?'

'I believe so, yes,' he said, though, in truth, he wasn't sure at all.

'I have to tell you, Danny, I'm beginning to regret my decision of bringing you on board. The meeting with Teddy ended up beneficial to us, but that had nothing to do with your contribution. I would say we got the information we did *in spite* of you. And I don't want my team to succeed in spite of any team member. I told you on day one I want us to operate as equals, each person bringing their own skills to every case. And right now, I'm asking myself: what the hell is Danny Murphy bringing except a hair-trigger temper and a ton of emotional baggage he hasn't dealt with?'

She downed her drink and poured another.

Danny had a sip of his.

'Drink up,' Tessa said.

He closed his eyes and poured the contents of the glass down his throat. Even with all the water he'd added, it burned.

'Good lad,' Tessa said and poured him another.

He thought about taking it to the bathroom for water but decided it was a pointless exercise.

'I'm sorry I messed up this morning,' he said instead.

'What happened?'

'It was... it was how casually he talked about the Connollys having to be dealt with. Human lives seem to mean so little to him. Here was a chance to help us find this little girl's parents, and he wasn't going to do anything, because as far as he's concerned, they needed to be taught a lesson. They'd somehow brought it on themselves.'

'Maybe they did,' Tessa said.

'Yes, but Ash didn't ask for that,' Danny said, and suddenly he felt angry, but not in the sense he might get physically violent.

It was more that he might cry.

'No, she did not,' Tessa said. 'And she's why we're here. To look after her. To be her advocates, to do the things she needs done but can't because she's just a kid and the world treats kids like shit. So we – you and me and Maggie and Pavlov – we need to think about her, put her first in everything we do. And sometimes that means sucking up our own feelings and making nice with a scumbag if it means we'll get some information that could help us.'

'I understand.'

'I don't think you do, you big fucking lug. Do you remember me telling you you're on probation?'

'Yes.'

'So what would you do if Teddy Moore lodged a complaint with the Garda Ombudsman that you'd laid hands on him? Where do you think you'd end up?'

'Back in the cell you found me in.'

'On your way to Wheatfield Prison' Tessa agreed, throwing back her drink again and pouring another. 'And where would that leave me? I'd promised the commissioner I could handle you, turn you into the good cop I believe you can be, but you'd have gone and proven the exact fucking opposite.'

'Tessa,' he said.

'What, Danny?'

He took a swallow of the whiskey. Somehow, this glass wasn't burning as much.

'If there had been a chance,' he said, 'even a small one, for someone to do something to pull my parents back from what happened to them, I would like to think they'd have done that. My life, it could have been completely different. That's been on my mind a lot.'

'I bet it has,' Tessa said.

'Ash has just started in the foster care system,' Danny went on. 'I remember what that was like. It was... it was *horrible*, Tessa. I felt so alone. I cried myself to sleep every single night for the first two months of it. Pushed my face into my pillow so no one heard me. I... if I can save Ash from that, I think I'll do anything. Maybe I took that in the wrong direction. Judged it badly.'

'The best thing you can do is be the finest cop you can be,' Tessa said. 'Ending up in jail won't help her or anyone else. Right now, you're starting to look like a man with anger-management issues you don't have under control. I can have you dismissed from the team right now and finish this case without you. I bet Dawn can recommend some people to help with those feelings, and I'll find someone else to take your place going forward.'

'I... if that's what you want.'

'No it's not what I fucking want! I want you to get your act together, Danny! See this as the chance to help not just Ash but lots and lots more kids. Whether you realise it or not, that little girl has really taken to you. I think she would be delighted to know you were one of the team sent out to bring her mam and dad home. I just need to know you're up to the job and aren't going to run amok on me when things get tough.'

'I won't. I give you my word.'

'Can you? Can you keep the anger at bay? Or even better, channel it. Use it to bring the Connollys off that island.'

'I can and I will.'

Tessa picked up her glass. 'A toast then,' she said. 'To tomorrow's mission. May we win the day and bring home all our people safe and sound.'

'Tomorrow's mission,' Danny said, and they both knocked back their drinks.

'I'm holding you to all of that,' Tessa said, standing. 'I like you, Danny, and I want to trust you. I almost do. Show me my faith is justified.'

'I will,' Danny said.

'Good. Now get some sleep. We've an early start.'

'I will, Tessa.'

She squeezed his shoulder once and left.

He sat for a long time, looking at the wall and wondering if he would be able to keep his promise to the woman he'd come to think of as his captain and mentor.

DAISY CONNOLLY

As the fourth day in the darkness ticked by, each second an eternity of misery, she began to believe she would die there.

She thought about her daughter, about their little family and the happy times, and tried to lift her essential self out of the pit and into the air and the sunlight and let herself drift on the wind, away from the pain and the misery and the terror.

Ash was a bright girl. By now, Daisy was certain Diarmuid didn't have her, and that meant her daughter, at least, was safe. She cried with relief at this knowledge. She had to assume the police had found her little girl, and that she was in foster care or in a children's home.

That wasn't ideal. But it did mean Ash was safe and had a future.

There was no doubt in her mind that she and her husband were as good as dead. It was simply a matter of slipping away by degrees now. She was resigned to it.

She wished she'd done more with her life. In most ways she'd been happy, blessed with a good marriage and a beautiful little girl. But she hadn't travelled much, and while she'd enjoyed working with Joe on the various projects they'd embarked upon, at first to support their parents' criminal enterprises and then when they'd broken out on their own.

It would have been so satisfying if they'd been able to make the leap into the world of real, legitimate business. But maybe that wasn't for the likes of them. It seemed the underworld of gangsters and assassins and smugglers just wasn't ready to let them go.

And now it had killed them.

Daisy grieved the fact she would never live to see her daughter become a woman.

She mourned that she wouldn't have the chance to grow old with the man she loved.

But somehow, the fact her daughter had escaped seemed a victory.

And as Daisy Connolly drifted into unconsciousness, she clung to that.

PART FIVE

LAKE MONSTERS

So lovely was the loneliness of a wild lake.

— EDGAR ALLEN POE

Men fear death as children fear to go in the dark; and as that natural fear in children is increased with tales, so is the other.

— FRANCIS BACON

68

The three-member assault team of Tessa, Danny and Bob O'Connor gathered by the shores of White Lake at 5.30 a.m., while mist still hung on the water and the cries of wildfowl echoed in the still morning air.

Afraid the sounds of their voices would carry across the lake to the community on the island in its centre, they worked silently, packing bags, weapons and finally themselves into an Osprey rigid inflatable boat. The vessel had an outboard motor, but they'd decided in advance that, for the trip out to the island at least, they would row, as the sound of the motor might cost them the element of surprise they were hoping would give them an advantage.

White Lake was situated about five kilometres south-west of the small town of Ballybay and sat in the middle of a patchwork of fields and marsh. The lough was 2.5 kilometres long and half a kilometre wide, and the unnamed island was situated five hundred metres from the eastern shore. From where the assault team stood, a thin funnel of smoke could be seen rising from the centre of the piece of land, but a line of dense trees obscured any view of the buildings they knew were in the island's interior.

The previous afternoon, Tessa, Danny, McEvoy and Garda O'Connor had sat with a rugged, weather-blasted man from the Irish Parks and Wildlife Service named Terrance.

'It's a strange one,' Terrance had said to the police officers. 'Technically, no one owns the lake. We look after it, and the Ballybay Fishing Club does a lot of conservation work too – keeping the reeds down, collecting rubbish that kids leave when they go there at night to drink and smoke pot, that kind of thing. But the island has been under the ownership of the Moynihan family since 1756 – it's believed they originally fled some kind of trouble in West Cork and settled here, heading out to the island and staking a claim.'

'Could they do that?' Tessa asked. 'It sounds very old-school colonial.'

'Doesn't really matter one way or the other,' Terrance said. 'They did. And they've been there ever since.'

'Do you know how many people are living there? What the layout is? If they have any firepower?'

Terrance blinked at the question. 'Detective Burns, my job involves finding where herons and reed buntings have their nests. I take water samples and I try to ensure otters are left alone by people's dogs. I have no idea if the Moynihans have guns out on their island. I'm... I'm sorry, I feel a little out of my depth here.'

'I apologise,' Tessa said. 'What *can* you tell us?'

'Okay. I took the liberty of sending one of our drones up earlier today to get a sense of how the island looks now.'

'The device wasn't spotted?' O'Connor asked.

'It's completely silent,' Terrance said. 'You can watch the footage it recorded. You'll see that no alarm was raised.'

He produced an iPad from his bag and played them a video that showed the island from above.

'I'm counting twelve buildings,' Tessa said.

These were laid out in a rough circle, with one large rectangle in the middle.

The place looked like a fortress. They could have been bunkers, weapons caches or blockaded dwellings. One seemed to be a boathouse, running as it did down to the lough. Three seemed to be communal work areas – people could clearly be seen coming and going, though from the height at which the drone had shot the footage, it was hard to tell if they were seeing the same individuals over and over again, or different ones.

'Looks like three boats moored near a cove there on the western side of the island,' O'Connor said.

'There's probably more in the boathouse,' Tessa said.

'Can we even estimate the numbers we're going up against?' Danny asked.

'Judging by the number of dwellings, the space on the island and the density of the figures moving about, I'd say no more than thirty,' O'Connor said. 'But I doubt we're looking at those kind of numbers.'

'My experience of the community is there's usually twelve men and two or three women,' McEvoy offered. 'I don't think they stray very far from that.'

'Jeremiah, any thoughts on weapons?'

'Once again, I can only speak to what they've habitually used,' the vice detective said, 'and I'm not sure how in touch I am with that anymore. But I would say a couple of handguns, two or three hunting rifles, usually small bore, .22s for shooting ducks and the like, as well as some bladed weapons: knives, machetes and slash hooks.'

'Any skilled fighters?' Tessa asked. 'Ex-military, ex-police, that kind of thing?'

'No, but Diarmuid is a wild card,' McEvoy said. 'He's nowhere near as stupid as he looks. If he has the Connollys, and if he is behind bringing in the' – he searched for the name, and gave up in vexation – 'those umm... those scar-faced lads, he'll have a plan in place in case someone comes out to try and take him on. You need to be prepared for that.'

'We will be,' Tessa said.

'We will?' Danny asked, clearly not so sure.

The plan, such as it was, was simple: go in fast, go in hard, locate the Connollys, extricate them and get out in one piece. It wasn't pretty, but it was what they had.

'We identify ourselves as police,' Tessa told the group that morning when they were gathered in the police station in advance of the raid. 'We give warning that we're armed and will use force if given cause to. And then we act on that.'

'They'll fight,' McEvoy said.

He wouldn't be joining them but insisted on being there to see them off.

'They'll fight and they'll fight hard.'

'It's a small area to search,' Maggie said.

She wouldn't be joining the assault team either, as the trip out in the boat and the uneven terrain on the island would be impossible for her to navigate in her chair.

'There aren't many places the Connollys could be, so approach it systematically, cover each of the structures and get out of there.'

'We will,' Tessa said. 'We'll be in touch by radio all the time.'

'Me and Jeremiah will be right here,' Maggie said.

'I know you will.'

'Be safe.'

'Right, my friends,' Tessa said, looking around at her team. 'Let's go and catch us some bad guys.'

. . .

As they silently rowed, their oars slicing through the dark water of the lough, Tessa prayed they would find the people they were looking for – and that she would be bringing her entire team home with her.

69

They reached the island within six minutes of launching the Osprey.

The shore of the island was largely overgrown, tree branches hanging down into the water, reeds and hanging weeds trailing into the lake like fingers or tendrils of hair, as if the island itself was a living thing, caressing the body of water that held it.

As they skirted the island's outline, they could smell the smoke they'd earlier seen but also what could only be described as the scent of humanity – it wasn't strong but it was definitely there: rubbish, a mild stench of human waste as well as animal droppings, obviously from livestock.

Rowing in a steady rhythm, they manoeuvred the boat around the shoreline until they reached a shallow sandy cove, just a small beach, that climbed out of the lake for five yards before meeting the vegetation of the island's interior. They hopped out and dragged the vessel up onto the shale, and once the boat was safely out of the currents, they donned their helmets – they were already wearing Kevlar vests and belts equipped with mace, tasers, batons and Sig Sauer P226s – and took stock of their surroundings.

The beach rose in a shallow slope, meeting an earthen bank overgrown with marsh grass and rosebay willowherb. Above this escarpment, and only about fifteen yards distant, they could see the shape of a man-made structure of some kind – it seemed to be made of boards of wood roughly hammered together. A path had been beaten through the undergrowth. This was obviously a regularly used thoroughfare, and they knew they couldn't hang around for long.

'Let's aim to preserve life where we can,' Tessa said, her voice just above a whisper. 'Danny, take the shotgun with the beanbag rounds. We try to immobilise unless we're given no choice. Am I clear?'

Danny picked up a Mauser shotgun that had green tape around the handgrip, identifying it as a weapon meant for non-lethal load.

'We good?' Tessa asked.

The two men gave her a thumbs up.

She nodded towards the start of the pathway through the scrub. 'Let's go.'

In single file, Tessa leading and O'Connor bringing up the rear, they moved quickly along the path and edged towards the collection of dwellings.

The path opened onto what looked almost like a village square, the footing hard, dry earth, flattened and worn solid by the passing of countless footsteps over many decades. The Moynihans' main dwelling area was probably five hundred yards long and the same distance in width. They'd seen this settlement from above in the drone photo, but in reality, Tessa was shocked by what was in front of her – the buildings looked as if they'd been constructed by a military engineering corps. All were of solid concrete, their roofs corrugated metal with grilles across the windows to further protect them.

Someone had planned it perfectly – Tessa's military experience told her the layout was designed for tactical efficiency. The Moynihans might look like a bunch of wild men, she thought, but they were far from stupid, and they were definitely not ill-equipped.

The only weakness the structures showed was their doors. The Moynihans clearly hadn't expected someone to infiltrate the settlement, and while the walls of the bunkers were all impenetrable, the doors were all made from what looked to be chipboard.

Which made Tessa and her team's job much easier.

A small goat was chewing on a patch of grass, and chickens clucked gently and scratched at the dirt.

Other than the animals, there wasn't a soul about, and the trio stood in a tight group, scanning the circle of buildings, which included what looked for all the world like a Viking longhouse in the middle.

Here, where these people lived and slept and worked, the smell of woodsmoke and human and animal waste was almost overpowering, as if the essence of the Moynihan experience was somehow concentrated.

Even with everyone asleep, there was a life force to the island, a sense of raw energy and threat. They all felt it.

'Okay,' Tessa said quietly, pushing any sense of nervousness aside. 'Shock and awe. We go fast, and we go hard. They'll be asleep and groggy, so we capitalise on that.'

And without pausing, she stepped back and kicked open the door of the bunker nearest her.

70

'Police! Hands in the air! *I said get your fucking hands in the air!*'

The building was a one-room cabin with a dry earth floor, a table that looked like it was made of sticks and woven reeds stood against the wall, and a bed that was really just a stained mattress was on the floor, upon which lay a long-haired man in a Pantera T-shirt and ragged boxer shorts. A naked girl lay beside him (the mattress was made for one person, and she was mostly on the floor), and Danny thought she looked to be little more than thirteen or fourteen.

When the door crashed open, the man sat bolt upright, a look of dumb surprise on his stubbled face. '*W-What the fuck...*' he stammered.

To Danny's horror, it wasn't him that produced a weapon but the girl, who suddenly had a revolver – an enormous handgun that looked like an antique from a conflict that had occurred long before she was born. With an unsteady grip, she pointed the huge weapon right at them.

'*Git outta my house!*' she screamed, pulling the hammer back on the cannon.

Danny didn't wait for the percussion and fired the non-lethal shotgun, catching her on the shoulder, causing her arms to jerk upwards. She fired a round from the revolver into the roof, blasting a hole in it.

They all heard the sonic boom of the gunshot echoing out into the clear morning air.

'Let's hope they think that's a hunter,' O'Connor said.

'They won't,' Tessa sighed. 'They'll know we're here now.'

As if to back up her point, the man on the mattress, staring in horror and disbelief at his stunned girlfriend, started to scream: '*Help! Help!*'

O'Connor was beside him in three steps and knocked him unconscious with one rap on the temple from the butt of his own shotgun.

'Take that blunderbuss and let's go,' Tessa said.

O'Connor did, shoving the revolver into his belt, and they headed back out into the sunlight. As they did, the door of a shack directly opposite them opened and a woman came out carrying a rifle.

'Police – stop right there,' O'Connor barked.

The island dweller – stick-thin, long dishwater-blonde hair, wearing an almost transparent shift dress – froze for a moment before scowling and opening fire. The shot went wide, punching a hole in a section of the house behind them.

'Put her down,' Tessa hissed at Danny, and he hit her with a beanbag round, catching her in the stomach and causing her to double over, then fall to her knees, but to their surprise, the impact didn't stop her. Gasping for breath, she levelled her weapon again, and Tessa shot her in the right arm, pushing her sideways and onto her back.

Doors were opening all around them now, and the three

police officers, forming a circle, covered the area with their weapons.

'We are members of the Garda Síochána,' Tessa said loudly. 'I am Detective Inspector Tessa Burns, and my team and I are on this island because we have been informed there are two people being held here against their will. I am requesting you hand those individuals over to us. If you do, we will leave peacefully, and the issue of how and why they got here can be discussed at a later date. For now, I just want Joe and Daisy Connolly.'

'Suppose we just shoot the three of you to pieces?' a voice bellowed from one of the houses.

'I don't know what kind of a firearm you've got,' Tessa said, 'but judging from what we've seen, you'd be hard-pressed to pierce our body armour. We've all got automatic and semi-automatic weapons, and there may be only three of us, but you don't stand a chance. Now be sensible and throw down whatever pop-guns you've got, and someone tell me where to find the Connollys.'

'We'll fuckin' see you dead first!'

A shot tore up the earth inches from O'Connor's feet. Tessa, without hesitation, fired three rounds in rapid succession through the wooden front of the house the bullet had originated from, aiming high with her shotgun, above the heads of whoever was inside.

She paused, waiting for the boom of the shots to echo out in the early morning stillness. When the impact had rung out, she called: 'I can go lower next time. Anyone want to take another shot?'

Silence reigned.

'I see I've made my point,' Tessa said. 'Now where are the Connollys? Who wants to tell me?'

A door opened in the longhouse, and a tall and painfully thin old man came out. He was dressed in a tweed suit over a collarless shirt, and his long hair was white but ran to yellow at the ends.

He was carrying a revolver not unlike the one O'Connor had confiscated from the underage girl.

'You'll have to pardon my family,' the old man said. 'They're simple people, and not used to visitors.'

'Diarmuid Moynihan?' Tessa asked.

'The very same.'

'Drop the piece.'

'You drop yours first.'

'Not happening.'

'Then it seems we've reached an impasse.'

He spoke in an educated non-accent, his tones rich and relaxed, as if he was completely confident in the situation in which he found himself.

'Why don't you step into my home and we can discuss this tiresome turn of events?'

Tessa eyed the thin man. 'My friends stay out here. Just in case any of your family decide to get clever.'

'As you wish.'

'Okay then. Lead the way.'

Diarmuid Moynihan turned and strode back through the door from which he'd emerged.

And Tessa Burns followed.

71

The longhouse was like an open-plan studio apartment, furnished and decorated by someone who thought they were guest-starring in an episode of *Downton Abbey*. One end was a bedroom – a king-size four-poster bed with purple drapes and an ornate dressing table, complete with a round, theatrical mirror – which eventually became a study that contained a roller desk and high-backed leather chair, which transformed into a sitting room (a red velvet suite of furniture that consisted of a three-seater couch and two armchairs, all equipped with recliners, all arrayed in front of a huge fireplace made of hand-hewn stones), which became a kitchen, the centre of which held a very impressive-looking Aga. Tessa stood just inside the door, her weapon still trained on the old man, who walked, seemingly unconcerned by her presence, to a leather armchair and sat down.

Tied to a wooden kitchen chair in front of the longhouse's empty fireplace, dressed in a foul vest and Y-fronts, was a man of a similar age to Diarmuid.

'This is Yves Blanchet,' the Moynihan patriarch said. 'You

probably know him as the Professor. Yves, allow me to introduce you to Detective Inspector Burns.'

The bound man made a kind of gurgling noise, his bald head lowered, as if he was so exhausted he could barely hold it up.

'Diarmuid, what the hell is going on?'

'It's a long and somewhat tawdry tale,' Moynihan said. 'A tragedy really.'

'Where are the Connollys?'

'Tsk, tsk. People these days are always in such a rush. All in good time. You do know who the Professor is, don't you?'

'He's the leading chemist for the international criminal underworld, from what I can gather.'

'Yes! That's it, and yet here he is, my guest, on my island. Don't you think that's wonderful?'

'No. Where are Joe and Daisy?'

'He's here because of them!' Diarmuid said. 'Joe Connolly's fame had spread, you see. His genius shone like a bright flame, and the Professor wanted to work with him. Isn't that right, Yves?'

The Professor didn't answer, simply emitting a long, pained sigh. It looked to Tessa as if he was being held up by his restraints – without them he'd have fallen to the floor. It was clear he'd been beaten badly.

'He doesn't look like he's in good shape,' she said. 'I'm guessing he needs a hospital.'

'I have people here who can tend his wounds,' Moynihan said dismissively. 'He wouldn't cooperate with me. I had to use certain... enticements.'

'How did that go for you?'

'As you see. The Professor and I are still negotiating. I may need to get less... gentle... during the next phase of our discussions.'

'Diarmuid, I have to tell you I'm losing patience. What is going on here?'

'Joe and Daisy Connolly had developed a plan to export exquisitely crafted artisan spirits to optimally located clubs on the continent,' Diarmuid said. 'A distribution system had been established and everything was in place but for one thing. And this was where the Connollys eventually discovered they needed outside help.'

'This is the whole drugs thing?' Tessa asked.

'Yes and no,' Diarmuid said. 'Joe refused to create narcotics. He considered it... ungentlemanly. He eschewed their creation and sale. No, he had an idea for something much more subtle.'

'You've lost me.'

'Joe designed what amounted to an Irish form of absinthe. A top-shelf Irish whiskey with a small quantity of opium mixed through it. Highly addictive, and completely unique, this was to be the crowning glory of the new line of spirits Joe was creating. The thing that made it extra special, the item completely unlike anything you could get in the pub down the street.'

'Okay,' Tessa said. 'The worst of both worlds.'

'I wouldn't put it quite like that, but I see your point. It was about this time when the Professor came to Ireland in search of Joe. From what I can gather, he had, quite independently, come up with an idea for a similar kind of beverage. And do you know what? And this tickles me.'

'What?'

'I didn't know it at the time, and neither did any of the other parties who were interested in getting in on this deal, but Joe was having problems creating his Irish absinthe. He couldn't get it to blend. The two components kept separating, and he believed it was the opiate part of the equation that was the problem. Yves here was having similar difficulties, but in his case, he thought it was the whiskey that was at fault.'

'A hilarious dilemma,' Tessa said, deadpan.

'So it made sense for them to join forces. Joe was a gifted distiller, Yves a talented pharmacologist – between them they could surely crack the code. And...' he paused, clearly for dramatic effect, 'they did! The two men worked side by side, day and night, for days on end, trying every possible approach to their problem, and finally, they had it. The correct blend of ingredients, the right heats and times for the distillation and filtration processes – they had...'

'They'd created the list,' Tessa said.

'Quite. They did indeed.'

'What went wrong?'

'Joe Connolly developed a... a strange notion,' Diarmuid said, and now Tessa could hear the jocularity was gone from his voice.

'He wanted to sell his creation to a reputable, *legal* liquor company,' she said.

'Even worse,' Diarmuid growled. 'He wanted to sell it to big pharma. According to what Yves has divulged, Joe began to get concerned about the addictive nature of his creation. As I said, he always had issues about drugs, and he felt he'd more or less created a narcotic with this. So he decided he wasn't going to persevere with its production on the black market but would instead try to do business with a legal drug company who could use it as an anaesthetic or a painkiller through controlled, medical distribution.'

'And you couldn't allow that to happen.'

'This would've been the jewel in the crown of his entire enterprise. I wasn't going to let him throw it away.'

'I take it Joe wasn't for turning.'

'He was not.'

'And he destroyed the list of ingredients and instructions for distilling it.'

'Perhaps,' Diarmuid Moynihan said. 'Or did he? People who worked with Joe in the past report that he was a habitual keeper of files and information. A custodian of his ideas and creations, if you will. I find it hard to believe he destroyed this one. It seems more likely to me he simply... put it somewhere for safe-keeping.'

'So you hired the Strígòil to bring the Connollys in so you could find out where?'

'I did,' Moynihan admitted. 'I'm afraid those three gentlemen proved to be quite the disappointment.'

'Okay,' Tessa said. 'We've established you've got Joe and Daisy. Now show me where.'

'And what if I say no,' Diarmuid said, levelling his gun at the prone Professor, 'and tell you I'll shoot Yves unless you turn around and walk away?'

Tessa chuckled in spite of herself. 'What if I tell you I'll shoot you in the kneecaps and drag your arse to the mainland if you do?'

'You'd never make it off the island.'

'Try me. I'm anxious for the challenge. I've got out of tougher scrapes.'

The two continued to eye one another.

'I believe we're in stalemate,' Diarmuid said.

'Looks like it.'

'Perhaps we can come to an agreement.'

'I'm listening.'

'I'll tell you where the Connollys are if you agree to let me walk away from here. I don't expect you'll let bygones be bygones, but you could give me a... sporting chance.'

'You *show* me where they are,' Tessa said, 'and then we'll discuss a deal.'

Diarmuid Moynihan chewed his lower lip and suddenly smiled. 'Very well. Let's go and say hello to Joe and Daisy. After you, Detective.'

72

Diarmuid Moynihan led Tessa, Danny and O'Connor away from the main settlement.

Some members of the community made to follow, but Tessa warned him: 'You want any chance of that head start you're looking for, you warn them to stay back. I don't want to have to deal with any more shenanigans getting Joe and Daisy out of here, d'you hear me?'

'No one follow,' Diarmuid called over his shoulder. 'The Gardai are to be allowed to carry out their duties unimpeded.'

There was a dull murmuring, but no one attempted to go against the patriarch's orders.

He picked a trail through dense trees, alder and elm, finally joining a game trail that brought them to a small concrete dock jutting out over what looked to be deep water. There was a mechanical winch, complete with chain and hook bolted to the concrete itself, which led Tessa to believe this was used to drop and raise some kind of fishing pots, and she wondered if there might be fresh-water mussels in the lake, or possibly crayfish. A few tools were strewn about beside it: an acetylene torch, some chisels and a few hammers.

Across the lake, Tessa could see the mainland – rolling green fields mixed with marsh. It seemed like another dimension to her, locked as she was in a battle of wills with this dangerous man for the lives of Ash's parents. She'd never felt further away from her home and things that were safe and familiar.

'All right, my dear detectives,' Diarmuid said, bowing to them all. 'I've fulfilled my end of the bargain. I bid you all adieu.'

'What are you talking about?' Tessa said. 'Where are Joe and Daisy?'

'Oh, I beg your pardon,' Diarmuid said, feigning embarrassment. 'They're down there.' He motioned with his thumb to the space beyond the dock.

Tessa walked to the edge and peered over. The water looked to be about four metres deep. At first she couldn't see anything at all, but as her eyes became accustomed to the murk, she saw that resting on the lake's bed were two long metal containers, both roughly coffin shaped. Squinting, she realised there were pipes coming from these metal boxes, tubes that ran to the surface. She followed their arc through the water and discovered they ended in what looked to be funnels that were floating on the surface, buffeted by the lapping waves of White Lake. As she watched, a wave sloshed over one, temporarily filling the plastic bowl of the contraption.

And that filled her with horror.

Because Tessa suddenly realised what she was looking at.

If she was right, Joe and Daisy were being held prisoner in those boxes, and the funnels were being used to pipe air to them.

'They've got walkie-talkies down there,' Diarmuid said matter-of-factly. 'All it takes is for one of them to decide to tell us where the list is, and we'll bring them up. The power really is in their hands.'

Tessa, fighting a growing sense of rage and revulsion towards the old man, said through gritted teeth: 'How long is it since you heard from either of them?'

'Maybe a day. Maybe a little more. When it became clear they were going to be stubborn, I decided to focus most of my attentions on Yves instead.'

'How long have they been down there?'

'Four days, give or take.'

Tessa grappled to comprehend the awfulness of that and couldn't. Her claustrophobia caused her mind to freeze almost immediately.

'How do you know they're still alive?'

'I'm pretty sure they are. Most people last about five days. They're both young and strong.'

'I don't believe what I'm hearing.'

'I suppose they might have passed out from hypothermia by now – that does happen when you're down there a while.'

'Shut up, Diarmuid,' Tessa said. 'Consider yourself arrested, by the way. I know it's going to take the three of us to bring the Connollys up, but as soon as we do, I'm coming after you.'

'We had an agreement.'

'Fuck the agreement.'

Diarmuid glowered at her and turned, disappearing back into the undergrowth.

Tessa gazed after him for a second, wondering for a moment if he might send the islanders to ambush them, but decided she couldn't focus on that and the job at hand, so went to the bundle of tools. The controls for the acetylene torch were attached to two gas cylinders, one of acetylene and one oxygen. She checked the regulator and saw the settings were correct, and that the torch had a cutting attachment.

'Do either of you have a lighter or matches?' she called to her partners.

O'Connor, without a word, tossed her a Zippo lighter.

'Thank you, Bob,' she said and switched on the gas, lighting the torch and making sure it worked.

Danny was stripping off his helmet, Kevlar and shirt. He sat on the edge of the dock and took off his shoes.

'Could you pass me the hook please?' he asked O'Connor.

The Garda grimly did so.

'I'll operate the winch,' O'Connor said. 'Once you get it hooked to the... the boxes, I'll pull them up.'

Danny nodded, took a breath and dived into White Lake.

73

Danny Murphy cut through the water with long, steady strokes.

With each sweep of his muscular arms, the coffins on the bottom drew closer and closer, and within ten seconds he was hanging above them. Thanks to the work of Terrance and his team, the lake water was clean and clear, and visibility was good. Fish darted here and there about Danny, not so much afraid as sensibly cautious of this large interloper in their domain. Reeds swayed about the two metal coffins, and Danny had to feel his way around them, to find the outcroppings of two handles, one on each side of the containers. Working quickly, he ran the hook and chain through the ones on the left, then made sure the hook itself was secured firmly, its barb through one of the links of the heavy chain.

Satisfied it would hold, he kicked off and allowed buoyancy to lift him back to the surface. Tessa and O'Connor were peering over the edge, waiting for him.

'I've got one rigged for lifting,' he said breathlessly. 'Winch it up.'

O'Connor released the winching mechanism and turned the handle. Thankfully the cogs and spokes were well oiled, and the device turned with ease. Slowly, inch by inch, the first of the metal coffins made its way upwards through the dark water.

Tessa, standing on the edge of the dock, watched it come closer and closer, seeing its colour change from a dark orange to a bright yellow and finally, as it broke the surface, she saw the container was actually white, flecked and mottled with rust.

Once the metal prison was level with the dock, O'Connor locked the winch in place, and together he and Tessa hauled it over so it was now above the concrete, after which O'Connor once again released the chain and lowered it to solid ground. Once it was down, Tessa removed the chain and passed it back down to Danny, waiting in the water below, who dived down to attach it to its still submerged twin.

Tessa took the torch over to the box and fired it up.

Before she started cutting, she knocked gently on the top of the container: 'I don't know if you can hear me, but I'm a member of the Gardai, and I'm about to cut you out. If you can keep low in there, try to do so. I'll have you free as quickly as I can.'

The torch cut through the metal like butter, and within a couple of minutes, Tessa was sliding the lid off.

The first thing that hit her was a smell of foetid water, which was followed by the sharp tang of urine. Then the lid was lying flat on the dock and the inside of the coffin was revealed.

'Oh sweet Jesus,' she said and called: 'Bob, get over here fast!'

The coffin they'd just raised contained an unconscious Daisy Connolly. Her face had a deathly pallor, her fingers a grey hue, their tips almost black, and the metal crate was half full of brown lake water. Tessa brought her cheek down so it was just below the woman's nostrils.

'She's breathing,' she said to O'Connor. 'Just. Help me get her out.'

They did, and immediately began rubbing her wrists and

ankles, trying to get the blood circulating again. Tessa moved up and started working on the woman's face, rubbing her cheeks vigorously, and suddenly, with a lurch and a cry, Daisy regained consciousness. Unfortunately, she didn't at first realise she'd been rescued and began beating at the air, screaming hysterically.

'Daisy, you're safe, you're safe,' Tessa said, catching her wrists and holding them. 'I've got you. You're okay.'

The woman stopped fighting, her eyes wide with panic, and Tessa saw reality dawn, and the nightmare recede.

'I thought I'd died,' Daisy Connolly said and began to weep.

74

Diarmuid Moynihan crept away from the little dock, beating a path through the trees along the island's perimeter.

He was fuming. It wasn't supposed to have ended like this. He'd put everything into this liquor-smuggling deal, and he'd genuinely believed it would pay off. And he *needed* it to pay off.

Diarmuid's family had been power players in the criminal landscape of Ireland's border regions for two hundred years, but in the past half a century, they'd fallen on hard times.

His father, Tim Jack Moynihan, had been a drinker and a womaniser and had drawn a collection of undisciplined vagabonds to their island, a bunch of wastrels who'd squandered what resources the Moynihans had once had on drugs, booze and whores. Diarmuid had understood when he was still a young man that if he was to alter the trajectory of his family's fortunes, he would first have to get away from it and secure an education.

This he did, winning scholarships to Trinity College Dublin and then to King's College Cambridge, studying business with a particular focus on human resource management. He wrote his thesis on grassroots movements, particularly within outsider cultures and, when he had his master's degree complete, spent five years in the United States, where he managed to acquire a role with a fraternal Italian American organisation who were inclined to have an antagonistic relationship with the law.

He learned more in those five years than he had in his entire seven years in university and returned to Ireland determined to set his family business back on track.

As soon as he'd landed on the island in the middle of White Lake, he'd discovered his father almost dead from alcohol poisoning and an obese man named Randall posing as his replacement. Diarmuid wasted no time in shooting Randall in the head and dumping his body in the lake, weighed down with rocks.

He then began the process of slowly rebuilding.

This he mostly did through investing wisely, hiring his men out as leg-breakers and enforcers, and keeping a weather eye on the comings and goings among the crooks and gangsters locally, to see if there were any voids that needed filling.

Over the years, he'd funded various operations that provided a steady stream of income, and all under the radar of law enforcement. Diarmuid believed the best way to succeed as a criminal was to make sure the police didn't even know you were in the crime game. He worked hard to have his men cultivate a reputation for being a group of hippies, freaks and freeloaders, more interested in getting drunk and stoned than committing serious criminal offences. He even insisted one or more of them got arrested for being drunk and disorderly or cutting some farmer in a knife fight at least every couple of months to keep the façade up.

That way, when the moment came to seize control, no one would be looking their way.

Someone, however, had squealed. There was a loose link in the chain, and he would have to find out who it was. He needed to go into hiding for a while, but when he came out, someone was going to pay.

The track he was following looped down towards the water, and there he found, hidden behind a low-hanging bush, a small wooden rowboat with an outboard motor.

Diarmuid sat in, primed the engine, pulled the ripcord and steered his little vessel out into the lake.

Things may have gone south on the deal, but he would live to fight another day.

You had to learn to take the rough with the smooth in this game.

75

Joe Connolly was blue when Tessa got the lid off his coffin.

The container was almost full of water, but somehow the young man, who was unconscious, had managed to remain floating near the top, breathing from the small air pocket.

Tessa and O'Connor repeated the exercise they'd done with Daisy, rubbing his wrists and cheeks, but colour wouldn't return, and when Danny came up from the water, he checked the man's breath to discover he had none.

'He's not breathing,' he said, resting his ear on the man's chest. 'No heartbeat either.'

Daisy emitted a wail, but Danny ignored her and began CPR.

'Oh God,' Daisy sobbed. 'Please don't let him die. Please don't!'

'Take a break,' Tessa said, and Danny paused as she listened for breath sounds.

She shook her head and he resumed, pushing down on the man's ribcage then releasing to keep the blood pumping.

'Break.'

Once again, no breath. Danny went back to chest compressions.

'How long has he been without a heartbeat?' O'Connor asked.

'I don't know. Maybe five, six minutes,' Tessa said.

'Look at his physical condition,' O'Connor pointed out. 'He's too weakened. You're wasting your time.'

'That's my call to make,' Danny said. 'Tessa, prepare to check.'

She nodded and did so but shook her head, and Danny kept pumping.

He'd performed four compressions in this sequence when Joe Connolly wheezed, coughed and spat out a lungful of water.

'Take it easy there, lad,' Tessa said. 'You've had quite the ordeal.'

'Where's Daisy?' the man rasped. 'And my daughter... where's Ash?'

'Your little girl is safe, Mr Connolly,' Tessa assured him. 'She's in a temporary foster placement with some good people.'

'And I'm here,' his wife said, and then the two of them were holding one another and crying, and the three police officers moved away to give them some space.

Tessa cast a look at Danny. He seemed to be trembling slightly, which might have been from the cold lake water, but she had a suspicion wasn't.

'You okay?' she asked.

'Yes thank you,' the big cop said, not meeting her gaze. 'I'm fine.'

She stepped around and took his chin in her hand, forcing her to look at him. 'You're *not* okay.'

He looked at her, and she could see pain and fear fighting for dominance in his eyes.

'It's okay to be upset,' she said gently. 'Now we're done and everyone is all right, it's *good* to be upset.'

'I... I thought we were too late,' Danny said. His breathing became rapid, and she could hear the anxiety in his voice. 'I tried and I tried, but I thought we'd lost Dad... I mean Joe... I...'

Tessa reached up and put her arms around the big detective and held him as he cried.

'It's all right, Danny, love,' she said gently. 'You saved him. You saved them both.'

76

Diarmuid steered the boat into the reeds on the shore of White Lake. There was a bog here, and after getting out, he artfully (and with no small amount of dexterity for a man of his age) picked his way from one solid spot to another, taking a circuitous route to safety.

The bog, he knew, would bring him in a wide arc around the western side of the long lake, where there was a network of paths and trails that crisscrossed the fields and pastures of the lowlands in this part of the county before eventually coming out onto a binary road, the R190, which would take him to Cootehill, in County Cavan, and from there to Kingscourt in County Meath, and from there to Navan, Dublin and beyond.

Making his way with great care, an hour later he came upon a pile of bramble and scrub. Pulling it aside, he revealed an ancient-looking Mercedes Benz truck. The key was in the ignition just where he'd left it. It turned over with ease, and the engine boomed and rumbled into life.

The truck, old as it was, handled the rough terrain perfectly, and fifteen minutes later Diarmuid Moynihan had the radio on, singing along to an old Dolly Parton song about a coat of many colours. He was on the final meandering path that would bring him to the road when he turned a corner and found his way blocked.

A long, black Lexus was parked right in the middle of the thoroughfare, and Teddy Moore, dressed in a grey suit, was leaning against the bonnet, an Uzi cradled almost casually across his arm.

The Irish godfather and the Moynihan patriarch's eyes met. No words were spoken, but everything that needed to be communicated was.

Diarmuid jammed the truck into reverse, but before he was able to get his foot on the accelerator, Teddy sprayed the front of the old Mercedes with bullets. The windscreen shattered in a hail of glass fragments, and Diarmuid was hit five times, the shells charting a progress of red ruin across his skinny chest.

He was dead before the sound of machine-gun fire died out.

Teddy Moore walked slowly over to the ruined truck, peered in at his old competitor and nodded once in satisfaction, then got back into his Lexus and drove away.

77

Bodahn, the detective from organised crime, came out to oversee the rounding up of the islanders. Despite their having already been unsuccessful in seeing off a team made of three armed police, to Tessa's disbelief they still mounted a defence against the ten-man armed response unit that arrived later that day to take the gang members in for questioning.

Despite being exasperated by the stubborn nature and intransigence of the group, the ARU took everyone without injury, and began combing the island and surrounding areas,

The body of Diarmuid Moynihan had been found by an early morning fisherman. Forensics took plaster casts of tyre tracks, which judging from the space between the wheels and the weight indicated by the depth of the indentations had come from a saloon style of car, possibly a Toyota or another luxury Japanese brand.

Of which there were literally thousands in use in the northeast of Ireland alone.

Bullets taken from Moynihan's seat and his left shoulder and collarbone only proved the weapon that had fired them wasn't on the system, and while ballistics could match them to the gun should one of the investigators come across it, that seemed unlikely, for the near future at any rate.

'I don't think we're going to see anyone brought to justice for the murder of Diarmuid Moynihan,' Bodahn said to Tessa as they stood outside the island's longhouse.

'I don't either,' Tessa said. 'But I have my suspicions.'

'Can't bring those to court.'

'Nope. Any sign of the Professor?'

'When we got here with the paramedics we found no trace of him, although a chair was located in the building behind us, and it did have traces of DNA – blood, skin and hair – stuck to it at various points.'

'So we can use that to identify him? Diarmuid called him Yves Blanchet, but I doubt that's his name.'

'The DNA was, sadly, not on the system,' Bodahn said. 'If that individual was the Professor, he's still at large. If he survived, of course.'

'What about the other islanders?'

'We'd planned to bring charges against the two who shot at you, but one of them has turned out to be a thirteen-year-old girl named Una Mulready, who was reported missing by her parents fourteen months ago.'

'Thirteen?'

'Yes. It seems unlikely those charges will hold.'

'Did you find anything else useful?'

'If you look in the boat moored down at the beach, you'll find a collection of twenty-two firearms of various vintages and dubious provenance,' Bodahn sighed. 'Oddly, none of the residents claim ownership or knowledge of them.'

'Funny that.'

'Hilarious,' the detective said without humour. 'The best I can say is that the investigation into where they came from continues.'

'Are you hopeful you'll find any answers?'

'Fuck no,' Bodahn said.

DAISY CONNOLLY

After they took her from the coffin, she drifted in and out of consciousness for a time.

It was disconcerting, as she kept forgetting she was safe, and she came awake in the boat and didn't know where she was, and thrashed and flailed about, terrified she was being taken to a new hell. She jerked into wakefulness in the ambulance, screaming for her daughter. She sat bolt upright on a gurney in A&E, crying wordlessly.

They must have sedated her, because she knew nothing for a long time.

When next she drifted into awareness, she was, for the first time in a very long time, comfortable, and she felt clean, and nothing hurt. She knew instinctively she was in a bed in a hospital, and when she opened her eyes, she saw a face she'd thought she would never see again.

'Ash,' she said and began to weep.

'Mammy,' her little girl said, throwing her arms around her mother's shoulders.

And then they were holding one another and everything was all right.

78

Ash was sitting beside Joe in his hospital bed, beaming from ear to ear.

While Daisy had required antibiotics and a few nights of rest, Joe had experienced far greater physical trauma. Three of his toes had to be removed due to having necrotised as a result of frostbite, and the doctors were waiting to see if the little finger on his left hand would suffer a similar fate.

This morning, Tessa was sitting in the guest chair in his room, Maggie beside her in her wheelchair with Pavlov at her feet, and Danny was leaning against the wall, looking happier and more relaxed than Tessa had ever seen him.

'The whole thing got out of hand really fast,' Joe was explaining to the team. 'My plan was, for sure, to make an Irish version of absinthe, and I still don't see anything wrong with that.'

'Except that it's completely illegal,' Tessa said.

'Well, except for that, yes. I mean ethically though. Absinthe contains wormwood, which gives it its aniseed flavour and provides its allegedly psychedelic effects. I had an idea to create something similar, but in a whiskey form.'

'So you didn't plan to add opium?' Tessa asked.

'I did not. That all came about when the Professor arrived at my home. He turned up one day, out of the blue. I'd heard of him of course, so I was excited at the idea of working with him. I told him about my plans to make an absinthe-like liquor, and he told me he'd been planning something similar. He suggested that if we worked together, and shared the credit for the finished article, people would go crazy to sample it. He said our reputations would mean it would be a modern distilling classic.'

'And you fell for that line,' Tessa said, shaking her head. 'You were believing your own press, Joe. That's never good.'

'It was all going so well until I discovered he was adding opium into the mix,' Joe said. 'We'd never discussed that, and I would never have agreed to it if we had. I was furious. And... and then I got scared. I investigated the impact of adding opium to a spirit like whiskey, and it can be wildly addictive, particularly for people with a propensity for alcoholism. I mean, this could have been *really* dangerous. So I decided to pull out.'

'That must have caused some consternation,' Tessa observed.

'Tony O'Neill, who I thought was a friend, tried to steal the formula and sell it to another gang, some Travellers from Galway,' Joe said. 'He'd hung out with me and the Professor a few times while we worked, but he only had half an idea of what we were doing. I tried to cover for him, make sure no one found out what he'd done. When I pulled out, he tried to tell the partners he could do the job instead of me.'

'That didn't work out very well for him,' Danny said. 'Or his wife and daughter.'

'We just wanted out of the whole thing at that stage,' Daisy said.

'Except you were in too deep,' Maggie said.

'I was,' Joe agreed. 'The various parties who were trying to buy in to the project weren't happy at my withdrawing. The

Moynihans, in particular, were enraged. They needed not just me but my production capabilities as well. My staff were all trained at this stage and very capable. I had equipment, a location... and they needed it all.'

'But you didn't want to give it,' Tessa said.

'I was given the choice – either go through with it or hand the recipe and my distilling production line over to the Professor so he could do it in my stead.'

'You knew that if you did that, they'd kill you,' Maggie said.

'Exactly,' Joe said. 'So Daisy and I stood firm.'

They all sat for a moment, thinking about what they'd just heard.

'Where's the list?' Tessa asked.

Joe grinned. 'Ash, can I have your bunny for a moment?'

The little girl passed it to her father.

He fiddled about with the seam on the toy's back until he found the section he was looking for, opening a Velcro seal and pulling out a small flash drive. 'It's all here.'

'If you thought this stuff was poison, why did you keep the details of how to make it?' Tessa asked.

'I had a notion there might be a medical use for it,' Joe said, confirming there had been some truth mixed in with Diarmuid's lies. 'I read somewhere that army medics sometimes used to use a blend of whiskey and morphine when they were performing operations in the field. It seemed reasonable that, if we couldn't make money from it in the traditional way, we might get something if we used a more creative approach.'

'By which you mean selling it to big pharma,' Maggie said.

'You are quite an individual, Joe Connolly,' Tessa said, although she wasn't sure she meant it as a compliment.

'I thought you'd be happy I wanted to go straight. How much trouble are we in?' Joe asked.

'Well, the local vice unit may try to prosecute you under the Illicit Distillation Act, but I doubt they'd succeed,' Tessa said.

'How come?'

'There's no product,' Tessa said. 'You didn't make any of this Irish absinthe, and your distilling plants have all been destroyed. I don't think they can get you on anything.'

'So we're in the clear then?' Daisy asked.

'You pissed off some very dangerous people,' Tessa said. 'Diarmuid may be dead, but someone will take his place, and I doubt they'll forget what you had on the table. I'd retire from the poitín game if I were you. Maybe take your beautiful family away somewhere nice for a while.'

'I might do that,' Joe said.

'I hope you do,' Tessa said.

Although she wasn't sure she believed him.

79

The attempt to bring charges against Joe and Daisy Connolly foundered quickly.

McEvoy had, by then, furnished his superiors with medical reports to show he was suffering from early-onset Alzheimer's, a condition with symptoms that included forgetting newly learned information, losing track of details like filing and chains of evidence, increasingly poor judgement, and getting mixed up about important things like the time, date and year, which called into question every case he'd investigated within the past twelve months, the time period his medics reckoned he'd been experiencing the rigors of the condition.

Any evidence he had on the Connollys within that time frame, which just happened to be when they'd been developing their new line of artisan spirits and its ambitious exportation plan, was considered unfit to submit to court.

And the work done by Tessa and her team proved none of the Irish absinthe had actually been made anyway.

The best the sergeant could hope for was a conspiracy to distil charge, which wouldn't even result in a custodial sentence, and was, within the space of fifteen minutes at a meeting with the Director of Public Prosecutions, deemed a waste of every-one's time and the state's money.

As Daisy had put it so artfully, the family was home and dry.

The Strígòil, now named John Doe on the paperwork in Mountjoy Prison (as he still refused to furnish the authorities with his name), pleaded not guilty to all charges filed against him – his story was he had accidentally driven into Tessa and Danny, had only approached their car to see if they were all right and had found the Glock on the roadside by their vehicle. His bail was set at five thousand euro, though no one had come forward to pay it – Tessa had been heard to comment that with his brothers dead and Diarmuid Moynihan, his employer, in a similar condition, it seemed the assassin had run out of friends.

John Doe's trial was pending.

80

Aisling Connolly looked at Maggie Doolan with a serious expression. 'You comin' back?'

'I'll check in on you for a bit, Ash, but you don't need me anymore. Your mam and dad are back now, and you're going to be going on a long holiday. So you won't be in Ireland for me even to visit.'

Pavlov was sitting on the couch beside the child in the living room of the Connolly farm. Ash scratched his ears, and he gave a satisfied sigh.

'Can we maybe do FaceTime now and again?' Ash asked after a while.

'Yes. We can FaceTime each other.'

'Promise?'

'I promise. But you'll find, as time goes by and you forget a little about everything that's happened, you won't want to so much. And that's okay. Don't feel bad about it.'

'I won't *never* forget about what happened here, or what you and Pav and Danny and Tessa done for me and my mam and dad!'

'I don't believe you will, but you know the way you think about it every day and lots and lots of times in every day?'

'Yeah.'

'That'll get less and less. And as it does, you won't miss me and Pav and Tessa and Danny so much.'

'Won't you miss me?'

Maggie reached out her arms, and the child came to her and climbed into her lap.

'Ash love, I miss you now, and we're still together. But me and Pav's job was to help you get through a horrible time, and we've done that, and now it's up to you and your folks to move on to the next stage in your lives. And I can't help you with that.'

'Pav can't neither?'

'Oh.' Maggie laughed. 'Pavlov the dog is very wise. He probably could, but I need him with me. There are other kids who need our help.'

'They be real lucky kids to have you come and help them.'

'Well I think we were very lucky to have met you, Ash Connolly.'

They hugged tight.

'Will we go outside and you can say goodbye to Danny and Tessa?'

Ash nodded.

The two detectives were standing in the front yard talking to Ash's parents.

'This little lady has come to say goodbye,' Maggie said.

'It's been a pleasure getting to know you, Ash,' Tessa said, extending her hand for the little girl to shake. 'You're one of the smartest and toughest kids I've met in a very long time. I know you're going to be a big help to your dad while he gets better.'

Joe would probably have to use a stick to walk for the rest of his life, and while he hadn't lost the finger, he had limited use of that hand, which meant doing certain tasks was difficult. The family were going to spend time with relatives of Joe's in Birmingham, and the hospital had arranged for him to have physiotherapy there. But it was going to be a long road, and recovery would take time and patience.

Ash had become his little helper, rarely away from her father's side.

'Thanks for finding my mam and dad,' Ash said.

Tessa grinned. 'You're welcome, sweetie. I was glad to be able to do it.'

Ash turned to Danny, who was standing a little apart from the group, looking out over the fields as if he was searching for something important.

The child reached out and took his huge hand in her small one.

'We never did go out for ice cream again,' she said, looking up at him.

'No,' he said quietly.

'Maybe we can when I get back from our trip.'

The big detective looked down at her. 'Would you like to?'

'If you wanted to come up for a visit.'

'Well...' Danny said. 'If your mam and dad say it's okay.'

'You saved their lives, silly,' Ash said, half-laughing and half-crying. 'I don't think they're gonna mind.'

Danny crouched down and put his arms around the child, making her almost disappear.

'Thank you for bringing my mam and dad back to me,' she whispered in his ear.

Danny wasn't able to answer.

He was laughing in joy that he'd helped Ash, but at the same time, he was crying, crying for the boy he'd once been, a little boy he felt he'd honoured, maybe for the first time.

EPILOGUE

MASKS

81

'I wasn't expecting visitors,' the Strígòil said.

He was dressed in the grey tracksuit most of the inmates in Dublin's Mountjoy Prison wore. Stubble was coming up patchily along his chin, but it seemed the surgeries he'd experienced interfered with his beard growth, as there were places that remained smooth and hairless.

The man seemed smaller and far less threatening in the cold light of the prison visitors' room. Tessa suspected that was exactly what he wanted her to think. And that letting her guard down would be a huge mistake.

He may have been a caged tiger. But he was still a tiger.

'I thought it was high time you and I had a talk,' she said.

'What do we have to talk about, Detective?'

'I think you know.'

'I'm a man who's had his freedom taken away from him. I live in this place, on a block with low men and sodomites. Outside of here, I'm considered a soldier. Here, I am less than nothing. If you want to talk to me, you agree to help me first.'

Tessa thought about that. She knew damn well the man in front of her, dangerous though he surely was, would be free within a year. It wouldn't take the most skilful of lawyers to argue that the evidence against him was purely circumstantial, and the strongest charge they could bring was possession of an unlicensed firearm.

Her agreeing to drop any charges against him wouldn't make a vast difference. She suspected Danny would be annoyed, but she would find a way to mollify him.

'I'll have all the charges I can dropped and I'll speak to the governor about having you moved to another wing,' Tessa said. 'Now tell me: what do you know about my parents?'

'I know nothing about your parents.'

'Bullshit,' Tessa said. 'You told me you know I dream of faceless men. Who told you to say that?'

'Ah.' The Strígòil grinned. 'I was right, wasn't I?'

'Maybe you were,' Tessa said. 'Tell me what made you say that. Who told you about what happened to my parents?'

The man sat back, his arms folded across his chest. 'Do you remember the night they died?'

'Some of it, yes.'

'You heard voices?'

'I heard shouting. My mother screaming.'

'You must have heard what they were saying, these voices.'

'No. I've tried to remember, but I can't.'

'Your father was an important man, wasn't he? He worked for the government. He knew the secrets and lies by which this country is run.'

'He was a security consultant,' Tessa said. 'I'm not sure what secrets he knew. They told me it was a robbery.'

'You never believed that,' the Strígòil said.

'No. I never did.'

The man sucked his teeth, as if considering what to say next.

Behind him, the door to the cell blocks opened and a stream

of similarly tracksuited men came in, all casting about to find the person there to see them.

'There are others like me,' the Strígòil said.

'Other killers? I'm a cop – I know that,' Tessa said, irritated.

'No. Others who *look* like me. My brothers and I, we're not the only ones who look... like this.'

'You're saying there's a group of you?'

'A guild, yes.'

Tessa began to feel excitement prickle at the base of her neck. 'Does this guild have a name?'

'It has many names,' the strange-looking man said.

As he spoke, one of the other prisoners walked behind him, on his way to the vending machine. As the inmate passed, the Strígòil stopped speaking, a look of puzzlement on his feature- less face.

'What?' Tessa said. 'Have you thought of something?'

The assassin opened his mouth, and blood poured forth, soaking into his tracksuit top and pooling on the table in front of him.

'Medic! I need a medic!' Tessa shouted, jumping up and moving around the table in time to catch the man as he slid forward off the chair, his body no longer capable of holding him up.

Tessa saw there was a hole in the base of his skull and knew he'd been stabbed, severing his spinal column, effectively breaking his neck and asphyxiating him all at the same time.

The dying man made an attempt to say something, but Tessa couldn't understand it.

'What is it?' she asked, leaning down so her mouth was close to his lips.

'*The Unattested*,' he said, his voice gurgling and thick with blood. '*The Unattested*.'

By the time the medics arrived, he was dead.

Tessa Burns sat on the floor of the visitors' room in Mountjoy while the medical staff made a futile attempt to revive him and wondered whether any of what she'd just been through was a coincidence.

Had she been sent to Monaghan for a reason?

Had the Strígòil known she would be there?

Had she, right back in the beginning, been led to rescue little Bettina Watson with the sole purpose of getting her in the line of fire?

Tessa didn't know.

What she did know, however, was that she had a team now: her, Maggie, Danny and Pavlov. Together, they would find out about the Faceless Men, and bring them and the people who controlled them to justice.

For the first time since her parents were taken from her, Tessa Burns didn't feel alone.

Two hours later, she was on her way home when her mobile phone rang.

'Tessa, can you come in to Harcourt Street?'

It was Dawn Wilson.

'What is it, boss?'

'A ship has run aground on the Wexford coast. I want you and the team down there.'

'Why, boss?'

'Because the only people on board the vessel are three kids.'

Tessa blinked. 'I'm on my way, boss.'

The Faceless Men and the Unattested would have to wait.

A LETTER FROM S.A. DUNPHY

Dear reader,

I want to say a huge thank you for choosing to read *Little Witness*. If you did enjoy it and want to keep up to date with all my latest releases and all other news, just sign up at the following link. Your email address will never be shared, and you can unsubscribe at any time.

www.bookouture.com/s.a.dunphy

I hope you loved *Little Witness*, and if you did I'd be extremely grateful if you could write a review. I'd love to hear what you think, and it makes such a difference helping new readers to discover one of my books for the first time.

I love hearing from my readers. I wouldn't be able to do what I do without you. If you'd like to, you can get in touch through social media or my website. I'm pretty active on social media, and value each and every interaction with my readers.

So thanks again, and I look forward to sharing more stories with you very soon.

Very best,

Shane (S.A. Dunphy)

KEEP IN TOUCH WITH S.A.
DUNPHY

https://shanedunphyauthor.org

facebook.com/shanewritesbooks

x.com/dunphyshane1

instagram.com/shanewritesbooks

AUTHOR'S NOTE AND ACKNOWLEDGEMENTS

I first visited County Monaghan when I was in my late teens, and I remember being awed by the beauty of its undulating countryside and the warmth and eccentricity of its people.

During my late twenties, I would live in the border region for several years, working in child protection in Navan and eventually running childcare courses at Monaghan Institute of Further Education and Training, which was, during my tenure, situated on the grounds of St Davnet's Hospital, where Paddy Dorney went to recover from his shock, and Danny interviewed him.

I drank in the pubs and ate in the cafés around those inter-linked squares in Monaghan's town centre, and I had occasion to spend some time in the town's police station through my child protection work.

I greatly enjoyed revisiting my old stomping grounds, and bringing Tessa, Danny, Maggie and Pavlov along with me.

I hope you found the trip satisfying too.

The idea for the Tessa Burns series was one I had many years ago, long before I had any aspirations to write. I was probably ten or eleven years old, and on a camping trip with my parents. We'd pitched our tent near the beach, but, this being Ireland, there was one afternoon of inclement weather, and I ran out of things to read. My mother passed me the newspaper, and I came across an article about a child who'd been murdered by an abusive stepfather. I remember becoming really incensed by the story and thinking there should be a team of police who specialised in such cases.

In those days, with the innocence and simplicity of a child, I envisioned an SAS-style team, abseiling down the wall of the unfortunate child's house to burst in through the windows so they could whisk him away to safety. Having now worked in child protection for most of my adult life, I understand that it rarely works like that.

Policing crimes involving children looks much like policing any other crime.

Although the emotional stakes are a little different.

In adulthood, I've met people who've dedicated their lives to protecting children. I want to mention two in particular who are no longer with us but who made a huge impression on me and my work. Ray Wyre, who was head of child protection for the British government, was a mentor and dear friend. He carried the weight of the dark work he did incredibly lightly, and was a font of wisdom and kindness.

And then there was Andrew Vachss, for whom this book is dedicated.

Andrew was a child protection investigator who worked mostly in New York. A qualified lawyer, he would only represent children in his practice. He was also the author of novels, comic books, journalism, poetry and even blues songs, all of which dealt with child-protection issues. Most importantly he was a crusader for children's rights without equal.

A man with a huge reputation (his appearance on Oprah Winfrey's iconic show brought about the first sex offender's register in the United States), I was deeply honoured when he reached out to me to commend me on my own books and to extend the hand of friendship.

To be referred to as a peer by a man of his standing was hugely humbling.

When I went public as a survivor of sexual abuse, Andrew

was incredibly kind and supportive, telling me I was not a survivor, but a 'transcender' – my decision to dedicate my professional life and my writing to child protection meant I had risen above the pain of what I'd experienced, and was bringing the fight to the enemy across several fronts.

Andrew left us at the end of 2021. He and I could go months without speaking, so not having heard from him didn't alarm me, and as was his wont, there was very little reporting of his death.

His wife, Alice, simply said when I contacted her: 'The loss cannot be measured and the debts only paid forward.'

Andrew left a remarkable legacy.

He is the only author I have ever known who told people *not* to buy his books.

'I only get about a buck for each one sold,' he told a surprised fan during an online forum we were both attending. 'If you want to do something real for kids at risk, give the eighteen dollars one of my novels costs to a child protection charity. It'd do a hell of a lot more good there.'

There was no one quite like Andrew.

The details of the illegal distilling trade in Ireland as I present them in this book are all completely accurate. If you're interested in knowing more, can I suggest *In Praise of Poteen*, by the delightfully named John McGuffin? It's a wonderful recounting, sometimes in rather dramatic terms, of the history of poitín-making in Ireland, not to mention a love letter to the spirit itself.

Each location I mention in this book is real and appears just as I describe it: County Monaghan is well worth a visit, and White Lake is beautiful. There's an island in the middle of it too, although it isn't home to a community of violent criminals.

At least, it wasn't the last time I visited.

I want to take a moment to thank my editor at Bookouture, Susannah Hamilton, who was instrumental in helping me draft the character sketches and plot points for this book and the ones to follow. We discussed many different aspects of the team, their lives, likes and dislikes. I knew they were all going to be broken people, in one way or another, but that coming together would in some way make them whole.

Susannah, very sensitively, understood that, and her input was hugely beneficial.

I also wish to thank her for her supreme patience as, for a variety of reasons, I had to push the deadline for completion of the first draft of this book back once and then twice. It's always a wonderful thing when an editor becomes a friend, and Susannah displayed all the traits of a very good one when I was deep in the weeds in the early stages of writing *Little Witness*.

Ivan Mulcahy, my literary agent, is not just a friend but has become a member of my family. I couldn't do what I do without his support. He is literally someone I can (and have) called at 11.30 p.m. on a Bank Holiday weekend seeking some superfluous piece of information. Don't get me wrong, he told me to fuck off, but he got me the information first.

We have that kind of relationship.

My kids are, as always, hugely tolerant of their father when he disappears for weeks at a time to get a manuscript finished: Richard and Marnie, I don't deserve your patience. My grandson Rhys is young enough that he's never known me *not* to disappear from time to time, but he also deserves a word of thanks for putting up with it.

Thanks as always to Emily Clarke for listening to me reading large chunks of the first draft as I tried to find the voices of my characters. Emily, you're a wonderful friend.

And finally, thanks to you, dear reader.

I couldn't do it without you.

PUBLISHING TEAM

Turning a manuscript into a book requires the efforts of many people. The publishing team at Bookouture would like to acknowledge everyone who contributed to this publication.

Audio
Alba Proko
Sinead O'Connor
Melissa Tran

Commercial
Lauren Morrissette
Jil Thielen
Imogen Allport

Contracts
Peta Nightingale

Cover design
Blacksheep

Data and analysis
Mark Alder
Mohamed Bussuri

Made in the USA
Monee, IL
09 February 2024

53200521R00215